AXREL

VRISHA WARRIORS

OLIVIA RILEY

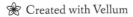

BEFORE

Axrel

"Do you think he'll die?" came a voice in the dark. A low voice, filled with apprehension and curiosity. Axrel couldn't see the owner of the voice, but he could smell them. A scent of iron, dirt, and fear.

"Leon will be pissed if he does," came another voice. A little more confident than the first. Axrel understood most of what they said though he was not versed in human tongue.

Something clicked sharply. There was a dim red glow followed by the scent of smoke. The scent blew in Axrel's face.

"Christ, he looks bad. They did a number on him. What do you think Leon will do?"

"He's already made up his mind. We're going to Larth."

"That's a Grayhart base." The voice sounded surprised. "What the hell does he think they can do?"

More smoke floated in the air. "There's someone there who knows a thing or two about these fuckers." Axrel felt something kick his side, shaking the cold metal brace that fixed him in place.

"Like an alien doctor?"

"Nah, she's human. She just knows alien medicine. Few people do who are out this far."

Axrel didn't move. He hardly breathed as he listened. They would have one of their own try to fix him. The thought of one of them touching him made him sick with fury. But he could not lash out. He was still too weak. He settled deep in himself, knowing what they said was true whether he liked it or not. He was near death. He could feel it.

And yet they were going to try to revive him.

He knew why. They needed him alive so that they could do what they'd always wanted since the beginning. Experiments. Tests. They wanted to see how he ticked. How he hunted and killed so easily. They wanted to know his weaknesses and study them obsessively. They wanted to understand what made him the predator that they feared.

They wouldn't need to do experiments to figure out why vrisha were better in every way. If he were freed and his body recovered, he would show them. With teeth and talons, he would show them.

"Leon honestly thinks anyone will work on this thing let alone go near it, he's nuts."

"She will. This doctor. Leon will persuade her. You know he will."

There was a hiss of breath. "Maybe we can convince her to not fix him up too good, huh?" There was quiet, nervous laughter.

"We'll see. Payton would have it that way if he could, but you know it's up to Leon."

"God, I just want to get to Fargis and be done with this shit already."

"Same, brother, same. Trust me, once we dump these prisoners, I'll be far away. Feel sorry for those guys who'll be stuck on Fargis with them."

"Sure do."

There was another puff of smoke, then something small and burning hit Axrel's leg. "All right, we've checked him out. He's definitely not doing better. Let's get out of here. Looking at this thing is making me feel sick."

The other agreed. Heavy steps turned away and grew quiet. Axrel took in the silence once they were gone. The air was chilly and dry, and he could hear the dull roaring of an engine nearby. The scent of smoke still lingered. The pain was there, but he'd grown used to it. It was another part of him now.

It was the rage that steadied him. The rage still burned like an unending fire in his heart. For the hundredth time, he thought of those who had put him where he was now. He thought of what he wanted to do to them. All the ways he could make them pay. There was nothing else for him now. All thoughts led to one thing above all others. He was close to death, yes, but the need for vengeance would keep him alive. For a time.

CHAPTER ONE

CHARLOTTE

The medical bay was quiet for once. On Larth, Grayhart station L58, medical staff lingered about, carrying on with the menial busy work that presented itself when there were few patients to attend to. They had received their last batch a few days ago when a small explorer ship had come into the docks, carrying an injured lygin cub and several adult lygin. Before that, there had only been a routine Grayhart ship, and none on board had needed so much as an exam.

The cub had gotten burned by one of the engines it had come too close into contact with. Charlotte was very familiar with burns. She also knew lygin anatomy well enough to know that some of their singed fur could spark an infection along the top of the skin if not cut and shaved. The little lygin's burns weren't too bad, but Charlotte still wanted to run tests and make sure no infection sprang up overnight.

Seated in a small corner of the recovery ward, Charlotte re-administered a powerful salve to the nearly sleeping lygin's arm.

"You did real good, Dycan." Charlotte smiled. "It doesn't hurt too bad, does it?"

The little lygin shook his head. "Just feels tingly," he said in xolian, lifting up his arm. His cat-like face twisted slightly, as if uncomfortable.

"You sure?" she replied back in xolian, the words clear despite her human accent.

The cub dipped his head. Charlotte carefully wrapped his arm in a fresh bandage. "You are very brave, you know. Your kin must be real proud to have a courageous man like yourself on board who can withstand fire."

The lygin smiled, showing small tiger-like fangs. He giggled. "I'm not a man. I'm just a kid."

"Yeah, but you are growing up so fast, aren't you? They'll be taking you on more excursions in no time. A human kid would be sulking for days, but you've kept your head up. Fire doesn't scare you, does it?"

The lygin seemed to think it over, then shook his head. "It was scary at first. But I think I'll just stay away from the thrusters next time."

"Smart boy." Charlotte finished wrapping up his arm and cinched it snugly in place.

"You know a lot for a human," the boy blurted as he looked over his arm.

Charlotte's smile widened. "I guess I do."

"You know about others too or just us?"

"I know others," Charlotte replied, capping the salve and packing away her kit.

The little lygin seemed impressed enough. "Like who?"

"Most xolians like yourself—grex, corax. The gyda too. And some other rarer types."

"Like the nillium?" the cub asked.

"A little."

"Wow. How do you remember them all?"

Charlotte grinned and drew the sheets over the cub. "Years of study and practice." She placed a gentle hand on his shoulder and could feel him purring. "Take a little rest. Your kin will come and grab you soon. You'll be out of here in no time. Here..." Charlotte took a small fishcake from her pocket and handed it to him. The cub cried out in delight. "Don't eat it too quickly, or you'll get a stomachache."

"All right. Thanks, doc!"

Charlotte stifled a laugh as she rose from her seat by the bed. He'd called her doc ever since his kin explained to him what she was. He had been nervous at first, and they wanted to put him at ease. She exited the small room, closing the curtain quietly.

"Dr. Lockley."

Charlotte twirled around and saw Mia walking toward her. The nurse looked concerned, her expression worrying. "Dycan is resting for now," Charlotte commented. "We can inform his group he can be released...What's wrong? Is it a patient?"

Mia shook her head, wringing her hands. "A military vessel just landed at the bay docks. They are asking for you."

Charlotte frowned. "Which military?"

"The governing systems. It's one of ours."

Ours as in a human vessel, Charlotte noted. Not associated with the Grayhart organization. Grayhart rarely worked with the military if they could help it. The organization was the head of exploration and discovery of new civilizations within the major systems. It was composed of scientists and researchers. They dealt with furthering relationships with other worlds and races not trying to dominate them. Or pick a fight. The alliance was the only thing keeping their fragile union together. The military stayed away from Grayhart affairs and vice versa. Aid between the two came reluctantly.

Charlotte looked over at the doors to the hall but didn't move. "How many injured?"

"I don't know. They wouldn't say."

Of course. She would have to go to them. Stubborn, inconsiderate...

Charlotte let out a slow breath, then started for the doors. "Do a round of check-ups for me, Mia. And tell the others to prepare beds. I'll be back when I can."

Down the hall, at the entrance of the hospital, Charlotte could see Grayhart security talking with a pair of soldiers. Their faces were hardened, bodies rigid. The soldiers' glares turned toward her as she approached.

"Char," called a voice before Charlotte could greet them. She glanced over and saw Grayson, head of Larth security, looking annoyed, his steel-blue eyes fixed on the other men. "A moment," he said to the soldiers.

The soldiers didn't say anything but glared back with impatience. Grayson pulled Charlotte aside.

"What's going on?" Charlotte asked softly.

"They won't say much. They docked not even twenty minutes ago and were asking for you before we even got talking," Grayson replied. "The ship is big. It must be carrying several hundred at least. It must be soldiers. Maybe there was an attack."

"Then why not bring their injured inside?" Charlotte inquired. "Why do they want me at the docks?"

"Hard to say," Grayson said in a low voice. He glanced over at the soldiers with a frown. "But I'll have a team nearby just in case."

Charlotte gazed at the soldiers, a bad feeling sitting in her gut. "Maybe you should come with me? You're head security, so they can hardly say no."

"I told them that. They said they only wanted to see you and weren't inclined to negotiate." His hand slipped to her arm, bringing her close. "But I'll be right nearby, all right? If things escalate..."

"They won't. I'll see them."

His hand dropped to her own, squeezing it gently before releasing. He stepped back, turning to the soldiers. "Fine, let's go."

They followed them out of the hospital and through the main corridor toward the docks. From the windows on one side, Charlotte could see the night sky and the two small moons in the distance. The land beyond was still dark save for the glow of lights from the city buildings. Larth was a rocky, dry place, and the air was stale, but it was growing, thanks to Grayhart efforts. It served as a base and trade-port just on the edge of the alliance territory. The neutral zones.

As they approached the docks, Charlotte wondered what a military vessel was doing this far out from the governing systems–Earth's territory. She supposed she'd learn soon enough.

As the wide metal door to the dock slid open, Charlotte was greeted with the sight of the huge ship and several dozen soldiers standing in groups around it. Some stood by, leisurely waiting, smoking blunts, while others rested their hands on the guns at their sides.

Grayhart staff stood nearby watching them, expressions twisted, as if they'd eaten something sour. She caught eyes with some of them, and they whispered between each other, a few waving at her. Their clean-cut gray uniforms looked well-kept while the soldiers didn't seem too concerned by their appearance as hardened as it was. Some were even wearing armored pads and battle-grade gear atop their dark camouflage-blue suits, as if ready for a fight.

Charlotte moved through them, following the pair of soldiers, with Grayson and his security team still behind her. They came to a tighter knit group beside the entrance of the ship, and the soldiers parted, revealing two officers and their commander standing beside large cargo carriers.

"Dr. Lockley." The commander, a heavy-set man with a wiry beard and graying hair, dropped the cigarette in his hand on the ground and smothered it with his boot. He grinned at her and put out his hand. Charlotte took it without hesitation. "I'm commander Leon Stride." He released her hand and pointed to a lanky, dark-eyed man with brown hair cut close to his skull on his left. "This is my second, Payton Ramsey. The other officer is Leslie Briggs." He gestured to the balding, beefy man on his right.

Charlotte looked between them. "What can I do for you?"

Leon lifted his gaze to Grayson and the Grayhart security team. "Think we can get a minute of her time alone?"

"You can," Charlotte replied instead. She turned to Grayson who glanced back at her with hesitance. "It's fine."

"Right nearby," Grayson mumbled before they stepped aside.

Charlotte turned back to Leon who gave her a confident grin. Between his narrowed lids, she could see blue eyes shining. He had crow's feet at the corners. His graying beard was well trimmed as was his hair. He had a polite air about him compared to the others, his expression less rigid, though he still held that edge of command.

"I appreciate your time, Dr. Lockley," he said sincerely.

I doubt it, she thought. Aloud, she said, "Why did you want to see me?"

"I've heard of your work. You're quite famous in the medical department, even within our base back home.

Charlotte's brows rose. "Really?"

"You bet. Your study of alien medicine back on Terra Centra, under Dr. Siera and her team, is talked of all the time. Your records on the alien patients are used by several staff."

"Do you get many otherkin on base?"

"Just gyda every so often." Leon shrugged. "But whatever information we can get helps."

"And I assume this has something to do with why you've called on me?"

Leon nodded as he sat back on a low crate beside him. "We have a situation on our hands, and we don't have the right staff for the job."

"They don't assign medical staff for soldiers on vessels now?" Charlotte said, barely hiding her sarcasm.

Leon laughed softly. "Oh, they do, they do. No, this is of the alien variety."

Charlotte glanced at the ship. "They are onboard?"

"That's right."

"How many?"

"About three hundred."

Charlotte looked back at him, nearly stunned speechless. "What are you doing with three hundred otherkin?" she asked, suspicious.

"Prisoners of the governing system. They got caught in our territory, broke our laws, and now we are taking them to Fargis."

Charlotte's throat tightened. "Fargis..." She was sure she'd heard that name before.

Leon crossed his arms and leaned back. "It's a newer base. Been built up for several years. Started as a working world, then turned into a closed off inmate camp. Now they have the largest prison base in the governing system. That's where we are headed and where our three hundred will soon be calling home."

"You brought prisoners to this base? Are you mad?" Charlotte said without thought.

Leon laughed. "Maybe. But trust me, they aren't getting loose, not on my watch. Even so, we wouldn't threaten this place with the possible danger if it weren't dire."

"Dire?" Charlotte repeated.

"That's right. You see, I need you on board, Dr. Lockley. We have a couple of wounded aliens, one badly so. I can't risk taking them off as I'm sure you understand, but we can't afford to have them die on us."

"Why not?" It sounded harsh, but she was honestly curious. Why did they care?

"Our mission is to get them safely to Fargis, that's all I am at liberty to say."

Charlotte crossed her arms. The idea of boarding a ship full of dangerous prisoners only made her mildly nervous, but her calling to help treat those in need was stronger. "I'll get my kit and a few nurses to come on board and have a look. If their injuries are great, you may have to stay for several days."

"I'm afraid that's not an option."

Charlotte shook her head. "I can only work so quickly. Even with our advanced equipment, I will need to run tests—"

"No. Sorry, Doc. No nurses, no staying. We leave tonight."

Charlotte's brow furrowed. She stared at him to gauge how serious he was. "You want me to come with you, is that what you are suggesting?"

"That's correct."

Charlotte blew out a breath of laughter. "I...no. No, I can't just leave everything here and come with you."

"I think we can convince you well enough."

"No amount of money is going to make me—"

"We aren't offering any. At least nothing impressive. You'll get paid with government coin."

Charlotte looked at him, annoyed. "Then what makes you think I'll just drop everything and take one step on that ship?"

Leon frowned. "Project Iris."

Charlotte stiffened. She looked to the other two officers who didn't so much as flinch. She turned her eyes back to Leon. "How do you know about that?"

Leon arched his brow. "Like I said, you're famous. In more ways than one, Doctor. The military doesn't have to search too deep to uncover anyone's secrets."

Charlotte's throat suddenly felt very dry. "That was a long time ago. Way before I was on Terra Centra. I was young and stupid and my father—"

"Got what he deserved, no?"

Charlotte clenched her jaw. "Yes, sir, he did. And I deserved the same punishment. If I had known how everything came to be..."

"That your father was dealing in the illegal transfer of alien organs and off the record experiments. Did he make you assist him, or did you do it willingly?"

Charlotte felt white hot anger burning in her chest, beginning to rise. "I didn't know about the transfers, not until after he got caught. As for the experiments...he had lied to me. I only worked with the dead bodies. He told me they were donations. If I had known what he had done to them before, I would have never..."

"I'm sure, Doctor. But you were a part of it, and, despite your record being cleared and your father jailed for good, I don't think the alliance will take kindly to the news, nor will your peers." Leon stood. He looked around and up at the ship. "I don't feel compelled to tell anyone. But I think you must have some guilt still stored up about it. These aliens need help. The trip isn't too long, and we will send you right back here as soon as the ship lands. So." He looked back at her and smiled. "I'll see you on board. We leave in ten minutes."

* * *

"Are you seriously going to do this?" Grayson asked as Charlotte began packing away her kit and a few belongings, mostly clothes and her ISpad, into a large duffle bag. "We need you here. And you haven't even spoken to the heads of base. They should know."

"They already do. I've sent word. They encouraged me to go as well," Charlotte said, stuffing her bathroom bag between two uniforms.

Grayson grabbed her hand and forced her to look at him. "You don't have to do this," he whispered, holding her hand tight.

Charlotte paused to study him. He was handsome. His steely eyes stared her down with concern, his lips set in a hard line. His black hair curled around his ears, making her want to trace her fingers through the locks. She liked him, she knew, and a part of her wished she had said yes to his offer of a date. "I'll come back," she said at last. "I won't be gone long."

Grayson placed something in her hand. Charlotte looked down at the slender black device with a speaker at one end and several buttons along its top. An advanced communications receiver.

"I have a wristpad," Charlotte began to protest. "If I need to call you..."

Grayson shook his head. "You'll be too far out for it to work. Keep that with you, just in case. Promise?"

Charlotte squeezed the receiver, then quickly placed it in her bag.

"I shouldn't be gone more than a week. Fargis is near the governing systems, but they claim to have jetline ships that will get me back in no time," Charlotte said, assuredly.

"Just be safe. If anything happens, call me." He leaned down and kissed the side of her head. She didn't pull away, but she didn't push for more. She didn't have time.

"Dr. Lockley, we need to go." A soldier stood at the door of her living quarters. Charlotte gazed up at Grayson one last time before picking up her bag and turning away.

They made good time back to the docks. When she entered to see the towering ship, she slowed a little. It was massive. The size of a cruise ship. Even the giant Grayhart deep space explorers weren't as big, and she had always considered those an impressive size. This was a fortress shaped like a ship. It was a wonder the dock had been big enough for it to land.

The soldiers who had been milling about beforehand were gone, already back inside the ship. Reluctantly, Charlotte followed the lone soldier toward the entrance. White, high-beam lights trailed down on the ground like spotlights. In the distance, she could hear the engines slowly firing up and the muffled sound of a woman's voice over an intercom, informing the docking staff of their departure. Air from vents blew Charlotte's golden blonde hair in her face as she stepped on to the platform and up a ramp into the ship.

All noise ceased as the locking doors shut tight with a dull thud and click. Charlotte looked back at the closed doors, a yellow stripe across the front. She turned and followed the soldier down a short passage. They stopped within a small room where a desk sat and a lone guard stood. There was a kiosk, and the soldier scanned an ID on his left wrist.

"Plug your credentials into the kiosk, and we will have an ID made for you," said the soldier.

Charlotte went over to the kiosk and typed in her name, Grayhart code number, and address. A moment later, the kiosk brightened, and there was a split-second flash that made Charlotte wince. The machine spat out a card, and Charlotte took it, looking it over. It had her credentials and a badly taken picture of her.

"Keep that on you. You'll need it to get into certain rooms and floors," the soldier informed her. "Leave your bag here. Someone will take it to your room. Let's go."

Charlotte stuck the card in her uniform pocket and placed her bag by the kiosk. Keeping only her kit with her, she followed the soldier down a passage to the left. The halls were bright–too bright–with a tinge of sickly green. It made her eyes hurt. As they started up a set of stairs, she could hear the roar of engines and feel the ground beneath her begin to shake.

"Shouldn't we take seats somewhere?" she asked, her hand tight on the rail.

The soldier didn't reply. The ship shook, and she could feel it beginning to move. Still, they continued upward. At the next level, the soldier took her down another long corridor. At the end of it, she could see several soldiers standing guard at a wide door with a red X across its front.

"Dr. Lockley to the medical sector," announced the soldier as they approached. One guard turned and scanned his wrist over a security pass, and the door slid open.

Passing through the door, Charlotte took a few steps inside, then froze. Her mouth dropped open, and she stared wide-eyed at the large central chamber before her.

The chamber consisted of three separate floors which she could see high above. Men walked along railed pathways to each side. On every floor were rows of doors, each with a small slit for a window.

"We need to keep going, doctor."

Charlotte looked at the soldier. "There really are prisoners," she said, stunned. "Are they really all...aliens?"

The soldier turned and started for another doorway at the end. Charlotte moved swiftly across the long chamber, hands gripping the strap of her kit. Her heart pumped faster even as she kept her nerves about her, trying not to think about what she was doing in such a place.

The soldier took her on to the next room which was clearly a security hub. Men sat at a C-shaped terminal staring fixedly at monitors while talking through headsets. None even glanced her way as she passed. Charlotte caught sight of a screen and saw a video feed showing several rooms including the large chamber they had come from. As they slipped into another wide passage leading downward on a low ramp, the lights flickered, and the pressure dropped. Then the gravity stabilizer kicked in, and the pressure returned to normal, making her ears pop. They were lifting off.

No turning back now, Charlotte thought. A twisting anxiety moved in her stomach and up her chest as they reached the end of the passage and stepped into a large, egg-shaped room with the bottom wide and the high ceiling narrow. Along the walls, there were no doors. Only curved glass containment pods. And most were occupied with a different race. Charlotte recognized them all. A corax with his shark-like head, long head fins, and gray skin, a grex with its reptilian physique and dark scales, a lygin with its feline features, several scars on its face, and—to her deep surprise—a fyrien, female if she wasn't mistaken, with several white stripes along her dark-purple arms, long white hair falling across her shoulders. All of them wore blue-gray prison uniforms and were in a deep slumber, fixed securely by thick metal cuffs at their legs and arms and a thick bar across their chests. Only two of the pods were empty.

At the center of the room, Leon spoke softly with two other men. He stopped and turned when he saw her.

"Welcome, doctor." He smiled, his blue eyes sparkling. "This is Michal and Kale. They are part of our medical division. They are willing to assist you if you need help."

Charlotte nodded to the men, and they bent their heads in return.

"I wish I had time to give you a tour, Ms. Lockley, but I'm afraid I don't. You saw most of what you needed to anyway, and someone will direct you to your temporary living unit when necessary."

"I don't understand, sir. Where is the medical station? You must have one on board," Charlotte said.

"The only medical facility we have is used strictly for our men. For the inmates you'll work here."

"Here?"

Leon nodded to Michal and Kale who walked over to a walled off section of the room. Charlotte had yet to notice the sheets of collapsible metal dividers along one side. "You'll have everything you need. We brought down some of the equipment, including a surgical machine if you need it. I'll leave Michal and Kale to show you."

The pair pushed back the metal dividers and began to move the equipment out into the center of the room. There was the surgical machine Leon mentioned, along with an x-ray machine, a computer, a metal table and scanner, and two large healing tanks, like metal coffins. They rolled them out, placing them in a single row.

"Your patients are resting inside. The tanks slow the rate of—"

"Of molecular and cellular damage, I know. We use them on Larth," Charlotte said, eyeing them warily.

Leon dropped a hand on her shoulder, making her look at him. "They are heavily sedated, so you should have no problems. But they are extremely high-risk, so if there is ever a concern, notify security immediately."

"Are these really the only two injured?" Charlotte asked.

"Currently, yes." Leon nodded to the pair. "Open them," he ordered.

They opened the first, cold clouds of vapor spilling off the side. Charlotte peered inside and thought she was looking down at a dog or a hyena. She had seen pictures of the race before but had never met one. They rarely ever left their own planet. "A drogin," she stated.

"Correct," Leon said. "He might be rabid, we don't know. He tried chewing his own arm off. You can see the damage."

She did. His right arm was a mangled mess of bone and fur, the sleeve of his uniform cut off to the shoulder. On one side of the shredded jumpsuit was the number 001. "Where did you get him?"

"He was caught on a freight ship. Killed several dozen. He must have been thrown off his own planet or was just a lone wolf. Who knows. Thankfully, he's really one of the worst here, and that's few of them. Most of the prisoners, though dangerous still, are at least manageable."

"Is that why these inmates are in sedation pods, unlike the rest?" Charlotte gestured to the sleeping aliens around them.

"You got it. Out of three hundred, these are the ones we worry about the most. These are what you would call high security prisoners."

Charlotte gazed back at the drogin nervously. "I guess it's nice to know they can't get much worse than him." And having to mend him made her stomach twist but, criminal or not, she would do what she could to fix his arm.

"Oh, they can." Leon laughed. "That would be your next patient."

Michal slipped over to the other tank and carefully opened it. Clouds of water vapor floated into the air with a hiss. Charlotte went over to the side and peered in, then let out a sharp gasp.

"It's okay. Remember, he's sedated. He can't hurt you," Leon reassured.

At first, she didn't even know what it was. All she saw was a pile of purple and red. With sharp points stuck at different angles. It took her a moment to even recognize the species.

"Th-that's...a vrisha, isn't it?"

"Hard to tell now, but yes."

Charlotte covered her mouth, feeling sick. "What happened to him?"

"A long story for another time, doc. All that matters right now is he's not doing too good. We're no experts but judging by the state of him...well, you can see for yourself."

She could. Most of what she'd studied about the vrisha was that they usually looked like some color or shade of red. This one was largely dark purple, even darker than the fyrien nearby. It was an unnatural shade for a vrisha, and she could see why. Most of his skin was charred or sliced away, revealing the color of his inner skin beneath the scaley exterior. The thigh of his leg was so bad she could even see a shiny black, like onyx. His bones.

She shook her head. "Who is he?"

"We just call him Prisoner Zero. He's a rogue caught on a trade world."

Charlotte's eyes shot up to him. "You mean..?"

"We are confident he's part of the group against the alliance. I'm sure you've heard about the Blood Guard. Hell, who hasn't?"

"Yes. I've heard of them. They follow a rogue queen."

"That's right."

"You're honestly telling me he's one of her guard?" She could hardly believe it. How could they even catch him, let alone take him down? It wasn't possible. Taking on a vrisha was near suicidal, and capturing one and keeping it was near impossible. The galactic devils were a deadly race, especially their warriors. They brought fear to many. Only Charlotte had studied enough about them to not get legends mixed up with the truth.

"You know about them, doc. You're his only chance of living," Leon said. "And we need him alive the most. Make sure he makes it to Fargis, and your work is done."

Charlotte glanced from him back down to the corpse of a body before her. Even being told what the vrisha was—an enemy to the alliance and therefore to her—she couldn't help the pity that slipped into her heart. He looked on the verge of death. He looked in great pain.

"I can't promise anything," Charlotte confessed after a pause, staring down at the vrisha, her heart skipping. "But...I will try."

Leon nodded. "Do what you can. Record everything. I will be monitoring the situation from my station." He turned for the exit. "Good luck, doctor."

CHAPTER TWO

CHARLOTTE

It took Charlotte a moment or two to regain her composure once Leon disappeared and she was left with the two medics who watched her from close by, waiting for her orders. She took a deep, slow breath, gathered her thoughts, then turned her gaze back to the alien before her.

The vrisha needed attending to immediately. So, the drogin would have to wait.

"Close the drogin up and place him aside for now. Make sure to monitor his vitals every half hour in case of a change." Charlotte placed her kit on a table, then went over to the control pad on the tank's side and began to power it down. Kale moved first, placing the drogin aside as asked.

Michal stood by. "What are you gonna do, exactly?" he asked.

"He needs surgery."

"The surgical machine is only programmed for human anatomy."

Of course it was. "Then start up the computer," Charlotte said.

She pressed through the screen, finding the controls to lift the vrisha's body from the tank. The slab beneath him began to rise.

From the corner of her eye, she could see Michal hadn't moved. She looked over at him and saw his mouth set in a hard line, his dark brown eyes shadowed. He was young, she noticed, and smaller than the other men she had seen. Scraggly, even. With a buzzed head and pale complexion, he looked worn and tired. Kale was similar in almost every way. In fact, she wondered if they could be brothers.

"Start the computer, please," she repeated.

Michal hesitated, then slowly made his way to the laptop on the metal table. He opened it up, and the screen brightened. He plugged in a passcode. When the vrisha's body was lifted high enough from the tank bed, Charlotte started for the back end and began to pull, moving the tank toward the surgical table with its machine hanging from two long metal panels above, which were connected by a pair of arms melded to the table on one side.

"You'll both have to help me lift him," she said, placing the tank right up to the table.

Kale glanced at Michal, then made his way over. Michal reluctantly followed.

"I don't think this is going to work," Michal mumbled as he took the vrisha's feet. Kale slipped to the opposite side of the surgical table, ready to pull the body on to it.

At the count of three, they lifted the body together. The vrisha was heavy despite how thin he looked. It took all of Charlotte's strength, and even then, she could hear his back scraping over the table.

When they had him firmly in place, Charlotte moved to the computer. She connected it to her Grayhart storage profile and pulled up their medical database. She plugged in her credentials and sifted through her storage of files under surgical codes and found the one she was looking for. With laptop in hand, she went over to the surgical machine's small display and connected her computer to it. She transferred over the files, and, as they downloaded, she placed the computer aside. Michal and Kale watched her carefully, the first looking annoyed, the second uninterested. There was a small bell-like noise as the download completed.

"The machine is programmed for alien anatomy now," Charlotte said, in case they were curious. "It just needs to scan." She lowered the machine from above, locking it in place.

The machine, which looked like a large camera with several lenses, began to move over the vrisha's body, a thin green light moving across his skin. When it was finished, the machine broke into several parts, each part placing itself over several areas of his body. A hot orange light covered the worst wounds. The vrisha didn't move an inch as the light sealed together sections of skin.

"Was an x-ray done at all?" Charlotte asked.

"No. Why?" Michal answered.

"To check for internal injuries. You must have considered there are some."

When they didn't answer, she glanced at them and saw Kale shrug. "Wasn't our job. That's why you're here. We don't work on aliens."

"Except now," Charlotte said aloud, irritation starting to rise.

"Only because Leon ordered us to," Michal said, crossing his arms.

Well, it wasn't like she'd expected that they'd volunteered. Who would?

Charlotte sighed. "Fine. I'll do one. You two can look after the drogin for now and clean this tank." She pushed the now empty tank away. It was stained red and black from blood. "Or can you not handle that?"

For the first time, she saw Michal smirk. Only a little and it was gone in a flash. "Yeah, sure. Whatever you say, boss."

The two men (boys really) took the tank away, placing it and the drogin back behind the metal dividers, where they went to work, speaking quietly.

Charlotte turned back to the alien, her attention now focused solely on him. Her eyes drifted over his body, and she felt that twisting feeling in her stomach again. He was so damaged she worried she might be too late. Her eyes fell to his torso where there were long gashes across his chest. Both arms had shredded skin, as if he had been defending himself against something sharp cutting into him. His legs also had deep slices at the sides, and it took her a moment to realize he had on some sort of thick leather-like pants, but they were so shredded they hardly covered him. Parts even seemed to be melded into his skin. She would need to remove them.

Her eyes lifted back to his stomach and chest. He was so still she would have thought he was already dead. She couldn't even see the rise and fall of his chest. Only from the machine's monitor could she see his vitals. They were dangerously low, even for a vrisha.

Her eyes finally drifted over his face, and a chill went down her spine. His outer lids were open but the inner ones, made of some filmy white sheen, hid his gaze. She had learned about their second lid before, back on Terra Centra. It reminded her of a snake. Many times, they slept with just the second lid, but it was said they could still sense their surroundings in their sleep. She had no clue how sedated or out of it he was, but she tried not to think too much about it.

The truth was, she had never actually worked on a living vrisha before. Nor a dead one. It was one of the only races she had little to no contact with despite studying them. The main medical headquarters on Terra Centra where she made her career had more information than anywhere else. Many years ago, they had the chance to work on a vrisha that had a mysterious illness. They learned all they could because, after that, they never got another chance. The vrisha refused to give them more information nor would they allow them to be studied and "experimented" upon. Even the head of the facility, Dr. Siera, couldn't convince them, and she had made a close friendship with Dr. Hart, the famed human turned vrishan queen.

So what little information they did acquire was only from that one encounter. It had been enough to at least understand their basic structure, but there was still much that could be learned. Charlotte realized she would be learning quite a lot in the next few hours.

She remembered her days back at school, when she had decided to take the course on the vrisha. Her college mates thought she was crazy. She'd never even get the chance to see one. It was a waste of time, they said.

Well, guess she showed them.

And secretly, she had always wanted to encounter one, to have this opportunity. Most people were too afraid. But she had found them rather fascinating.

So, she'd gotten her wish. And remembering Leon's words, she wasn't sure she was thankful for it. As she watched the vrisha on the table, her heart began to race.

If he recovered well enough, he'd likely try to escape. Even Leon and his men couldn't be so foolish as to think they could contain him. And if he was part of the Blood Guard like Leon mentioned, he'd try to kill them too.

Charlotte stifled a shudder. If they got him to Fargis, hopefully she would be long gone before anything like that happened. For now, she just needed to do her job. Not think about who she was working on.

The lights darkened as the machine sealed up the last major gash on his front side. Charlotte went over to the display monitor and plugged in the controls that allowed the machine to carefully turn him over so that they could work on his back side. Rollers along the table slowly turned him until he lay flat on his stomach. The machine readjusted its position, and the lights brightened as Charlotte watched the long slashes across his back slowly seal up. His back was so badly marred, parts of his skin were shredded, as if someone had sliced or cut repeatedly and violently. Even some of the spikes along his spine were missing. His horns along his head were broken, asymmetrical, some long, others short. Once again, she felt pity fill her chest. Maybe she shouldn't feel any compassion for him if he truly was who they said, yet she couldn't help it. Perhaps it was just the healer in her.

When the machine had finished its work, she had him set on his back again. Even with some of his major external injuries covered, and his blood loss halted, it would still take time for the skin to mend naturally, and he would be heavily scarred for life. Nothing could be done about that.

Charlotte brought over the x-ray machine and grabbed a scanner attached to its side. Carefully, she traced over the prisoner's body with the scanner until the machine began to compile all possible internal damage. After only a few seconds, it confirmed her suspicions. He had some damage on the inside as well. His intestines were bruised, and he had a small rib crack in his left side. His knee joint was dislocated as well, and, curiously, he had tiny fractures in his hands. His tail, which lay limp to one side, also had a few minor tears in the muscles, and the sharp tip at the end was split on one side. Still, compared to his outer injuries, she was impressed by the little damage on the inside.

The surgical machine couldn't mend bones like skin or organs, but she could administer a medicine that could quicken the process.

First, to examine him by hand. He was caked in dry blood, the fresher kind dripping off the sides. He would need to be washed too.

Charlotte looked at his vitals from the monitor. Despite her work so far, nothing had changed. His heart rate was still low. If it got too low or stopped, she would have to jump him.

Working as quickly as she could while still remaining careful, Charlotte lifted up the surgical machine so that she could lean in and take a better look. She took out a pair of gloves from her kit and put them on before standing to one side of the table. Hovering above the terrifying specimen, she cautiously lowered her hand down to him. Even though he was heavily sedated, and clearly too weak to try anything, she still felt a pang of fear in her heart. She couldn't let it stop her from touching him, but it made her pulse race all the same.

Gently, she placed her hand on his chest, feeling the roughness of his scale-like skin. She waited a moment to see if he would react. His body didn't move, but from the monitor, his heart rate rose, if only a little. She paused for a moment longer, then let her hand slide across his arm. Carefully, she lifted his hand and examined the knuckles. They were black with bruises.

Charlotte brought up her wristpad. "Record. File number one. Vrisha," she started. "Patient has several minor breaks. The external damage is more severe. Will need to cast his hands and wrap torso." She lowered his hand and pressed softly on his throat. She took out a small light and shined it in his eyes. No reaction. "No damage to throat or eyes. A few marks across the face, from jaw to brow." She carefully cupped his jaw and went to pry open his mouth when a set of black fangs slipped from his upper lip. Charlotte flinched. With the lightest trace of her fingers, she pulled open his mouth and quickly looked inside. "No damage to the mouth." She cleared her throat to stifle a gasp as the jaws shut on their own as soon as she released him. Ignoring the thumping of her heart, she turned back to his lower half. "Patient has a dislocated knee which I will have to reattach." She set her light down and moved to his leg, taking hold of each side. She gazed over at his face to watch his expression for any change. Then, with a gentle, swift movement, she extended the lower half of his leg with one hand and applied pressure to one side of the knee with the other, pushing gently until the kneecap righted itself back into the groove. It might have been painful, but the vrisha didn't so much as wince.

Charlotte exhaled and rubbed her forehead against the back of her hand where a few beads of sweat had formed. She gripped his leg again and bent it carefully, making sure it moved with ease. "Knee is set. I will now administer a mending agent to help with the fractures."

Once Charlotte had injected the agent into his body using a thick needle poked into his side, she waited again for a reaction and found none. Leon and the others must have pumped him with a lot of sedatives and possibly painkillers, though she didn't think they would be so merciful as that. After all, he looked malnourished from lack of food and care.

She observed him for a moment, wondering if he was in a coma but remembered his heart rate going up from her touch. That was a reaction that wouldn't be possible under those circumstances. He was alive, if only slightly aware. For whatever reason, the pain didn't move him.

She called over Michal and Kale. Only Kale came to her side.

"I need antibacterial soap and warm water, a splint, and several feet of gauze. And a towel," she said.

Without a word, Kale disappeared. Several minutes later, he returned with a small green block that must have been soap, luke-warm water, no splint, a crumbled layer of bandages, and a dirty rag.

"This was all you could find?" she said.

"This was all that was available," he replied.

Charlotte turned away, exasperated, while Kale returned to his place behind the dividers. She set the bucket of water at her feet, then took a rag from her kit (a clean one) and set it and the soap into the water, rubbing both together until the crumbling green block dissolved partially into the rag. Then she set to work.

She started at his shoulders, gently scrubbing and rinsing away the blood and dirt. Then she worked down his torso and his stomach. When she got to his bottom half, she hesitated only for a second before finally taking out a pair of scissors and cutting off the pants. She set them aside, then returned to her washing. She had no real shock when she saw his fully naked body. She'd seen drawings and pictures many times before. And currently, there was nothing to see. She imagined if the vrisha knew humans had that sort of knowledge about their anatomy, they wouldn't be too happy.

She washed each of his legs, starting from his feet then up his thighs. He was filthy, and another pang of remorse filled her, especially at the thought that he had been sitting in the tank as he was for so long. Even if he was dangerous, it was shameful to keep him in such a state. Like an animal. She kept her touch as light as possible, then dried him off gingerly, grateful that he had yet to wake. She could imagine his reaction. A hissing, snarling, violent reaction.

When all was finished, she did her best to bandage him, even without the splint. Then she called for her medic boys so they could place him back in his tank.

As they were maneuvering the tank around, Charlotte touched at his side one last time, finding it starting to warm. It wasn't her best work, but it was all she could do for now. She looked at the monitor with a frown. The vitals had hardly changed.

"Sorry, devilman," Charlotte whispered to the vrisha. "I did my best."

CHAPTER THREE

AXREL

The dark seemed endless as he lay inside the tank. Rarely were there any sounds save for the muffled voices outside and the hiss of vapor that slipped within, pumping some kind of drug into the air to keep him out. The drug's effects were lessening, yet he still found it hard to move, to stay focused for long periods of time.

The setting hadn't changed. He was still locked away. But his body felt different. For the first time in what seemed like forever, he felt unwithered, undying. The pain had lessened considerably in some places, and he could even feel his strength beginning to return. Though it was slight.

Such changes didn't spontaneously happen from nowhere. Someone had tried to mend him. As he lay quietly in the tank, he recalled being moved. Feeling the cold air on his torn skin. He remembered there was light passing through his eyelids, an orange glow, followed by a heavenly heat across his body. That light, and heat from it, had taken away some of the pain. He no longer felt like he was losing bits of himself. He almost felt whole.

He remembered a voice too. Gentler than the others, yet confident. A female's voice. She had brought him just on the edge of wakefulness. Like a serpent coming up from deep water, nearly breaking the surface. Not just her voice drew him from sleep, but her scent, an exotic aroma, like a dark flower or fruit. It intrigued him. It was not like the stink of the men, though fear still permeated the room, coming from her as well as the others.

She was afraid, yet she still treated him. She had even dared place her hand on him. He distinctly remembered that too. A warm, soft, delicate touch. He hadn't been sure how to feel. He had loathed the idea of one of them touching him. But, to his astonishment, he did not feel the rising violence like he thought he would. No. He was cautious, to be sure, but the anger in him didn't linger. He instead focused intently on her hands and where they went. She examined him, but not in the way someone would study a specimen. Instead, she wanted to see if he had further injuries. Her touch was steady. Her hand didn't even shake.

He could have risen out of his stupor and snatched her arm if he had so wished it. The humans thought just because he looked broken that he couldn't still move. He might be weak, but he could still scare them off. Scare her off if he wanted to.

But he didn't want to. Not yet. She was healing him, for one. And that, he needed if he ever wanted to escape. But also, he was too fixated on this doctor and what she was doing. Astonished by how easily she touched him. She had even bathed him. He felt the cool water on his bare skin, her palms reaching across his naked body. Perhaps he should have stopped her then. A human touching a vrisha, especially one of the warrior class such as himself, without permission was taboo if not forbidden. Yet, he had felt no desire to halt her. She was helping him. And as upset as he was at being imprisoned, he was grateful she took the time to clean him, even if it should be unnecessary to her.

After all, the others hadn't cared for him like that. They hadn't even attempted to fix him. They didn't come near him if they could help it. Only to check and make sure he was still alive.

Everything was quiet now, like before. He had been in and out of sleep, uncertain sometimes if he was awake or dreaming. His thoughts slipped back again to before he had been placed on the ship. Anger seethed and bubbled once more in his heart. He could think of nothing else, as usual, imagining those who had wronged him torn apart and broken by his hand. Crushed under his feet.

Footsteps approached and he heard that voice again. Hers.

The tank opened with a hiss, and the darkness faded.

"I told you, the surgical machine only does so much. I still need to make sure there's no infection," he heard her say to someone unseen. He couldn't see her either, only the thin, foggy shape of her through his thin lids.

Another voice—a male's—responded but wasn't heard. There was a soft whirring sound as he felt the slab underneath lifting him out of the tank.

He heard her stepping around to him and, after a short pause, felt her touch him again, her fingers lightly pressing on his shoulder. She lifted his arm as if to examine it, then grazed a hand along his torso and stomach. The wounds there were still sensitive but not painful.

"I'm seeing no sign of infection so far, but I'd still like to administer the salve to keep the scabbing clean. It will help soften the scarring too."

"We're not here to make him look good as new. Just good enough to survive," responded the male dryly.

"Leon appointed me to keep him alive, and I'm going to do everything possible to help make it happen. Which means treating him like I would any other patient. If you don't have any salve—"

"Not for him."

"—then I'll use what I have with me," she snapped. She walked off, then came back a moment later. He heard the pop of a lid and clacking of metal on metal. "You can go," she said, sounding irritated.

Footsteps faded and the woman sighed. Her scent caught in his nose again—a lovely flower—as she bent over him.

He felt the cool sensation of something oily and strong, smelling like icy pinewood, along his thigh. The woman's fingers carefully smeared whatever the oily substance was on his skin; a delicate, soft touch like before.

His seething anger ceased momentarily as he turned his focus solely to whatever she was doing. She had mentioned a salve. For cleaning. That was what it was.

"Sorry if this is uncomfortable for you, devilman," she said, softly. "I know you aren't fond of anything cold."

She was speaking to him. That was astonishing to say the least. None of them had ever tried talking with him.

And she knew his kind didn't like cold things. Interesting. So she did know something about them.

Her fingers trailed up his thigh to his hip. She took her time, slowly dabbing each tear that had been sealed up by the human's odd machine. Axrel remained unmoving, the drugs still keeping him in a sedated sort of state. He didn't care to move yet, anyway. He felt oddly relaxed by her touch and was certain if he moved and scared her, she wouldn't come so close to him again. Perhaps that was how it should be. He shouldn't want her near. She was still one of them. And she'd likely react to him the same as the others did if he 'woke up'.

When she finished smearing the salve on his body, he felt the slab under him lift his upper half so that he sat up at a slight angle. He heard her move around, and, before he could even wonder what she was doing next, he felt something poke at his mouth. His heart pumped a little faster, worried she was trying to administer some other drug. But when he felt a rush of warm liquid trickle between his lips, he tasted water and nothing more.

"What are you doing?" came that male voice from nearby.

"He's dehydrated, what do you think?" she replied. "He probably hasn't had a sip of water for who knows how long."

"They can go a long time without it."

"Well, I say it's been long enough." The water stopped as she placed the bottle aside. Then there was the sound of something tearing open.

"You're seriously going to feed him too?"

"Yes. He is also malnourished, or can you not see that?"

"He can go a long time without—"

"Please," she started. "Go check on the drogin."

"I already did, fifteen minutes ago." The male sounded annoyed.

"Check again."

"You're spoiling him. He's a bloody monster, you know. He doesn't need or deserve our food. He can make it just fine without until he gets to Fargis."

"I am his doctor, and I say otherwise. Now go."

The male slipped away. This time, Axrel felt some sort of metal stick poke between his lips and tasted salty mush on his tongue. It wasn't good, but it was sustenance, and that too would make him stronger.

"Sorry, this was all I could get," the human female said suddenly. "I know it's no tender slab of meat."

The mush slid down his throat, and he nearly choked it up. At least it was meat, even if it was of the worst consistency.

"That's it," she cooed. She gave him water after, and he let that slide down his throat as well. Grateful for it. His throat constricted as he swallowed. He heard the woman inhale, as if the movement surprised her.

She cleared her throat, then attempted to give him more water. "You probably never thought you'd end up in this situation, huh? Having a human tend to you. It must be humiliating."

It was. But at least she wasn't one of the men.

And it wasn't like he could do much about it. Again, he could scare her, but he didn't want to lose the opportunity to heal. If she left and the men came, he would likely degrade.

And he needed to get better. If he wanted any chance of revenge.

"I know it's not much," she mentioned. "But we will take it one day at a time." She gave him another portion of food, and he let it slide down. "And then you'll be all better and..."

She trailed off, saying no more. He heard weariness in her voice and wondered the cause. It didn't matter. He knew wherever they were taking him was no place good. He just needed to be ready when the time came to fight his way out.

"We're leaving for now," said that male voice. "Shift ends in twenty and starts again in six hours. Are you staying or what?"

He heard the woman place the food and water away. "I'll stay a little longer to watch his vitals. And start working on the other one."

"Fine. We go to the medic ward first at beginning of shift since humans are obviously our main priority. We'll be back after."

"All right."

"I'd also make sure he's tied down properly. He's sedated well enough, but per safety protocols, he needs to be secured. Especially now that he's been treated."

The woman hesitated. "I understand. I'll do that."

The scent of the human males dissolved as their steps faded. The woman cleared her throat, and he felt her hands on him again. This time checking his now bandaged hands. She let them slide against her own before setting them down gently. "One day at a time," she whispered.

He felt cold metal settle across his arms and legs to lock him in place, then the slab beneath begin to sink, laying him back down. Slowly, the light disappeared, shutting him in darkness as the tank door sealed shut above him.

CHAPTER FOUR

CHARLOTTE

The room was small but comfortable enough. It was a single unit with a twin bed on one side and desk and chair on the other. There was an even narrower bathroom with a showerhead and a toilet with access at the foot of the bed dividing the room with a thin sliding door. It was nothing grand, but Charlotte had stayed in worse. At the back of the room was a small window, no bigger than the size of her head. Beyond was nothing but black.

Why put windows on ships, Charlotte wondered, *when there is nothing to see?* She supposed it was so people didn't feel claustrophobic. Even if they were boxed in, they could at least know there was endless space just beyond thickly laid glass.

She lay down for about two hours, then slept for only two more before she woke in the dark and couldn't fall back asleep. She wasn't prone to insomnia, but being in her current situation changed that.

She sat up from her bed and went over to the desk. She rummaged through her bag till she found a small pouch. From the pouch, she took out a pillbox. She uncapped the lid and stared down at the little red pills inside. She didn't have many left. She took the medicine only when necessary, to keep the edge off. To dull the anxiety. As she popped one of the pills, she thought she'd likely have an empty pillbox before the end of their journey. She drank from a water bottle she had set on the table next to her bag, then went into the bathroom. Even with the medicine, she knew sleep was unlikely. She washed her face in the sink, then slipped back into the little room and put on her uniform—a light blue, long-sleeved shirt and pants with the Grayhart insignia on the left breast. It was just five stars surrounding a planet. Simple.

Staring at it in a small metal mirror on the wall, she thought of her home, Larth. She was the head doctor there. A station serving as a transport for Grayhart vessels, while also a port city for alliance members and tradeships alike, and a base for medical research and biomedic discovery. It was one of the larger bases on the terraformed planet.

She had been with Grayhart for five years, three of which had been on Larth. With all their amazing advancements in technology and highly regarded as professional space-faring scientists, they still had the ugliest uniforms she'd seen.

Charlotte smirked at herself in the mirror, fixing the collar of her shirt. If she wasn't going to sleep, she might as well work.

Before she headed back for the alien holdings, she made a point to take a different route to get a better idea of her surroundings. The ship was large and had many rooms and passageways. Even with the map they had sent to her ISpad, she wanted a better view. She took out the small ISpad from her bag and tapped the screen, bringing up the map. Most of the rooms were either prisoner holdings or soldiers. The soldiers were around the outer and upper decks while the prisoners were middle and lower. The high security prisoner chamber—and her supposed medical hub—was located nearly at the center of the ship.

Judging by the number of rooms on the outside, she could say there were about fifty soldiers tops. That wasn't a lot, but most of the space had been made to carry the prisoners. She assumed, like a Grayhart ship, the men all had different duties like security, kitchen, maintenance, and piloting.

Along with the units, there was a break room and small cafeteria, the captain and commander's quarters, a warehouse for storage, and saferooms with escape pods at the back. The engine and warp reactor lay at the very bottom. She hadn't felt them make any jumps, but newer ships made it almost so seamless you hardly felt it. They were likely short and few with a ship of this size.

Charlotte put away her ISpad, then left her unit, slipping down one hall. She didn't pass a single soldier as she turned for a set of stairs. There were no elevators on the ship. Just one lift used for equipment that might need to be transferred to a different floor. The bright greenish lights, the whitewashed or steel gray walls, and endless networks of piping above showed just how much of a military vessel it really was.

At the next level, through a wider passage, she came to the ship's medical bay. Through a set of wide windows at either side of the entrance, she could see it was relatively dark within. The twins, as she liked to call them (though she wasn't sure if Michal and Kale were really brothers), hadn't awakened, leaving the place empty.

Charlotte peered through one window and could see several machines sitting to either end, along with bedpods and healing tanks like the ones being used in high security. To the back, she could see another room with a surgical machine. Beside it was a large metal cabinet. She was willing to bet there was a surplus of supplies inside.

She went for the door and pulled out her card. As she pressed it against the security scanner, she was both shocked and relieved when the door opened. Leon must have given her permission to enter in case she needed something, like a tool or extra supplies.

And she did. Or at least she knew she would eventually, and she feared it was going to be hard convincing the twins to let her have anything more. Her kit only held a limited number of items and wouldn't last long. The vrisha needed better, cleaner gauze when she rewrapped him, and he could use some heat and ice pads for his various breaks. The twins would think the pads were a luxury, but Charlotte didn't care. If they weren't being used by the staff, there was no harm in it by her standards.

Charlotte slipped inside and went straight for the cabinet. She tugged it open and searched through the various shelves. By the dim light, she found what she needed and snatched each item up, placing what she could in the pockets of her uniform. Before she closed the cabinet door, she saw a small storage freezer at the bottom. On it was a chart. She bent her head, and her eyes narrowed as she saw several names listed. Grex...lygin...fyrien...vrisha.

Before she could drop her hand to open it, she heard voices behind her. She closed up the cabinet and left the medical area, stepping back into the passage. The door closed behind her just as a pair of soldiers came up the stairs. She stiffened when she thought it was the twins. It annoyed her to feel like she had to prepare for a verbal fighting match when she had perfectly good reason for taking the things she needed. It wasn't the twins, anyway. The soldiers peered at her curiously as they walked by, and she gave them a nod and a smile. When they disappeared around a corner, she made for the stairs.

She went to the cafeteria and the break room next. Few sat around, mostly drinking black coffee and reading. They hardly looked up at her as she passed. She went over to the open window between the cafeteria and kitchen and saw a large man with a bushy mustache cutting a set of tan blocks into small cubes at a wide metal table.

"Excuse me, are you serving?"

"Not really. We have coffee," he said. He glanced over at her. "What do you want?"

"I was hoping you'd have some kind of meat."

He stopped what he was doing to give her a sharp look. "All we have are provisions. Jerky or canned fish."

"I'll take both," she said.

The man's brow furrowed. "Who for?"

"Myself."

"Where's your ID card?"

She flashed it at him, and he stared at it, his frown deepening. The man grunted but didn't argue, even though he looked like he wanted to. He dropped his knife before stomping away toward a storage room at the back, Charlotte craned her neck to watch him open the door and disappear inside.

The meat (if you could even call it that) she had given Prisoner Zero hours before had been disgusting in her opinion. It was nothing but sloppy mush that looked more like cat-food than anything else. It was what Kale had brought her when she asked, though it had taken some persuading. Like Michal, he didn't think the vrisha needed any real sustenance, but he was willing to help her out by giving her an expired can left in the medical bay. She was surprised the vrisha had even been able to swallow it.

The large man returned and set the food in front of her. "Don't think I can give you two of these every day. We don't have enough."

"Thank you." She took the wrapped jerky and tuna and put them in another pocket, then headed out of the cafeteria. This would be better.

* * *

She unlocked the tank lid, then lifted it slowly. Her heart did a little flip as the vrisha appeared before her, as if her mind instinctually turned to fight or flight despite her remaining outwardly calm. He looked no different than a few hours ago, his eyes covered in those thin lids, his body rigid and unmoving.

"Fancy meeting you again," she said, forcing a smile. "Hope you slept better than me." She glanced at the screen of her computer where she had linked it up to the tank in order to better read his vitals. They were still low, but that was to be expected. Vrisha had low heart rates to begin with, yet his wasn't quite normal by their standards. His temperature was down too, likely from the cold airflow of the tank. It wasn't good for him, but the tanks were meant for humans, not vrisha and so started at a lower temperature. Charlotte raised it to a more comfortable setting using the controls on one side of the tank.

She began to unpocket her supplies and set them aside on the table beside the tank as the temperature warmed. "I have something you might like more than that awful junk I was forced to give you before." She started to reach over for the metal clamp at his arms, then hesitated. She probably shouldn't untie him. Even though the readings showed that he was highly sedated, her mind turned back to what Leon had said. The vrisha wasn't a nice alien or so they say. He was one of the rogues who wanted her kind dead. She was so used to treating every patient with trust and care it was hard to remind herself of what he was.

She checked his bandages instead and the sealed wounds to see how they were progressing. There was some improvement even in the last few hours.

As she touched lightly at his marred skin, she saw his pulse rise slightly. She froze, watching. She lifted her hand not even an inch and hovered it over him. The pulse began to lower until she touched him again, then it rose. He was reacting to her. Even in the state that he was in, he could sense her, knowing she had her hand on him. Her own pulse began to race. She drew her hand back, then inched closer to the monitor.

Maybe he didn't like her touching him, and the heart rate was a stress reaction. That must be it. Perhaps she should be more careful, but she had to check him and eventually rewrap him. If he could complain about it, she would back off. But as it were...

"Sorry, devilman. I don't mean to upset you," she whispered. "But I'm going to have to redress you at some point and wash off the salve. Sorry if that bothers—" Charlotte froze again, a chill running down her spine. Did she just see what she thought she saw?

Slowly, she moved closer to his side. She watched him intently until her heart did another little flip.

His hand moved.

It curled once, then twice, then lay limp. Her eyes shot over to the monitor again and saw he was already getting a near fatal dose of sedative. It couldn't go any higher without putting him in a coma. Yet how...?

The vrisha as a race had always been a mystery. There were still many things they didn't know—even she didn't know, and she had studied them extensively. Some things could only be theorized. Right now, she theorized that the sedative was wearing thin, even at such a high level.

He was growing used to it very quickly. Like alcohol or other drugs, he was losing sensitivity.

And that would explain why he could react to her. If he felt her, he also likely could hear her too.

Charlotte watched the monitor for a long moment, watching as his heart rate fluctuated. She turned her eyes back down and waited, but he didn't move again. Still, she didn't take her eyes off him as she reached for the heat pads. "I'm going to set these on you. They will help with any minor damage and reduce swelling. I think you won't mind...but if you do, you can move your hand again and let me know." Charlotte took two heat pads and carefully set one on each leg. Prisoner Zero's heart rate went up and remained that way, but his hand didn't move. She couldn't help the little smirk that followed. "I had a feeling you'd like that."

She tapped at the controls along the tank and had the vrisha lifted up, the slab underneath him rising slowly. His upper half rose at an angle, putting him in a near sitting position, the steel clamps still keeping him secured. She stared at them for a moment and felt the sting of pity again. It was hard for her not to. Even if he was a monster as Michal said, seeing someone tied down when they were trying to heal from massive injuries just felt...odd. It wasn't something she was used to, and she'd been through many strange scenarios before.

Maybe things would be different if she understood who he was. She could be cold like the others and give him little attention, but it just wasn't in her nature. No matter who she was treating.

Charlotte took up the canned tuna and peeled away the lid. The scent of sea and fish hit her nose. This far out from the governing systems, it surprised her that it was authentic. She placed it down and took up the small water bottle she had left on the table from before. She brought the long, narrow straw topper to the vrisha's mouth and squeezed gently, letting some of the water trickle between his lips. Most of it spilled down his jaw, but she was only trying to give him a taste.

His throat constricted, and she placed the bottle aside, then took up the fish. It was slick enough he wouldn't have to chew. She used a narrow utensil like a metal chopstick to only stick small bits into his mouth.

"There you go. Not too bad, is it?" she said softly. "I'm not a fan of fish myself, but it can't be worse than what you had before." He swallowed it down but only a little. She took her time feeding him tiny portions, then giving him water.

"I don't know why you are here." She spoke as if they were talking in secret. "I wish I knew. I can't blame your hate for my kind. Whatever they did to you...it's unspeakable. I've seen many bad injuries in my time, and I can tell when someone has been mercilessly attacked. Even if you attacked first, wounds like these aren't the result of someone who was trying to defend themselves. Otherwise, you would have been riddled with bullets, and I would have been spending hours trying to pull metal from your skin. No. Several people did this to you. Perhaps torture of some kind, I'm not sure. Some might think you deserve it, but I don't. Whatever you might have done, I don't think you deserved this." Charlotte placed the food and water aside, then took a rag and wiped away what hadn't made it into his mouth. As she gently dabbed at his throat, she began to examine the slender holes between his neck and shoulder. She understood they were like a natural vent for absorbing oxygen and other molecules in the air.

"I know you probably won't believe me when I say it, but we're not all bad. Maybe that doesn't matter to you though," she said as she touched the vents lightly, making sure there was no blood coating them. "I wish things could be different, regardless. Fargis is known to be a harsh place. Maybe even for someone like you. It shouldn't be a place for anyone. Even prisoners."

Her gaze focused on the scales along his neck. They were almost violet in color, with a tinge of red. It was a lovely shade really, and she was sad to see such vibrant scales scarred so badly. He must have been stunning, even in his deadliness, before he was ripped apart. Like a viper, lethal yet beautiful. She imagined the way he moved was akin to one as well. Though he was too thin, he still had tight muscles that at one point must have made him look lithe and powerful. She could nearly see it. Even beyond all the ugly scars. It really was an utter shame.

Charlotte trailed her fingers along the scales at his shoulder. Unable to resist. "I wish..." she began to say. Then stopped and went still as a mouse. Her gaze floated up to his face, breath catching in her lungs.

His eyes were open. The thin lids gone. He leered back at her with eyes the color of a red sunset on a dark horizon.

Charlotte turned rigid at the sinister glare, as if held in a tight grip, heat draining from her body. Her hand still rested on his shoulder, and she feared if she moved an inch, he would strike at her, just like a snake, his dark fangs slicing her skin.

She licked her lips and swallowed, then cautiously slid her hand from him. He didn't turn his head or bare his fangs to bite her. He just stared at her. She let out a slow breath and placed her hand at her side, curling it tightly into a fist, the knuckles going white.

She opened and closed her mouth a couple times, unsure what to say to him, then eventually went with, "Do you understand me?"

Vrisha weren't known to understand human tongue nor did most care to learn, so it would surprise her if he honestly caught on to her words. They were more likely to know xolian–the common language–than any other language other than their own.

He blinked at her with his thin lids, then bowed his head. It was a subtle movement, but it was enough for her to notice.

So, he did understand her. How fascinating. She turned to the table and placed the rag on top. "Your cuts are mending quickly, and I see no sign of infection," she said in her most stern voice. She started placing the food away in her kit, keeping the jerky for later. "You'll still need a lot of rest. I've administered a healing agent for your broken bones, but it would be best for you not to move too much. I couldn't find any splints." He likely didn't know what those were, and she realized she was mostly just talking at him like she did sometimes to patients when they asked how bad off they were. She dared glance back at him and saw he was still watching her.

"*Xi rishes il sarifes,*" he hissed softly.

Before she could react or respond, he closed his eyes and fell back into his stupor.

Charlotte stood there, hovering over him for a long time, her mind flipping over vrisha words and phrases she had been taught at school on Terra Centra. She was sure she had heard him right.

For your aid, he'd said, *I'm grateful.*

CHAPTER FIVE

CHARLOTTE

She didn't tell the twins what happened. She knew she was taking a risk in not doing so. The more desensitized Prisoner Zero became to the drug, the more he might start regaining focus or movement. He was still secured with the clamps, but vrisha were notorious for escape. Eventually, she would have to say something, but she wanted to make sure that Michal and Kale's first response wasn't to administer more sedative. Even if Prisoner Zero was becoming used to the drug, if they pumped him with any more, he would likely never wake up again. For now, he would remain tied down, and she would talk to Leon once she deemed him repaired enough to be moved from the tank.

Thankfully, he remained in his resting state while the twins worked around her. When she wasn't caring for Prisoner Zero, she was working on the drogin—or Prisoner One as she sometimes called him. The dog-like man looked in poor shape, despite his arm being wrapped and healing. His fur was matted, patches of it gone.

He had crooked fangs and one damaged eye, leaving it looking white and faded. He'd clearly been in some bad fights. He had old scars and bullet wounds. Some medic had done a shoddy job of trying to fix him beforehand, leaving disfigured skin. At times, he seemed to wake in the mending process but still remained unresponsive, drool trickling down his jaw as he stared at her with half-lidded eyes.

"Commander Stride is coming down," Michal announced as she did one last check over Prisoner One and deemed he was healed enough to be transferred. "He wants to see the progress you've made."

Charlotte ripped off a pair of gloves and threw them out before washing her hands with wipes. "I should have expected as much." She was about to clean the healing salve from Prisoner Zero, but she supposed it would have to wait. She looked over at his tank, anticipation tightening in her stomach.

Not more than ten minutes later, Leon appeared down the entrance ramp with his head officers, Payton and Leslie. He saw her and fixed her with a smile.

"I heard things have been going well?" he said.

"As well as can be expected," was her reply.

He gestured to the tanks. "Let's open them up and take a look."

Michal and Kale moved toward the tanks before she could and opened both at the same time. Leon moved over to the drogin first and peered down.

"Sad, ugly, bastard," he mumbled. "How's his arm?"

"He didn't reach the bone," Charlotte answered, coming up beside him, "So, there were no breaks. Just badly mauled flesh. He was already scabbing over when I checked him, ripped out a good amount of hair, leaving the flesh wounds shallow. He's lost a lot of blood, but a cell generating agent kept him from the dying state."

"Sounds like he'll survive just fine then," Leon stated. "I think he's ready to go back in the pod."

The twins moved toward the tank at Leon's nod. They untied the drogin and moved him to a gurney, swiftly strapping him in. As they rolled him over to the nearest empty pod for transfer, Leon turned toward the vrisha.

"This poor devil looks a tad better than the last I saw him. I take it he's past the possibility of death?"

"So far," Charlotte said. "I've sealed most of the major wounds and gave him the cell microbial agent to help mend some of the broken bones."

Leon's brow furrowed as he stared down at the alien. Charlotte stood rigid, fearing the vrisha might wake in Leon's presence. "Why's he so shiny?"

"I've administered a topical salve to help the skin heal and keep away infection."

Leon grunted. "And I see you've wrapped him up pretty good too."

"To keep—" *him from moving*, she almost said "—the body parts in place, so the bones can mend right."

"I see," Leon said.

"She's been feeding him too," Michal commented as he and Kale locked the drogin in the pod and returned to stand close by. Leon's eyebrows rose, and the other officers looked at her squarely.

It was Officer Payton who responded first. "That's unnecessary. The pods keep them nutritionally stable. Plus, vrisha can go a long time without feeding."

Charlotte tilted her head up and clasped her hands together. "I disagree, officer. The vrisha is clearly malnourished. They may be able to last weeks or possibly months, but in his state, he needs energy to grow stronger. He's too weak."

Clearly, she'd spoken the wrong words. The officers frowned at her, Payton's dark eyes narrowing.

"He doesn't need to get stronger, Ms. Lockley," Payton explained. "He just needs to be stable enough when he's moved from the ship to the encampment."

"You asked me to keep him alive. He needs food and water in order to do so. He might not be human, but he is a person, and, despite what you might think, every creature, no matter where it comes from, needs to feed."

Payton crossed his arms. "It's not going to die from that. It will remain weakened, but it won't die. It can absorb water molecules in the air, if I've read correctly, from the vents at its neck."

"That's true but—"

"And therefore, it gets water through those means as well, if only a tiny amount."

"Except you've had him sedated, and so he can't properly absorb anything within the tank," Charlotte countered. "And when's the last time he's had any real sustenance? Weeks? By my observation, he's been in this weakened state since before he even arrived on the ship."

"Even so, the pods keep him from losing any more nutritional—"

"Except he hasn't been in the pod. He's been in here." Charlotte pointed at the tank. "Wasting away, being pumped with sedative that nearly puts him on the brink of a coma."

"If he gains any real measure of strength, he'll become a higher risk of harming someone when transferring him to Fargis."

Charlotte opened her mouth to ask how the hell that was even possible once he was secured well enough inside the pod, when Leon put up his hands to silence them both.

"Now let's just take a moment," he said in a gentle command. He looked to Payton first. "Ramsey, I don't think giving him a small amount of food is going to significantly change anything. Besides, from what I can see, he looks about ready to go into the pod. What do you think, doctor?"

Charlotte glanced up at him in surprise, then down at the vrisha lying in the tank. "I still need to clean off the salve and rewrap him. I also want to do a few more examinations, in case I missed anything."

Michal muttered something nearby, but Charlotte didn't dare look over at him. She turned back to Leon instead, who was watching her closely.

"I understand this is probably a huge opportunity for you, Ms. Lockley. But Payton isn't wrong. Keeping the prisoner out much longer poses a risk. If he's in stable condition and has no chance of dying on us, it would do well to get him secured tightly in that pod."

Charlotte glanced over at the others, then back at Leon. "I understand. But you should know if there is any other underlying issue that pops up or he suddenly worsens, I will need to work on him immediately."

Leon rubbed his fingers along his short beard, as if thinking.

"I don't think it's a bad idea, if you don't mind me saying," Kale said suddenly. Charlotte shot her eyes over to him where he leaned against the gurney, hands in his pockets. His face was expressionless as he locked eyes with Leon. "I've seen patients start to get better, then the next moment, crash and die out of nowhere." He shrugged. "Don't know about vrisha, but it can happen to anyone. Might be good to just let her keep an eye on him. Only for a little while."

Michal whispered something to Kale, and he merely shook his head. Leon regarded his suggestion, then turned to Charlotte. "Is that a possibility?" he asked.

Charlotte straightened. "Yes. It is possible."

Leon gazed at her for a moment, then nodded his head. "All right. But only a day or two to keep an eye on him. If nothing has changed by then and he isn't getting worse, we put him in the pod. Got it?"

Charlotte nodded back. "Fine."

"We'll be back down." Leon started for the exit. His officers moved to follow, Payton's cold gaze catching her own before turning away. "A few more days, Dr. Lockley," he called back. "And Fargis will be in sight."

Charlotte stood beside Prisoner Zero's tank, watching the monitor, observing his heart rate, which had risen.

Behind her, Michal and Kale scrubbed out the drogin's now empty tank. Michal had remained quiet since Leon and the officers left except every so often when she heard him muttering or talking quietly to himself. She didn't bother to try to understand. Kale didn't say much, but he seemed less irritable. She was still surprised he had agreed with her about keeping the vrisha out for a little longer. She didn't think much about why. She was only grateful for the extra time.

Because Leon hadn't been wrong. She did see this moment as an opportunity. Back on Terra Centra, when she had studied the vrisha, she had been one in ten who had taken the class, with two dropping out midway through. Because, to many, it had been a waste of time. They only saw vrisha sparingly in the cities and never in the medical sectors.

But it wasn't just the opportunity of fixing one up. Some part of her wanted to understand this vrisha.

They said he was a monster. A killer. She shouldn't be so curious. But she was.

Without a word, Michal and Kale rolled the empty tank toward the lift. The door opened, and they pushed it inside, then disappeared, taking the tank back up to medical. She didn't expect to see them again for a while, so she turned back to the vrisha.

"Alone again. At last," she said. She took out a thin box of cleaning wipes from her kit and set it on the table. She wouldn't bother trying to get a clean rag and hot water from the twins. The wipes would have to do.

She took out a small pair of scissors and the newer gauze she'd swiped in the medical bay. She had seen Kale give her an annoyed glare when he had noticed the heat pads, but thankfully, he didn't say a word. She'd likely hear about it later, but she wasn't feeling worried about it.

She tapped at the tank's controls, lifting Prisoner Zero up into his usual seating position, then unraveled some of the gauze. Picking up the scissors, she turned toward the tank and heard a low growl.

She went deathly still. Prisoner Zero leered at her again with those devilish eyes. His black fangs slipped from his mouth as if to bare them at her. He looked defensive and angry, like he didn't want her to come near.

Charlotte slowly put up her free hand and backed away. "I'm not here to hurt you, devilman. I just want to help. I need to change your wrappings."

His eyes slipped downward, and Charlotte followed his gaze. He was staring at her hand gripping the scissors.

"Oh," she said softly. He thought the scissors were a weapon. Either someone had used them on him before or anything sharp brought on the reaction.

Carefully, she placed the scissors down on the table. "It's all right, see? I'm not gonna hurt you."

His teeth disappeared back behind his lips. His gaze lost some of its sharpness, whether from him calming or from the sedative, she couldn't be sure. The clamps against his arms and legs had creaked and groaned as he pushed against them but were now silent. He continued to glare at her but with a little less menace and perhaps now with a little more curiosity. Still, he was cautious. His tail, which had been crushed underneath him, moved as if to weave, but it was too stuck to do so.

"May I take off your wrappings?" Charlotte asked, watching him carefully.

He didn't say anything at first, and she wondered for a moment if he really understood her at all. Then he bowed his head.

Charlotte took up the scissors again and turned back, waiting to see his reaction. This time, he didn't growl at her, but his eyes did follow the scissors with intense focus. Charlotte started to reach over to cut at the wrapping on his hand, then hesitated.

"You should understand, if you try anything I will be forced to put you under," she warned. "The sedative working on you now is already dangerously high. It's a wonder you can see me and move at all. But if I press at this display here," she pointed to the screen beside the tank, "it will pump you with enough to possibly kill you. And I really don't want to have to do that."

He stared at her for a long minute, a glint in his eye.

"*Erisa lis na fisa,*" he hissed quietly back. "*Esa nif shisia li nif haash.*"

And if you try anything to harm me, I will be forced to strike. And I don't want to have to do that.

Or something along those lines. Her vrishan wasn't amazing but she knew enough to understand.

Charlotte smirked. "I'm glad we are on the same page." She moved closer and placed her hand on his arm, then began to cut the band of cloth. "You were able to move your hand before. Was there little pain or discomfort?"

He tilted his head as he watched her snip then peel the wrappings off. He seemed fixated on her hand touching him, though he didn't recoil or show signs of displeasure. Maybe he was even fascinated. "Little pain," he said in his vrishan tongue.

Charlotte nodded. "That's good. It means you're healing fast." Really fast actually. It took humans a week to mend properly when using the regenerative healing agent. Longer without it. Yet for the vrisha it had only been a few hours.

Granted, he had been healing naturally for some time within the tank. She could imagine how far worse he had been before that.

She glanced at him several times as she worked from one hand to the next. It was truly astounding that he understood her tongue. "Where did you learn to understand human language?" she asked, too curious.

His eyes lifted to hers. "I have heard enough of it in my time being here. Humans come and go, talking around me." His body tensed, the clamps straining. "And I am a quick learner."

Charlotte's eyebrows rose. "But you do not speak it?"

His expression darkened. "I wouldn't try. I wouldn't disgrace my tongue lest it fall to ashes at the first word."

Fair. Dramatic, but fair. Charlotte started cutting the bandages on his leg. She gripped the shin carefully as she did so. With him tensing, his muscles were tight and as hard as the steel beneath him.

"How is it you know *vrishan*?" he asked suddenly, a drop of venom in his voice. A suspicious tone.

"I learned it on Terra Centra," she answered honestly.

He grunted. "I should have figured as much."

"You don't care for that place, do you?"

He didn't respond at first, then said, "I don't trust such a place."

"Why? Because it's the most diverse world within the known systems? The only planet to house every race within said systems? Or the capital for the alliance?"

"There are too many packed in one place. It is a fool's hope to think it could work out forever. With all the attacks—"

"By the Blood Guard?" She eyed him intently.

A fire set in his gaze. "Of other sorts."

Charlotte peeled the bandages off his leg. "Every place will have its issues."

"Experimenting on others is a serious issue."

Charlotte nearly flinched. "There are those fighting to stop that. And the attacks too. The alliance does its best to keep things peaceful."

Prisoner Zero snorted. "Or to keep things in control. And hide what they cannot. They trust too easily and punish too little for the sake of their so-called *peace*."

"I think they've done all they can," Charlotte argued.

He looked away from her and scowled. "You are ignorant to think so."

"So be it." She ripped off the last bit of tape on his skin and let it fall to the ground. She tugged a few wipes from their box and squeezed out the excess water.

"It seems to be a common trait in your kind," he said in a low, quiet voice. "When you humans aren't scheming or plotting to capture one of us or dissect us, you're creating problems everywhere you go. You infest a place and act noble, then betray those who trust you. A barbaric lot who still see themselves superior even though you are by far the weakest cowards." His tone went from calm to seething, hissing anger.

"I'm sorry you think that. I'm going to have to clean this salve off you. Think you can handle that, or am I too barbaric and distrusting?"

He looked back at her, a flicker of surprise in his expression that was gone in an instant. He dropped his gaze to the wet cloth. He seemed to think it over, then said, "I will allow it."

Charlotte went slow so as to not startle him as she gingerly wiped the shiny topical salve off his skin, starting with his arm. The tension in his body began to disappear, and his breathing slowed as his anger calmed. He watched her quietly with narrowed eyes that looked more tired now than suspicious.

"I'm sorry you think that about my kind," Charlotte said, cleaning up one arm. "I'm not going to lie to you and say we are all good. But we aren't all bad either. Some of us do bad things. Some of us regret them. Some don't. Some want to do better—be better—try to make a difference. It's easier said than done."

He studied her through half-lidded eyes. "Is that why you learned to treat otherkin? You want to make some kind of difference?"

She slowed in her washing. "Yeah, I guess it is."

"Not to learn in order to get inside us and see how we tick?"

Charlotte clenched her jaw. "No. Not that."

He stared at her as if waiting to find fault in her. When she didn't expose any, he relaxed again.

He remained silent as she cleaned his arms, then moved to his legs. At one point, his eyes closed—not just the inner lids this time but the outer as well, as if he were just taking a moment of meditation.

Or maybe to enjoy your touch, said a voice at the back of her mind. Charlotte nearly laughed out loud. Yeah, right.

As she came to his torso, however, she paused. He growled softly again, almost like a low purr. But he didn't look at her angrily or distrustingly. Eyes still closed, he looked more on the verge of sleep than anything.

Maybe he was going back into himself. Into that near-sleep state. Her hand drifted down his chest to his stomach, seeing his scales glisten. It really was an utter shame he'd be so scarred.

There was a soft hiss of breath as her hand drew lower, gently dabbing across his hip. She didn't bother to look up at him. If he didn't like it, he could tell her to stop.

When she was done cleaning off as much of the salve as she could, she threw away the wipes.

"You're healing really fast," she commented. She picked up the clean, elastic gauze and began separating it into pieces. "But I want to wrap your hands and knee, since there is still bruising and tendonitis...that's swelling in your hands." She glanced at his face when he didn't respond. He still had his eyes closed.

Taking it as an invitation to dress him, Charlotte lifted his right hand. He was warming, she could tell; the heat radiated off his body, from his hand to hers. Gently, she wrapped his hand, twining it around his wrist to the lower half of his long fingers.

"Why are you being nice to me?"

Charlotte looked up at him in surprise. His sleepy gaze fixed on her again.

"I'm sorry?"

"You're doing all this...more than they have asked you. Why?"

Charlotte turned back to her work. "It's my job to give the best care possible to those who need it."

"A lie," he whispered. "You could have been done with me that first time. You could have agreed that I should be placed back in that glass cage on the wall. You are stalling. What do you want from me?"

She taped his hand, then started on the next. "I don't want anything."

"Another lie."

"I'm not lying." She stopped, fixing him with a sharp glare. "I'm not. I don't want anything from you. I just..."

His eyes narrowed to mere slits. "What?"

Charlotte shook her head. "Nothing. It's nothing. I just want to take the greatest possible measure so that you don't die."

He snorted softly. "I wouldn't worry about that."

Right. She wrapped his other hand slowly, knowing he still watched her. "You won't be treated kindly on Fargis," she said after a short silence. "They want to keep you weak for some reason."

"They fear me."

"Of course."

His head tilted back. "They know if I gain too much of my strength, I won't hesitate to escape."

Charlotte shrugged. "Yes. That's likely."

"Still. There is no reason for you to help me more, is there?"

She frowned. "No, I guess not."

His hand curled around hers in a sudden tight grip. Firm, not enough to hurt, but only to hold her still. She froze, her heart jolting a little in her chest.

"You pity me. That's why you treat me like you do, unlike the others." His eyes glowed like twin flames, burning into her. "Even though I could kill you. And the other humans. I could rip you and them all apart. Your soft flesh stripped from bone. I could taste your blood in my mouth. How sweet it must be."

He was trying to scare her, she knew. And it was working.

Charlotte didn't try to tug away. She locked eyes with him, trying to keep the shaking out of her voice. "Yes. You could do that."

He stared back at her for a moment longer, though it felt like forever, then he slowly loosened his grip. "Don't pity me."

Charlotte straightened, her hand tightening around the gauze still in her hands. "All right," she said. "I won't." Not wanting him to see the fear in her eyes, she shifted over to his bad leg and quickly wrapped it, cinching it tight. When she finished, she turned back to him. "But I won't treat you like an animal either."

"It's what I expect," he said, "from your kind."

Charlotte studied him, then went over to her kit and tossed the extra gauze inside. Her eyes drifted down underneath the table, and she saw the vrisha's leather-like pants lying there, where they must have been kicked aside. Thankfully not thrown away by the twins. She'd forgotten about them herself. She leaned down and grabbed them, setting them on the table.

Without a word, she tapped at the controls on the tank and watched as Prisoner Zero was laid back down, the metal slab beneath him sinking.

His eyes never fell from her face, as if he expected some kind of emotion from her but couldn't find it.

"Be ready to be disappointed," she said without breaking his gaze. She reached for the lid, then closed it down to shut him within.

CHAPTER SIX

Axrel

The woman was vexing to say the least. Even after his attempt to scare her, to tell her he didn't want her sympathy, she still came to him, helped him, as if the near threat hadn't fazed her.

He knew she feared him at some level (everyone does, no matter how hard they try not to), she was just too stubborn to show it.

When he lay in the dark, he thought of her. At first, it was mere suspicion. Surely, there was some ploy. She wanted something from him. She had to. Humans didn't go out of their way for nothing. They wanted something in return.

But she claimed she was only doing her job. Either she was lying to him (and a good liar at that), or she was already gaining something. The more he thought it over, the more he wondered if that something was him. Just him. She wanted to help him because she'd never experienced a vrisha. It was her chance to examine one up close. To actually work on one like no human doctor had ever done before.

If it had been any other doctor, he would have been pissed even by that possibility. He didn't like the idea of aiding them in anything or giving them such an opportunity. But, for whatever reason, he couldn't feel anger toward her. He would have almost said it was because she seemed too innocent. And in a way, she was. But she was also much more brave and exceedingly more caring than the others.

It wasn't just that, however. Even just being brave didn't warrant respect. And her caring nature could be a front for some other goal. It was something else. Something he wasn't completely clear on. He wanted to believe she was just a very good faker. But, in truth, she came off more genuine and honest than any human he'd ever met. He found it hard to see any kind of sinister side in her. Any sort of dishonesty. Somehow, as absurd as it appeared even to him, she wanted to help him.

And he, despite how little he trusted humans, began to think she would have done it even if she had nothing to gain from it at all. Which was...insane. It confused him and at times even made him more suspicious.

Yes, she was very vexing.

His mind turned her over, as if she were a puzzle he needed to solve. He thought he'd encounter enough humans to understand them all well enough. Everything he had told her before, he considered the truth. That humans were an inferior, barbaric race who couldn't be trusted.

Yet, when he had said those things to her, she hadn't gotten mad or defensive. She didn't agree with him, of course, but she didn't turn from him either, or shut him away to silence him. Or call him a monster, which she surely must think he was. She listened and heard. Talked to him like any other person. She didn't treat him like he was a beast, to be ignored.

It was strange lying in the dark, thinking—almost obsessing, really —over some human. He should be thinking about what he was going to do when he got out. About how he would find and kill those who had betrayed him. Those *traitors*.

Rage rose in him again as he contemplated everything that had happened and everything he hoped would come to be. He focused on that pain and fury—until he heard soft steps just outside the tank, and the thoughts instantly scattered into oblivion as the woman's image returned.

Then the steps dissolved away, and there was silence again. No, perhaps it wasn't her. Just another soldier walking by. Sometimes, they came to take a peek at him. Other times, they passed by without a word.

It was no matter. It was silly of him to anticipate her return. Better to rest.

And he did for some time. He even dreamed. Of black blood on white snow. Of teeth and talons sinking into skin and dark shadows embraced by fire. Of a soft hand on his shoulder and a whispered promise of life.

When he woke, he smelled that flowery scent again. Her scent lingered, confusing him, until the lid above him opened, spilling in the light.

Her face hovered over him for a moment, and her lips curled. "Morning," she said in her human tongue. He stared up at her, too focused by the sparkle in her eyes to respond. They were a deep blue in color, like the gems one sometimes found in deep caves on Tryth. Around the iris was nothing but white. They were odd, he decided. But...not awful to look at.

He watched her with his usual caution as he was lifted up and seated at an angle. She turned and went to her bag on the table beside his tank and began rifling through it. "Hope you slept well because I didn't. I don't know how anyone can on these hunks of metal."

His eyes drew down to her hand where she pulled out an item from the bag, wrapped in some kind of cloth. She took a chair and sat down near to him but not close enough to where he could touch her, he noted. She too was still cautious. Smart of her.

"Where are your helpers?" he asked, his eyes shifting around. Usually those two other men stayed nearby when she worked.

"It's early. They probably aren't even awake." She began to

unwrap whatever was in the cloth. "And I've mostly relieved them of any help at this point." Another scent drifted into his nose as she unraveled the cloth and tore a piece of what he knew now to be dried meat. The spicy aroma hit him, and he immediately began to salivate. By *Veradis*, he hadn't had well-cooked meat in forever.

She held up the piece to him. "Hungry?"

She knew he must be, and yet he didn't want to take from her so easily. His nostrils flared, but he turned his head away.

"It's good, I promise. See?" She ripped off a portion with her tiny white teeth and chewed slowly.

"I told you not to give me sympathy, and yet you want to feed me," he growled.

"I'm not giving you sympathy. I'm giving you one last good meal before you're thrown onto Fargis and will likely never have anything this good ever again."

He glanced back at her. "That's sympathy."

"No, it's tradition."

He gave her a confused look. "Tradition?"

She rolled her shoulders in a shrug. "Well, a very old, mostly ancient tradition now. But back on my home planet, Earth, when prisoners were sentenced to death, they got one last good meal before they died. Usually they could pick whatever they liked. Steak, seafood, ketchup and pancakes—you dont' know that one, but trust me when I say it's gross. They got to enjoy something one last time."

"I'm not going to my death," he stated matter of factly.

She took another small bite. "Maybe not. But I've been looking into Fargis when I can't sleep." She chewed the meat carefully, then swallowed. "It might as well be a death sentence. The planet is mostly islands surrounded by an unforgiving sea. It's always dark there, the thick storm clouds covering the sky." She locked eyes with him. "They hardly bother to keep the prisoners locked up. They roam freely within the grounds and therefore they fight—they kill. They...eat each other."

He looked away, annoyed. "If I must survive, then I will. I fear no one. Nothing."

"Even if many of these prisoners ganged up on you? Beat you?"

He turned back to her, stunned. She was eyeing the cuts over his body. Did she know?

"They wouldn't be able to overtake me," he said, confident still.

Her eyes lifted again to his face. "Three hundred to one is terrible odds. Even for you."

His fangs slipped from his upper lip. "You'd be amazed."

"Maybe." She offered him the meat again, and he turned away. "Suit yourself." She got up, and to his great, shocked frustration, he saw her moving toward a waste container.

"You would waste good meat like that?" he said, perplexed and troubled.

"I ate my portion. This was yours. But since you don't want it..." She opened the container top.

Damnable female.

"Stop."

She paused and looked at him squarely, her furry brow arching.

He growled softly, baring his teeth. "Come back."

He took her expression for smug as she sauntered back over. She sat back down, sliding her chair a little closer, near to his shoulder. She stared at him as she tore a piece off, then, with it between two fingers, began to reach toward his mouth.

Was she really going to risk feeding him like that? Careless. She trusted too much. He could slice her fingers in half with just the edge of one fang.

She stopped just out of reach, then shook her head and smiled. "Not likely." She grabbed a pair of tongs beside the table and transferred the meat from her delicate fingers to the metal ones. With the meat gripped with the tongs, she lifted her arm the rest of the way, letting the meat touch at his lips.

His eyes narrowed on her—clever girl—and he snapped up the meat in one swift strike. She flinched back despite herself but recovered quickly. As he tasted the sweet, spicy meat on his tongue, she tore another piece and took it up with the tongs.

"How is it?" she asked, casually.

He let the meat slide down his throat before he said, "Good for one last decent meal."

She laughed a little, the sound surprisingly pleasant. "I'm glad." She brought the other piece up to his mouth. "Not as sweet as my blood, though, I'm willing to bet," she said in a strange, almost bitter tone.

"I don't know." He took the other piece and chewed thoroughly before swallowing. "I would need to taste and see."

A shadow passed her gaze, though her smile remained. She shook her head. "Too bad. I guess you'll have to leave it to your imagination."

She offered him a few more tender bites, and he took them hesitantly. Deep down, whether he cared to admit it or not, he was grateful once more to her. The meat lifted his spirits and made him feel stronger.

She was playing a dangerous game, allowing him to regain what strength he had lost.

When he'd had enough, she put the remaining meat away, claiming to save it for later. She took up the container of water next and let him drink his fill.

"You're odd," he said after, when she was packing some of her things away.

"Am I? I always thought I was pretty normal."

"Normal is a human staying far from me, not nursing me like a newborn fledgling," he stated.

She laughed. "I don't think you know what normal in a human is."

"Maybe not."

She closed up her bag, then turned to face him. She seemed to be hesitating on something, but he couldn't gauge what it was. She stared at him for a long, hard moment, and he did the same.

"Why did you learn about us?" he asked. "When you were on

Terra Centra?" Suddenly, he was curious. And doubt about her intentions began to eat at him.

She blinked at him, as if she had been woken from a trance. "I wanted to understand you."

"That's all?" he asked, doubt growing.

She shook her head. "As a part of my studies, I was required to take a class on one of the uncommons—that's what they called the less seen races. Nillium, fyrien, vrisha, drogin...to have better knowledge of one specifically, in case of some rare circumstances where they need medical attention."

He tilted his head at her. "And you picked vrisha."

"Yes."

"Even though your chances of ever seeing one let alone treating one were a billion to one."

She gave him a timid sort of smile. "Not the worst odds after all, considering the situation."

He grunted in agreement.

Her smile faded. "Truthfully, I was fascinated by the vrisha. I had read all of Dr. Hart's journals and data. You know of her, I'm sure."

"There isn't a vrisha who doesn't at this point," he said dryly.

"I was intrigued by the vrisha's power, their astounding survival and hunter instincts. It's not just a mere rumor when everyone says they are the galaxy's top predator."

He felt a sense of pride swelling in him. "Because we are."

"Though I'd counter to say the fyrien and even nillium are formidable foes."

The pride sank away and was replaced by bitterness. "The vrisha's true foe are themselves," he said with a hiss. "But yes...there are many others who we must be cautious of."

She said nothing. He studied her face, her expression appearing worried. She was hesitant again, before she spoke. "I want to know. Can anything change your mind about us? About humans and the alliance?"

His eyes met hers and didn't look away as he said, "No."

She nodded her head, as if expecting his answer. She went back to her bag and opened it, then took out a dark-red fabric. He recognized the make as vrishan.

"These were the pants you wore when I was first treating you." She held them up for him to see. They were no longer ripped and dirtied. "It took some time to find a clothing machine on this ship to mend them. I figure you'd like to have the extra protection when you're on Fargis. It's not a warm world."

"I would like them, yes," he said with honesty. Though he had no issue with his nakedness, the air was cold, and the scales around his abdomen were finer, more vulnerable than he cared to admit.

"I thought maybe I could hide it in your pod somewhere, so someone would allow you to put them on when they placed you in a holding. But knowing these soldiers, they wouldn't bother with remembering or care to let you cover yourself."

His eyes dropped to the pants, then back to her. "Probably true."

"So, that means I'd need to put them on for you. Which means I'm going to have to unclasp your legs."

He understood what she was trying to say. And why she was so worried. "I swear not to kick you."

"If you do, you know what I'll have to do," she warned.

Put him under, he got that. "Yes."

She moved around to the front of the tank toward his legs. "I need to do it quickly. And you need to be still."

"Fine."

He felt her loosen the clasps at his legs. Thankfully, kelva—the fabric of which the clothing was made—was durable in most situations and stretched to fit many sizes. She placed each foot through one pant leg, then began to slip it upward, struggling a little when she came to his thighs. There was a slit in the back for his tail, and it took her some time to slip it through.

Throughout the ordeal, she had made herself vulnerable to his attack. He could have broken his promise easily and thrown out a leg or cut her with his tail. But he didn't. He was still strapped down at his upper half, for one. Though he could have hurt her badly despite that fact, he had no desire to do so. Maybe it was an honor thing. That's what he told himself.

"There." She fastened the tie to tighten the fabric around his waist. She gave him a quick glance, then set the clamps back over his legs. "Better?"

He bowed his head. "Better. Though I could do without the restraints."

"Yes, I'm sure you would." He thought he caught a flicker of something—disappointment?—in her gaze, then it was gone. "You'll have to go back in the pod soon. There isn't much more I can do for you."

"I figured as much." Suddenly, he wished she were closer. He had an insane urge to touch her, to trail his fingers through the lock of golden-brown hair that had fallen across her shoulder. But she didn't come closer, and he brushed the desire quickly away. Instead, he tried to shift in place, hoping to sit up better, but was unable to. "I can't deny you've impressed me, human. One of very few. Perhaps if I feel inclined, I'll speak of the great Dr. Lockey who revived me."

She smiled, then laughed. "*Lockley* not Lockey. You overheard the men call me that?"

He tilted his head in a shrug. "I overheard many things."

She nodded, then, after a small pause, said," Charlotte. You can just call me Charlotte. That's my first name."

"*Shharlot,*" he repeated, not exactly as she had. She laughed again, and he still liked the sound. He felt a heat stirring in his belly and in his chest. An odd reaction but he didn't think much of it. "Axrel," he said. "That is mine."

Her eyes appeared to brighten. "Axrel."

He grunted. He liked the sound of his name on her lips too. It didn't bother him that she should know it. What did it matter at this point? Once off the ship, he would never see her again. But at least he knew her name and so could remember the woman who saved him. The only human who cared. She certainly had proved him wrong in that small way. She would be his little secret. He'd keep her in his thoughts.

She closed the distance between them and pressed the unseen display so that he sank down into the tank. "I will be there when you are transferred," she promised. She looked as if she wanted to say more but didn't. Perhaps it was for the better.

CHAPTER SEVEN

Charlotte

Charlotte took the stairs up to the bridge, knowing that was where she would find Leon and the other officers. They would want to know her work was finished. She could do little more for the vrisha. His vitals were stable, the fractures were already healing fast, and the scabbing and peeling of his skin meant new skin was forming. By the time they got to Fargis, Prisoner Zero would be strong enough at least to survive.

No, not Prisoner Zero. Axrel.

Charlotte smiled, if sadly. She did what she could for him. Even if he was an enemy of the alliance, she felt there was some good in him. He could have attacked her before but hadn't, despite his threat. He could have refused to speak to her, spat at her, called her derogatory names. But he hadn't. She would be sorry to see him thrown on that wasteland of a planet. Perhaps if things had been different...

She stepped onto the landing and across to the door where a lone soldier stood guard. She showed her ID to him, and he nodded, allowing her to enter.

Inside, co-pilots and navigators sat at a long terminal facing a set of wide windows looking out into nothing but stars. At one side, Leon and his officers stood around a display table, the holographic image of a map in front of them.

"Doctor," Leon greeted as she joined them. "We were just wondering how things were going down there."

"They're fine," she said.

"So, the prisoner is stable?"

"As stable as can be expected."

"Good, that's good." He nodded. He leaned against the display, blue light glowing across his face. "He should be ready for transfer then?"

"Soon, yes." A sudden shiver ran down her spine, and she glanced over to see Payton fixing her with a cold glare.

"Don't need to feed him again, I hope?" he asked.

"No. I think I gave him all I could at this point," she said, glaring back.

"Commander, we have a response back from Warden Cain," a young private interrupted from beside the terminal.

"Play the message," Leon ordered.

The map before them disappeared, and the image of a man took its place. He was no older than Payton, who looked to be in his thirties, only the dark circles under his eyes and gaunt paleness of his face made him appear as old as Leon.

"Commander Leon," he began. "We are prepared for your arrival and ready to receive the prisoners. However, due to some unforeseen circumstances, we cannot allow you to dock at the main landing port. Please see the map I've sent in regards to where you should land instead. The prisoners will be transferred in the same fashion. When your ship is in atmosphere, we will guide you at communication controls. Until then, safe travels." His image faded, and a different map appeared.

"What do you suppose that's about?" Officer Leslie asked.

Leon rubbed at his chin, his eyes meeting hers briefly before looking away. He tapped at the map and brought Fargis in closer until a marker popped up on a large island near to the size of the United Kingdom. At least if Charlotte gauged it right.

"They want us to land within the prison sector itself? Even across the shield barriers?" Payton said, looking confused.

"Where do you usually land?" Charlotte asked, curious.

"Here." Leon pointed to a smaller island almost touching the larger. "The port in and out is located on this small island. Prisoners are then transported either by sea ship or by air ship; there is no bridge, in case of extreme circumstances where there is a break."

"More like impossible," Payton said. "The walls and barriers along with round the clock guards keep any from possibly escaping."

Leon shrugged. "Anything is possible, Officer Payton. It's good to use precaution in any case."

"So, the warden wants you to land the ship within the actual prison?" Charlotte said, staring at the marker on the map.

"No, just an emergency dock near the facility," Leon answered. "Right beside it, in fact. Within the city."

Charlotte's brows rose. "The city?"

"The central base where the prison workers and guards live. It's a small city but secure," he said. "There are working sectors for prisoners and guard stations scattered around the prison also."

"What exactly do they have the prisoners working on?"

"Whatever they can to keep them busy. Mining mostly, but some field work and factories."

So, exploiting them for slave work. No surprise there, even if laws on Earth forbade it. But on other worlds, such laws didn't stand. And even if they did, they didn't extend to non-human folk.

Charlotte thought about Axrel working away in some mine, his marred skin dirtied even more by dust and grime. Her heart sank a little at the thought.

If it was in her to ask whether they had any counseling and suitable medical treatment in the prison, she would, but she already knew the answer. She could imagine their laughter.

Leon sighed as he blinked at the map. "Well, we'll deal with landing when we get into Fargis' orbit. The dock is big enough for it, but transport procedures are going to change."

"Commander, a moment of your time?" called a pilot seated at the front terminal. "We got a few obstructions ahead."

Leon put up his hand to his officers to wait for him, then nodded to Charlotte before turning away.

Payton crossed his arms and looked over the map, shaking his head. "I'm going to try to call one of the head officers on Fargis. See what this is about." He left for one of the communication consoles, leaving her and Officer Leslie alone.

"You guys have been doing this for a while, I take it?" Charlotte asked, only partially curious but mainly wanting to study the map a little more. There were markers indicating the prison, the city base, the guard stations, and the working sectors Leon had mentioned. She had a similar map downloaded on her ISpad, but it had shown nothing more than the prison and the main dock. This map in front of them now, she noticed, had other markers Leon hadn't spoken of.

"If you mean transporting prisoners to Fargis, Leon and Payton have been for several years. This is only my second," Leslie said. "The first time being a few years ago, before I was placed within the elite tactical units and RAID duty."

Charlotte observed the map, only half-listening, nodding her head. "So, you went on some heavy missions, I take it?"

"Some of the heaviest. Half these prisoners were taken by my team, in fact."

Charlotte tore her eyes away from the map to look at him. "You mean you arrested them?"

He shrugged, crossing his arms. "More or less. Or caught them in the middle of a run, whether drugs or other illegal hideouts. Some were from rescue missions."

Charlotte frowned. "What do you mean? Rescuing them?"

He glanced back at her and laughed deep. "Not them, hell no. Rescuing others from them. Citizens and the like."

"Oh." She looked back down at the map. "So, like the drogin, when he attacked those people on the freightship."

"Exactly. Him, the lygin in the pod next to him, and the vrisha, among others."

Her eyes shot back up to him. "You were there when he got caught?" she said in a low voice.

"I was there for all of them."

"Right, but...the vrisha. You saw what happened?"

He nodded once, his expression grave. "Yeah, I was there. Horrible stuff. Some of the worst I've ever seen."

She wondered if she should even ask. But she had to—needed to—know. "Will you tell me what happened?"

His brow furrowed. "I wouldn't want to scare you with any of that."

"I'm a big girl. I've seen and heard my share of awful things."

He looked her over, his forehead wrinkling below his bald head. "It was in one of our manufacturing towns on one of the trade worlds. Cold as hell, farther from the others. Called Obilis Zero. Not much to the place except that it was used as one of the main ports for transporting various materials needed for our ships and...other necessary items which we traded."

Charlotte didn't need to ask. Weapons, tactical gear, or any of the like were probable items she could assume. The town was clearly used to trade, house, and ship such materials for the military or other Earth-based companies.

"And that's where he attacked?"

Leslie's gaze darkened. "Where *they* attacked."

Charlotte's throat tightened. "The Blood Guard?"

"A whole pack. Destroyed more than half the town. The fires could be seen from the next town over, more than twenty miles away. We got the distress call, but it was too late. I'll never forget, the smell of iron was so strong that day it made some of my team gag. The bodies were near unrecognizable. Men, women, children. A mass slaughter."

A shiver ran down her spine, and her stomach twisted. "No survivors?"

"Few. Those who did will never be the same."

Charlotte stared off toward the window. She tried to stop the thoughts from coming but couldn't. She saw Axrel, slicing through an innocent man with his powerful taloned fingers, saw him cutting down screaming women and children with his mighty tail. Saw him against the fires, roaring into the night.

"How did you capture him then?" she asked, barely hearing herself. "How did you catch Prisoner Zero?"

He was silent for a long moment, and Charlotte forced her gaze back over to him.

"The pack had fled when our forces moved in, toting our biggest weapons. The vrisha were there to terrorize, not fight a battle. But Prisoner Zero...he must have gotten too cocky and stayed or got left behind."

"Then how did he come to be so injured?" Charlotte said, still trying to understand. "He had no bullets in him, no signs of being shot at or burned by throwers."

"Truthfully," he glanced away, troubled. "Someone or something else got to him before we did."

Charlotte's eyes widened. "He was already in that state when you found him?"

Leslie nodded. "Can't say what happened. Didn't care to mull it over, to be honest. He was there, he was one of them. Maybe someone was trying to protect the town, and he got into it with them. Someone actually equal to their strength. Who knows."

"So, you didn't torture him?" she said, still with an air of suspicion.

Leslie laughed. "Didn't have to. He was already in such bad shape and likely in a lot of pain. All we had to do was dig a finger into the wounds, and any prisoner would be talking."

"And you tried?" She didn't bother keeping the anger from her voice.

"We did. But if you know anything about the vrisha, as you claim to, you know they are tough bastards. He didn't talk. Didn't move. We figured he was almost too far gone to tell us anything yet."

"Yet." Charlotte let out a breath of air. "But when he's on Fargis...?"

"If he can tell us where to find the Blood Guard, you better believe we will do all we can to get it out of him."

Right. So, they hadn't tortured him like she had thought. But they were planning to. All her work, just so they could hurt him some more.

But maybe she shouldn't care. Now that she knew the truth. Now that she knew what kind of monster he was.

Her emotions were a whirlwind inside of her that she couldn't yet grasp. She should hate him then. Feel guilty for giving him far more attention than he deserved. And yet a small part of her still wanted to believe he wasn't completely evil. That she could find that better piece of him.

"Just be thankful one of them will pay," Leslie said. "And trust me, he will."

Charlotte didn't respond. Didn't know how to. "I should get back," she said. "Tell Commander Leon I'll be down below." She glanced at the map one last time, seeing the prison, then turned away and left.

She returned to the high security room and found Michal there. Most of the medical equipment was gone now. Only her kit and computer sitting on the metal table beside Axrel's tank remained. As she made it down the ramp, she could see Michal had the lid open to the tank and was hovering over Axrel. He reached in and ripped at the bandages on Axrel's leg. Some of the torn gauze was already piled on the floor.

"What are you doing?" Charlotte cried as she rushed toward him.

Michal looked over, and his expression made her almost pause. Almost.

"This is new gauze. The best we have." He shook it in his fist, then threw it on the ground. Then he picked up one of the heat pads. "And this is meant for the medical bay only," he hissed. "You snuck in and took these things without permission. Giving it to this fucking creature." He smacked the pad on the table. "You're going to be reported for stealing and overstepping your treatment."

Charlotte stopped a couple of feet from him. Her eyes glanced over at the tank, at Axrel lying inside motionless, then back at the medic. "I didn't steal. The ID card worked on the bay door which meant I was given access. As for overstepping my treatment, I did what I felt was necessary. If you want to report me, go ahead. I won't stop you." She picked up the gauze on the ground and went around him to set it on the table. "But I think you are done here. I don't require your assistance any longer, and if I see you messing with my patient again, I will report *you*. And something tells me Commander Leon will consider my issues over yours."

Michal's mouth twisted into a snarl. "You're just one of them, aren't you?" he said, eyes flashing.

"I don't follow," Charlotte said dryly.

"You studied these things, specifically. That's why they asked you here. You treat it more like a sad pet that needs delicate care and mending than the dirty criminal that it is." His mouth tightened into a wide sneer. "You feel sorry for it, don't you?"

Charlotte lifted her chin and refused to move even as he stepped closer. "You're like that other doctor who got with one of them. You think you can mend this one in more ways than physical. And then maybe after, it will give you a good alien fucking."

She nearly slapped him. Instead, she placed her hand in the pocket of her uniform. She would remain calm even if inside she felt the heat of anger rising. "You're right, I do feel sorry for him. But you're mistaken if you think there's anything beyond that."

His eyes told her he didn't believe her. But she could care less what this man thought. "Did they tell you what he did?" he said. "About what happened on the planet where they found him. Hm?"

Charlotte didn't turn away from him when she said, "Yes. I know."

"And yet you still wanna help him out?"

She let her eyes drop this time. "My treatment is finished. There's nothing more I can do, whether I'd like to or not." She looked back at him. "But I'm not sorry for doing my job the best way I can. Criminal or no."

He nodded his head, as if he expected as much. "He'd kill you the first chance he got regardless of your treatment. Just so you know. And he'd like it too, I'll bet. He'd eat your insides right up and then go on about his day."

Charlotte wanted to roll her eyes and sigh deeply. "Maybe so, but that isn't the point," she snapped. "I was brought here by your commander to fix him up. To keep him alive so he can be thrown on Fargis and tortured. So, if anything, maybe you should be congratulating me. Not only will he stay alive, but he'll be well enough to know the agony of getting ripped apart yet again by your superiors."

Michal actually seemed to consider her argument. He laughed. "Good point. Even though I know that's not why you gave him better treatment than he needed." He took another step closer, nearly touching her. "But listen. You don't need to try to get attention from one of them. It's pointless. Seriously, he'd eat you before even considering being your friend. But if you're that desperate and lonely," his hand came up, his fingers trailing down a lock of her hair, "you know where to find me."

Charlotte grabbed his wrist and flung it away. "Get out."

He laughed again, taking a few steps back. "I'll even tape a picture of one of them over my face, so you can at least have a visual." He turned from her. "See you later, doc."

She watched him go, her hands turning to fists beside her. It was all so absurd. Leon had brought her here to fix him, but all the others hated her for it. All because, what? She was a little nicer than she needed to be? Ridiculous.

And she really did mean what she said. Criminal or no, she wasn't about to be careless in her work all because Axrel was...who he was. Yes, she'd been a little more careful and considerate, but what did that matter? Why be cruel because of someone else's cruelty? Why stoop to their level? She was better than that.

And she still believed, deep down, that if Axrel saw her kindness, it would show that not all humans were the same. Maybe it was pointless. But maybe it wasn't.

Regardless, he was going to be punished, wasn't he? For his crimes. Justice would be served.

CHAPTER EIGHT

Axrel

He listened to their conversation intently, keeping deathly still and silent, until the male left. He got lost by some of the words, but he understood enough. He had remained calm, even when he had felt the man tearing at the bandages on his leg, tearing away Charlotte's work. It would have done no good to open his eyes and snap at him. It would have only gotten him forced into the pod sooner.

But the conversation had bothered him. Not just how the man had talked to her, and the awareness that he was to be tortured on Fargis, though even that was of no surprise. He focused on the fact that Charlotte knew something now about what had happened on Obilis Zero. And by the way her voice wavered a little, he imagined it deeply disturbed her.

What did they say? He could only guess. Whatever it was, he wondered what she must think of him now. He suspected she had been blissfully unaware of those events before, but the humans would tell it like they saw it. For their own benefit.

Perhaps it was for the best. This strange little occurrence between them couldn't last. They were meant to distrust one another.

He told himself this, yet he still felt a layer of ice slipping around his heart. He opened his eyes, wanting to see her, wanting to see the cold hate in her stare that must have now settled there. She was still standing by the tank, only she was looking away at something else, or maybe at nothing. But there was no anger he could tell. Her head was bowed and her eyes shadowed. She didn't look angry. She looked...sad.

He should say something, should tell her the boy was right. That she should stay away from him. But the words refused to leave his throat. She didn't need to be told. She was tough, he could tell. And she wasn't stupid. She didn't need to be told.

Her head turned, and she saw him watching her. They stared at each other for a long moment, neither able to look away.

Charlotte reacted first. "I'm going to guess you heard all that?"

"Yes," he said.

She nodded her head. She took up the gauze on the table and, to his shock, began to rewrap his leg with it.

"Why are you—"

"There's no reason to waste it," she said, her eyes now focused on his leg. She wouldn't look at him now. He could hear the tension in her voice.

"They told you about what happened when they found me?" He wanted her to look at him, but she wouldn't.

"Yes."

He closed his eyes, trying to find what to say. He thought about asking her what story they told, but he didn't think it would matter. She spoke again before he could consider asking anyway.

"You warned me too, didn't you? And it's not like I couldn't have guessed. I know what the Blood Guard are about. I've heard about their attacks." She taped the bandage up, setting it almost exactly like before. "It only makes sense that you..."

"Look at me, Shharlotte."

She did, her eyes wide with wonder.

"I told you not to pity me. And now you understand why."

She frowned. "Fine. I don't, then. But I don't regret fixing you." She finished up and appeared ready to shut the lid on him but stopped. "I know this might mean nothing to you, but I'll wish better for you. I have no hate for you. I only hope maybe someday you'll remember we're not all out to harm you. Some of us want better."

He wasn't sure how to respond, so he didn't. She started to lower the lid but paused again.

"Can I ask one thing? Just one."

"Yes," he said.

She looked hesitant, then said, "I know you have no reason to promise anything to me. But you said you were grateful for me saving your life. Is that still true?"

He wouldn't lie. "It is."

"Then would you honor a favor in return?"

He looked at her curiously, then bowed his head. "If it is possible for me to do so."

"A life for a life, that's all I ask. If you do escape—and I'm not in any way uncertain that you can't—will you spare a life in the process? Even if it's just a soldier or a worker, will you?"

He blinked at her, shocked. "Spare one?"

"Or all of them if that's what my aid is worth. But even just one. Even from you. Would you?"

He stared at her for a long moment, then felt himself dip his head. Her face relaxed a little, and her eyes brightened. "Thank you," she whispered.

The lid closed down on him, and he let the darkness sink in. He thought over what he could have told her, but there was no explaining himself. Nothing that could have painted him in some better light. Not even for her.

Because he had been with them. With his brothers and sisters. He had followed them. He was responsible too, no matter how everything had played out.

* * *

He slept for some time. Afterward, he lay for many hours, wondering about Charlotte and their conversations. He didn't think he'd see her again. Not after their last talk. He wished he understood why he felt disappointed by it. It should be no surprise to him. But for whatever reason, he would have liked to have parted on better terms. Maybe that was why he agreed to her favor. To not have to see the look of disappointment in her own face and have it be the last.

He wondered why he hadn't just ignored her or why he talked to her at all. He theorized it was because he hadn't expected...her. Hadn't expected a human to talk to him like a friend. Though they barely knew each other. It had been so strange and so different from what he expected that he couldn't have helped saying something to her.

But then he didn't know many humans. He only ever saw their fear and apprehension. Even she had some fear. But she had pushed past her fear to engage with him. And not in a hostile, violent manner. That's what had surprised him. She had put her hands on him to heal him without a second thought. Even when she knew he was a threat.

If he wasn't about to be caged and thrown onto some hellish planet...if he weren't hellbent on revenge...maybe things could have been different.

Maybe she could have gotten through to him more.

But as it were, he only had her favor to honor. A life for a life.

He heard footsteps nearby and woke to them, hoping to smell that flowery, familiar scent. To his disappointment, he smelled the bitter tang of iron and dirt.

The lid opened, and through his thin lids, he could see the shape of a man. He stifled a hiss, assuming it was that same male from before, come to tear off the bandages again.

But no, there was something different about this one. He was calmer, quieter. The other mumbled and cursed a lot. This one held less fear of him. He was more collected.

He heard something drop on the table next to him, then the snapping of gloves.

"You there?" came a voice, smaller, with a static tone.

The shape of the man lifted his arm to his mouth. "Yeah, I'm here."

"He's out?"

"Obviously. He's been sedated since he's been in the tank."

"You got five minutes. Guard change at the stairs. Make it quick."

"Fine." He dropped his hand, then shuffled around for a moment. Axrel watched his shape closely, remaining still.

The man's hand touched him, gripping his shoulder. Something sharp sliced across his forearm, digging into the scales of his skin. Pain shot up his arm, but he hardly noticed. He was focused intently on what this man was doing to him. It only took him a second to realize it was a knife digging into his skin, and the man was extracting one of his scales.

He was taking pieces of his skin. And Axrel didn't have to think far as to why. He could imagine the price each of his scales went for.

"Don't forget we need one of the spikes too," demanded the small, static voice.

"I know, shut up." The man's hand lifted from him, and he moved toward Axrel's head. He could feel the man hesitating before he fumbled for some other tool, then quickly grasped Axrel's shoulder, letting his head fall to one side. Something burned at the back of his neck as the man sawed at one his spikes.

Rage filled him. How dare this human take something from him. His own flesh. Experiments flashed into his mind. Of his own kind lying on beds. Pieces of them. Samples. They were taking samples.

The man's arm holding his shoulder was too close. And he was going to regret it. Charlotte appeared in his mind for an instant, but he couldn't stop himself. He saw red.

He woke fully, then snapped his head around, his teeth sinking into the man's flesh. Blood filled his mouth, and the man screamed.

The blood was bitter. Not so very sweet, he'd bet, as...

The man cried and pulled at his arm, and in turn, Axrel tugged his head back, ripping flesh from the bone. Blood poured down one side of his jaw and down his neck, warm and bright. The man continued to scream, holding his arm with his other hand. He slipped and fell, tripping over some small container with a handle, the contents inside rolling out. Vials and glass jars. He crawled away, moaning in pain as blood splattered all across the dark floor.

Axrel watched him and knew what came next. The other men would come. He would be put out for a long time. When he came to, he'd be on Fargis for sure.

Only a few hours and he'd broken his promise. But, in his rage, he noted, this man's life wasn't worth saving. He'd live anyway. But he wouldn't touch Axrel or another like him again. He'd learn the price of a vrisha's skin wasn't worth the risk.

CHAPTER NINE

CHARLOTTE

There was a knock on her unit door. She hadn't been sleeping, rather researching on her ISpad, going through her files on the vrisha and the reports she'd made on Axrel.

She looked over some of the pictures she had taken with the surgical machine and some she'd shot when he was sleeping in the tank with her wristpad. She could easily see the difference. He looked less like a pile of shredded skin on bones and more like a recognizable being.

Despite her best efforts and knowing she'd accomplished her job with success, she still felt defeated about...well, everything. Sad at the circumstances and disappointed that she didn't have more time. Maybe she could have done more, could have understood Axrel better, tried to make him understand her.

She was sure that knock on the door was the end of the line. The timer had run down, and there was no more time left. They were going to transfer him to the pod. She had asked them to let her know when they were going to do it, so she could at least say goodbye. She might not have gotten to know him much, but he was still her patient, and she wanted to see the job done through to the end.

She got up and pressed her hand to the door, letting it slide open. A young private in security uniform with short dirty blond hair frowned at her, his green eyes bright and alert.

"Dr. Lockley, sorry to wake you," he started.

"It's all right, I wasn't asleep. Is it time for the transfer?" She craned her neck behind him and saw several men running down the hall. The lights above were flashing orange. "What's going on?"

"We need you in the medical bay immediately."

Charlotte frowned back at him. "What's happened?"

"No time." He stepped aside, waiting for her to exit the room.

It was good that she hadn't bothered to change out of her uniform yet. She looked back at her room, then stepped out into the hall, letting the door slide shut behind her.

She followed the young private down the passage and to the stairs. When they came to the medical bay, there were several soldiers standing by the doors. They gave her a cold stare as she walked by. As they entered the main medical room, staff were running from one side to the next as she saw Michal barking orders beside a gurney. She approached the gurney and saw Kale there, unconscious, eyes rolled back into his head, his face ashen. Her eyes trailed down his body and saw the bloodied arm wrapped in thick cloth.

"What happened?" she asked. Without a thought, she checked his pulse and his temperature. Both were abnormally low.

"What do you think?" Michal hissed. "Look at his arm and see for yourself."

Charlotte did just that. She carefully unwrapped the cloth and stared down at the torn arm, several long gashes going deep to the bone.

Her body turned to ice. Not because of the injury itself (she'd seen worse) but because by the shape of the wound, she could tell it was a bite mark. And she knew there was only one who could bite like that.

Her jaw tightened, and her throat constricted, but she didn't have time to ask how it was possible. He had lost a lot of blood. "He needs a blood transfusion and I need—"

"I've ordered the others to get everything ready," Michal said.

"Let's get him on the surgical table then."

Several minutes later, Kale had his arm cleaned and wrapped and was lying in one of the beds with an IV hooked to his arm. Charlotte gave him a small dose of a cell generating agent to help speed the process. Kale had awoken when they hooked him up but had barely moved. He eventually fell back asleep as Charlotte moved about the room, checking him over.

"It's impossible. How could the vrisha have bitten him?" Michal said, standing nearby. "He was sedated. And clamped down."

Charlotte shook her head but couldn't answer. She should have said something before. Warned them not to go near. She didn't think they would. But she still should have told them the vrisha was awake, and the dose of sedation no longer kept him under. She had been careless. And she had been a fool to think he wouldn't have attacked them unlike her.

And why had Kale been so close in the first place? She had told them the work was done. They had no reason to go near him.

She froze, her heart dropping to her stomach. They had to know now that he was awake. Which meant...

"I have to go. Watch him. If there are any signs of reaction, let me know." She turned and raced out of the medical bay with Michal calling after her.

When she got to the security level, there were soldiers everywhere. Guns out, waiting. That whole part of the ship was on lock-down, and it took a great deal of convincing to let her pass. When she finally made it down the ramp to the high-security chamber, she could see Leon with his officers and several other men, guns raised. Her eyes shot over to the tank, and it was closed shut. Red stained one side and dripped on the floor. There were little splatters everywhere, along with red footprints from the men walking.

Charlotte rushed to Leon who was speaking to his officers. When they saw her approach, Leon turned and quieted.

"I thought I ordered them to take you to the medical bay," Leon said, frowning.

"They did. Kale is recovering now." Charlotte eyed the tank behind him. "Is he...?"

"Tied down still. Had to shock him to get the lid shut." Leon gestured to Payton who held a taser gun in his hand. "We just pumped him with more sedative, hoping it will knock him out. We're just giving it some time."

Charlotte felt her chest tighten. *Dammit, no.*

It was as she'd feared. Though she was glad no one else was hurt, giving him more sedative meant he was...

"You shouldn't have done that. He was already given a near fatal dose," Charlotte said, trying to keep her voice from cracking. "He might be in a coma as we speak." She moved toward the tank, but he put out his hand to stop her.

"Too much of a risk for you to check, doc, I'm sorry."

"I guarantee by now there's no way he's—"

"If you want to check that badly," he said, calmly, "you can see his vitals from the monitor."

Charlotte pursed her lips but didn't protest. He put his hand down, and she walked over to the monitor beside the tank. She held her breath as she looked over Axrel's vitals.

His pulse was still stable, and his brain waves were still active. He wasn't in a coma yet, but he definitely was unconscious judging by the low energy waves.

"He's out. You should move him to the pod as soon as possible. And don't give him any more sedative."

"We'll pump him with drugs till he sleeps for a decade for all I care," Payton said, his grip tightening on his gun.

"Then you'll kill him."

"At this point, I couldn't give a shit."

Leon gave him a mean look, then turned back to his men. "Let's get this done quickly. Move," he ordered.

The men did as commanded. They stepped closer, guns still drawn, while Leslie came around with a strange device that looked like a muzzle. Another man had a pair of thick steel cuffs while two guards held strange guns with vapor spewing from the tips.

"What are those?" she asked.

"Iceshockers," Leon said.

Charlotte looked at him, mortified. "You mean to burn him with ice? You could give him frostbite."

"The cold is the only thing that might keep him at bay, Dr. Lockley, or would you prefer the electrical approach?"

Her mouth twisted, and she shook her head. "This is unnecessary. He's out."

"Then hopefully we won't have to use them."

The men circled the tank, and from the side, one soldier gripped the lid handle. He lifted it up, and instantly, the men aimed their guns toward the inside. Charlotte blew out a breath when she saw Axrel lying within, unmoving.

Leslie took up the metal muzzle and quickly secured it around Axrel's face. Then he stepped aside as the man with the cuffs reached down to free Axrel from the tank's restraints and transfer his hands and feet to the cuffs. In the process, Axrel's wrappings were torn.

Leslie tapped at the controls, lifting Axrel from the tank. Charlotte watched as the men without guns moved around his body and grabbed hold, readying to slide him on to the gurney placed beside the tank. As they lifted him, Axrel's tail dropped to the floor, and some of the men flinched, causing Axrel to almost be dropped on the ground. Some of the men backed away as he slid on the gurney, his body twisted in an odd position.

"It's all right," Leon said, lifting his hands. The men stared at the tail, with its deadly tip, like it was a snake ready to strike. "Start rolling him out."

The men hesitated but didn't refuse an order. They slowly stepped back around, making sure to keep far from the tail.

Leslie started to put his hand on Axrel's shoulder, but he froze. He was staring down at something, and when Charlotte followed his gaze, she saw he was looking down at Axrel's hands. They were twitching.

"Fuck," one of the men cursed as Axrel's body began to shake, his limbs jerking.

Immediately, Charlotte shot forward, pulling away from whoever's hand tried to grab at her. She smacked against the gurney and tried to pull Axrel's body up herself, but he was too heavy. "You gave him too much sedative. He's having a seizure. Help me!"

The men helped her roll him to his side as his body stiffened, curling into itself. Charlotte clawed at the muzzle but couldn't get it off. "We need to take this off. He might not be able to breathe!"

As Leslie reached over to unclasp the muzzle, Axrel suddenly jolted upward. A snarl ripped from his throat, and he began to flail. The men backed away, Leon shouting for them to stand down.

"Axrel! Axrel, it's okay," Charlotte cried. "No! Don't hurt him!"

Payton aimed his gun and shocked him, hitting Axrel on the chest. "He's awake, dammit!"

He shocked him again, and the men with iceshockers came forward, ready to blast him with icy vapor. She tried to grab Payton's arm, but he shoved her off. "Get her the fuck away!"

Axrel twisted, another snarl ripping from his throat. His tail whipped up, slashing toward Payton. Charlotte reached to push him away.

Axrel's tail missed Payton. But not her. The small spikes sliced her palm clean across, leaving a deep gash. The pain cut hard like a razor.

Charlotte stared down at her hand, in shock as blood pooled and spilled, falling in droplets across the floor.

She couldn't react quickly enough to anything else that happened next. Her eyes lifted in time to catch Axrel's own just before the men swarmed in, pulling her back and blocking her view.

She was too stunned to speak, to tell them to stop as they struck Axrel with electric bolts and the icy vapor. Her eyes stung as they hit him again and again until he was knocked out for good.

They rolled the gurney toward the far wall and quickly lowered down the pod, opening the glass door and dropping Axrel's limp body inside. Once they secured him with the restraints, they locked the door tight and lifted the pod back in place. Vapor within the pod thickened until he was no longer visible.

"You're bleeding," a voice said beside her. One of the soldiers who had his gun up, ready to fire with a single command.

It took Charlotte a second to pull herself together before she turned away. Her kit still laid on the metal table to one side. With a shaky hand, she opened it and took out spare bandage pads with a wrap and disinfectant gel.

"How bad is it?" Leon asked, coming up beside her.

"I'll be fine," she said, her tone short. She took out the wipes and wiped at the blood. She smeared on some of the gel, then pressed the pad into her palm.

"The tail is poisonous, isn't it?"

"Just the sharp tip," Charlotte corrected, wrapping her hand tight. "It looks like it was only one of the spikes though."

Because if it had been the tip, she'd know by now. She'd feel the poisonous effects already. Fever, chills, followed by violent puking and unconsciousness. They learned about that the hard way when an altercation had happened on a trade world. A man got too close, and a vrisha sliced his leg. The man had died not even an hour later.

Only vrisha were immune to their own poison and were the only ones with an antidote. Some theorized they could control the range of poison that secreted from the end, but no one knew for sure.

"Get to the medical bay. Have someone clean it better for you," Leon ordered.

She nodded, knowing there was nothing more she could do. Axrel was in the pod. She got to see him transferred but never imagined it going like this. She picked up her kit to take it back with her, the rest belonging to the ship. As she went to turn away, she eyed a cooler on the ground next to the table. Her eyes narrowed at a small label on the lid. She paused to pick it up as well.

"I'm sorry it had to go this way," Leon said, putting his hands on his hips. "But it's done. And he'll live at least. You did good, doc."

Charlotte nodded again but said nothing. She turned away with kit in her good hand and cooler under her arm, her eyes drifting to the pod before starting up the ramp to medical.

* * *

"Looks like you got taught your own lesson too, huh?" Michal said, eyeing her hand as she walked past him into a small exam room. He let out a short laugh. "What'd you do to get on his shit list then? Did you make a pass?"

She dropped her kit and the cooler on top of a cabinet and turned toward the sink. She began to unwrap her hand, the end sticking to her blood-coated skin.

Michal whistled low. "Yeah, he got you real good."

Charlotte started the water and placed her hand underneath, pain shooting through her hand and fingers, making her wince.

"Here, let me look." Michal reached over.

Charlotte blocked him. "I'm fine. How is Kale?"

Michal frowned, dropping his arm. "He's fine. Transfusion is done. He's just sleeping it off. You're gonna need to seal that."

She knew. The wound was too deep. "I'll take care of it."

"Gonna have a nice scar at least. Now you can tell everyone what happens when you get too close." He shook his head and laughed quietly as if to say I told you so.

Charlotte didn't bother telling him what actually happened. He'd find out soon enough and feel sorry for it. Or not. It didn't matter.

She knew it was an accident. She had seen the brief look in Axrel's eyes. There was no elation or satisfaction there when he saw what he did. But she couldn't say what he felt otherwise. There was no chance.

Michal left her alone as she cleaned the wound as best she could, then moved to the surgical machine. She placed her arm inside and let it scan her hand before sealing it up. After, she put on some healing salve and wrapped it up once more. She stared down at her hand, flexing it. Her heart sank a little.

Hers had been an accident. But what about Kale? Why had Axrel attacked him? She didn't want to believe it was only because he'd gotten too close. She didn't want to believe he just saw an opportunity to hurt him and took it, even after their conversation.

Was it so stupid of her to have trusted his word?

She tore her eyes away from her hand to search the room. She stopped on the supply cabinet, then turned her gaze to where she had placed the kit and cooler. She walked over and looked down at the cooler lid, at the label taped on top.

Samples.

She opened the lid and peered inside. There were several vials and a pair of glass jars at the bottom. She took up an empty vial with no label, the glass stained red. It was cracked in half to one side, the contents gone.

She placed the vial back and shut the lid, her brow furrowing. When she left the exam room, most of the other staff were gone, including Michal. To one wall, Kale lay in his bed. She approached his side and checked his chart.

"Looks like we both are gonna have a good story to tell, huh?" he said.

Charlotte looked down and saw Kale watching her. She turned back to the chart, pretending to scan it over, so he couldn't see her expression. "Yes. But I'd say yours has a darker twist than mine."

"What makes you say that?"

Charlotte turned back to him. "What were you doing down there, Kale?"

His mouth twisted, and he looked away. "I was...just checking him over."

She crossed her arms. "You shouldn't be doing that without my supervision. If I had needed your assistance, I would have told you."

He merely shrugged, as if it were of no consequence.

She eyed him warily, knowing he was keeping something from her. "I found your cooler that was left behind. I left it in the exam room."

His gaze shifted back to her. "My cooler?"

"The one labeled samples?"

His jaw tightened, his eyes dropping.

She was certain she could put two and two together. The cooler, the freezer at the bottom of the supply cabinet. "How much were you hoping to get for each scale or horn, hm? A few million credits?"

When his eyes turned back to her, she could see by his expression she was right. "It was just a tiny piece of him," he hissed. "You of all people should know how desperate we are to have anything on those guys. Just to have a leg up when they eventually attack us."

She arched her brow. "Is that really what you think?"

"He's one of them! Against the alliance. Of course I think that." He rose into a sitting position. "And you think this job pays well? Fuck, one scale would get me a ticket to a civilian world and living off the credits the rest of my life." He shook his head, gritting his teeth.

"Sorry it couldn't work out like that," Charlotte said. She almost felt bad for the relief that was pouring through her. So, Axrel had attacked him in self-defense. Just like he had tried to attack Payton only to hit her.

Kale's hands balled into fists at his sides. "So, you gonna report me then?"

Her eyes fell from him. "I probably should."

He shook his head, scowling. "Bullshit," he whispered.

"They have the right to know why he attacked you," she said matter of factly. "Why you shouldn't have been there." She grabbed his empty drinking cup by the bedside table and started for the sink nearby to refill it.

"Yeah, why he attacked me...you know I'm wondering about that," he said. "Because, you see, he *shouldn't* have attacked me at all. You know, seeing as he was supposed to be out cold from the sedative."

Charlotte didn't turn back to him right away as she filled the cup and shut off the faucet. When she did finally look back at him, he was leaning forward, glaring at her.

"If there had been a hint of him being that active even on the drug, you would have known, right?" he said in a low voice. He tilted his head, eyes narrowing. "Even if he wasn't asleep, he should have been too lethargic and weak to do anything like that. Did you know the drug wasn't affecting him anymore?"

Charlotte stood there, clutching the cup tight. She casually walked back over and set the cup down. Kale reached out with his good hand and gripped her wrist, forcing her to look at him.

"Maybe I have something to report as well then," he growled. "A safety breach. And neglect of protocol." His grip tightened. "You let that thing wake up and have a clear head. You knew, but you didn't raise the level of sedative."

"Let go of my arm, Kale," Charlotte said, keeping her composure. He glared at her for a second longer, then released her. Charlotte straightened. "If he had been given any more, it could have killed him or put him into a coma. He had a seizure just from them putting him out again while I was down there. He's out now for sure, and I don't even know if he will wake up again." She shook her head. "I wasn't going to risk that after everything I did to keep him alive. He was clamped down, and I felt I could take the risk to be near him."

"Trusted him, you mean. And you were crazy to do so."

"Maybe I did," she confessed. "But then I wasn't extracting from him. I was trying to heal him. There's a big difference, Kale."

He snorted, looking away from her. "Whatever. You still should have told us. Told me."

"Maybe so. But then I told you I no longer needed your assistance, and you snuck down anyway. So, I guess we both made mistakes."

His face twisted. He mumbled a curse under his breath. Charlotte watched him for a moment longer before stepping to the end of the bed. "I am sorry, Kale, that this happened. We will keep an eye on your arm for infection, but I'm confident it will heal fine in a few weeks, given you keep it clean and use a regenerative agent every few days." She'd turned to leave when he called to her again.

"You know it was pointless caring about him, right?" he said. "Did you think he was just getting thrown on Fargis to live out his days working in one of the factories or mines? And that you gave him some kind of chance to survive?" He shook his head and laughed quietly. "They got a lot more plans for him than that."

Charlotte frowned. "I know about the torture. I know they'll try to get him to talk." She turned away, once again not wanting him to see her expression.

"Oh, yeah, they'll try that for sure. But it's not all they'll do."

She looked over at him, suspicion tightening in her gut. "What do you mean?"

His lip curled to one side. "Let's just say I was getting a leg up on any part of him before there were nothing but scraps."

She turned to face him. No. She couldn't believe that. Not after everything. "So, he's to be taken apart after they torture him? Seriously?"

"Not after the torture. After the experiments."

Charlotte went still, eyes widening. Kale laughed again.

"Really?" he said, through his laughter. "You honestly didn't think they weren't going to try, did you? Come on." He leaned back. "He's going to a government-controlled prison. For aliens. What did you think they did there?"

Charlotte clenched her jaw. "That's illegal and against alliance—"

"Do you think they care?" Kale lay back. "They don't. And, for the record, if you attempt to say anything, they'll have government officials ready to speak against you, and they'll destroy your reputation for even considering it. The aliens were either caught in our territory or attacked our people. All bets are off. Sorry, doc." He placed his hands behind his back. "You're in the governing systems now, not some neutral territory. These aliens belong to us."

CHAPTER TEN

CHARLOTTE

She sat on her small bed in her unit, staring out at the nothingness that was deep space. It looked like how she probably felt inside at that moment. Dark and empty.

She couldn't see it now, but she knew based on the updates she received that Fargis was in sight. They were within its system now.

She should be relieved. She would be going home soon. She did what they asked, and she could put it all behind her, return to Larth, continue her work there with Grayhart. Forget everything.

But she knew she couldn't. She couldn't go on pretending everything was fine. Axrel never left her thoughts. Whatever he'd done, he didn't deserve this. No one did. Now that she knew his fate, she felt betrayed, lied to, scammed.

And powerless.

Because, despite hours to contemplate it, there was nothing she could really do. Yes, she could go to the alliance council and tell them, but what evidence did she have? Her word meant nothing.

And she believed Kale when he said the heads of the governing systems would deny any accusations. Of course they would.

She had a mind to go off on Leon and the others, reputation be damned, though it would do nothing. Nothing to save Axrel from his fate.

Hell, she even contemplated attempting to free him and assisting in his escape. Just for a brief moment. But that would put other people's lives at risk. Even if he swore not to harm another for her sake, she couldn't know for sure he wouldn't. And afterward, who's to say he wouldn't go back to the Blood Guard, to his mad queen. To plan out another attack.

Maybe he was better off imprisoned just for that possibility alone. But to be tortured and experimented on...No, it was unspeakable.

And humans wondered why some vrisha hated them.

Charlotte's hands curled on her lap. She looked down at her wrapped hand and could feel a headache forming. She just wanted to show him that not all humans were the same. To show him a better side. But everything she had tried to accomplish would be thrown out the window. Not in just physically healing him, but mentally. If he had even a sliver of thought to see them differently, to see the good, that thought would be lost as soon as they took him into the prison and destroyed every piece of him.

Charlotte shut her eyes tight, then opened them slowly. She got up from the bed and went over to the dresser. She went through her bag and took out the receiver given to her by Grayson. If she thought it possible, she would call him then and there and tell him to send a ship out with a team. Maybe they could infiltrate this ship before it landed and steal the pod...

Charlotte dropped the receiver into the bag and sighed. Even their fastest ship wouldn't make it in time. And what could Grayhart security do against government trained soldiers? Grayhart's security was made up of some of the best in their field, but so were some of those aboard this ship. And to pick a fight over a hostile vrisha? All for what? So she could take him home like some pet that needed disciplining?

It was insane. She wasn't thinking clearly. She was just emotional and wanted to do something. *Anything.*

She reached back into the bag and took out her pillbox. She opened the lid and popped one of the tiny red pills into her mouth. She swallowed it down with some water, then closed the bottle up and threw it back into the bag.

Maybe I can't do anything. Maybe it is too late, she thought bitterly. *But damn if I won't at least say something.*

She turned for the door and exited the room, making her way down the hall to the stairs. Even if it was fruitless, her anger was too great. Those of the governing systems or even the alliance might not believe her. But Grayhart would. And she'd do all she could to make sure they never worked with the military ever again.

She didn't go to the bridge right away. She had started to—determined to go off on Leon and his crew—but her feet took her another route. She went through the prisoner level into security and down the ramp until she stood in the high-security room with the six glass pods surrounding her.

She looked up at Axrel in his pod. His eyes were closed, no thin inner lids covering over this time, just his outer, shut tight. Now he appeared to actually be sleeping—a deep, dead-like sleep that she wondered if he would ever wake from.

A part of her hoped he didn't. If only because he at least wouldn't have to endure everything that came after.

"I'm sorry I ever came aboard this ship," she whispered. "I'm sorry I ever let them convince me to keep you alive. Your death would be a mercy compared to what they have planned for you."

He was silent in his pod, no hint of a movement, just the wisps of vapor hovering around him. She sighed. Why did she come down at all? She knew he wouldn't be awake. Knew he'd never be able to hear her.

Maybe she just needed one more glimpse before he was gone for good.

She opened her mouth to say more, as if it mattered, when the lights flickered overhead and a bell-like noise echoed through the room.

"All crew to their required positions," called a monotonous voice. "Prepare for arrival."

Charlotte scanned over Axrel one last time, finding it hard to move. "I guess this is goodbye." She backed away slowly, then forced herself to turn away.

She made for the stairs, up to the bridge. When she got there, she was stopped by the guard.

"I need to talk to him right now."

"We are about to dock. You should be in your unit," the guard said, not budging.

"Then tell him I'd like a brief chat before I do," Charlotte said, unwavering. "Otherwise, I'll stand right here and wait to be escorted."

The guard glared at her for a second longer before he turned and went inside. Charlotte waited a minute more before the door opened, and he stepped aside to allow her through. She didn't hesitate as she entered onto the bridge. She made for the front of the room where Leon stood watching Fargis draw closer.

"Commander Leon, I need a word."

Leon gestured for her to come closer. Charlotte came to his side.

"Ugly place, isn't it?" he said, nodding toward the planet.

There wasn't much to see to make that judgment just yet, but the thick cloud cover and the deep navy—almost black—oceans certainly didn't make the world seem like a pleasing vacation getaway. Every few seconds, there were flashes of light as storms raged, scattered across the planet.

"I want to talk about Prisoner Zero," Charlotte said, watching the clouds move.

"Now is probably not the best time, doc."

"Now is a better time than any." Her eyes shifted over to his face, but he didn't turn to meet her gaze. "What you plan to do to him is a crime against the alliance. It's bad enough you plan to torture him, but I refuse to stay silent about any experiments. You knew how I felt about that, about my past, and yet you tricked me into coming here to heal a prisoner you were only planning to break. It's sickening," she said through clenched teeth. "Once I get home, I'm going to make a full report to the head of Grayhart. We won't have any part of this. I'll make sure Grayhart never aids the governing military, ever. Do you understand?"

His mouth turned up into a smile. "Sorry to hear that, doc."

She waited for more, but it never came. "Damn you and your whole system. This prison is a hell, and I will do whatever it takes to tell others what you and the military are doing."

He side-eyed her, his smile fading. "You know what that entails," he said. "Don't be a fool, Lockley. You are a brilliant doctor and surgeon. Would be a waste to lose your career over it."

"At this point, I don't know if I could care less!" she nearly yelled. "You had me fix him, knowing what was going to happen. You deceived me."

He laughed. "What did you think?" He turned to her. "What other reason would we need him alive?"

Her throat constricted, not wanting to say she believed they wanted him alive to carry out the justice they saw fit. To have him spend his days in prison like any other criminal to serve out his punishment. And she saw now how foolish and naive that was. Damn him. And damn her for not considering their motives sooner.

"Commander," Payton appeared, glaring at her before turning to Leon. "We've established communication."

"Took them long enough. We are almost in the atmosphere. Pull up the tower communications overhead," Leon ordered.

Payton directed a crew member to do so, and Charlotte saw from a screen above the terminal a set of coordinates and a call number.

There was a brief clicking noise, like someone repeatedly snapping their fingers, as they established the call.

"This is *Tarus* 301. We are set to dock at city sector. Are we clear?" asked one of the pilots.

There was silence for a long moment, just hushed static on the other end.

"Tower, do you hear me?"

The static lessened to a low hum. There was another pause, then a voice, deep and grating, responded. "Clear to dock."

A slow chill ran down Charlotte's body, the voice felt in her gut. She couldn't place why, but the tone made her feel on edge. The dark swirling clouds drew closer as they began to descend.

She glanced at Leon, nervously. "The storm will make landing rough, won't it?"

"The ship has dealt with worse." He gazed back at her. "But you should return to your unit. Wait there for someone to escort you off. Once we are fully on the ground, we'll get you on the first transport back home."

She wanted to protest, but she'd already said what she came to say and there was no reason for her to linger. Arguing more with Leon would get her nowhere. "Fine. But this isn't done with. I'm not going to keep quiet, just so you are aware." She felt a hand on her shoulder, and she brushed it off. "If I have to talk to every head in charge, every reporter, every official, alliance or otherwise, I will. I will do whatever it takes to stop whatever is happening here, career be damned!" She turned from him toward the exit, knowing whatever soldier was escorting her followed close behind.

She didn't look back, only forward, with nowhere else to go now but to her unit. Back to waiting and letting the anger stir, slow and hot. But this time, she had a plan. She would make promise of her words. She'd start a campaign if she had to. She was still certain Grayhart would defend her.

As she made for the stairs, the ship trembled. They must have hit the atmosphere. She paused as the lights flickered again overhead and the pressure dropped. She could feel the ship slowing.

"We need to keep going," said the soldier behind her.

Charlotte continued on. They stepped off the stairs and started down a long corridor, soldiers moving every which way. When she got back to her unit, the soldier escorting her disappeared, and she began to pack her things.

She paused again as the light from the planet's sun began to fade. They finally dipped into the thick dark clouds. She could see the flashes of lightning out her small window. The ship trembled again as she closed up her kit and zipped her bag. There was a flash of red that blinked through the window.

Interesting. She rarely ever saw red lightning.

She turned to the window and looked out, curious to see the rare phenomenon. She leaned into the curved glass, looking every which way, hoping to get a glimpse of the ground once they broke through the clouds.

Another flash of red—a small sprite—flickered through the dark. Her brow furrowed, eyes narrowing.

Did she just see...?

They must have ships guiding them to the dock. Though why they would hover inside the clouds was odd.

She drew closer, watching, waiting. Another flash came, and her eyes widened, a small gasp slipping past her teeth. She straightened and backed away.

She was sure she saw it this time. A ship. But it didn't look like any human ship she'd ever seen. It looked alien. It looked like–

Her room shook violently, and a loud boom roared in her ears. Charlotte fell back on her bed, then to her knees on the floor as the ship tilted.

There was a deep red flash and another thunderous boom. She felt a surge of heat surround her, as if a wave of fire had swept across the exterior of the ship. A siren went off, and the regular lights went out, bringing the flashing, orange emergency lights on.

It took her only a second to realize they were under attack and only another second more to get up off her knees onto her feet. She grabbed her kit and threw her bag over her shoulder, then bolted from her unit.

She slid into the wall opposite, hitting her shoulder against the metal siding. She pushed off, pushing her legs to run, run as hard as she could. The hall was leaning to one side, making it difficult, but she kept going. As she flew down the corridor, the ground shook again, and pipes broke over her head. She slipped a few times but refused to stop. Her mind raced, trying to recall the map of the ship in her mind. There was an emergency escape room not far. She just needed to keep going.

Steam blasted from the broken pipes into her face. The hall grew hot as she heard the roaring and crackling of fire nearby over the sirens. Her stomach felt like it was rising into her chest as gravity took hold, and the ship was falling.

She ran blindly, fearing at any moment, she would run headfirst into someone, another crewmen or soldier running for their life. But she didn't. The crew were gone somewhere else on the ship, either in position to fight or having already escaped.

When she saw a sign pointing toward the escape room, she turned the corner, then was blown off her feet as the ship lurched back, the engines roaring. Someone was trying to halt their crash, still holding on.

Charlotte tumbled and hit a wall. Her bag was crushed against her back, her kit landing at her side. Her hand throbbed, a burning pain slipping up her arm. Her shoulder and neck ached. She groaned and attempted to rise again, using the wall for leverage. Slow, but determined, she lifted herself to her feet, grabbing her kit off the ground, ignoring the pain in her hand.

She stumbled forward, then took off down the passage until she smacked into the escape room door. As she slipped inside, a wind whipped out from a tear in the hull. She looked around for anyone injured and found the chamber empty. Several of the escape pods along the walls were already gone, and one was on fire. She lurched toward one that was empty, passed a computer terminal, and nearly tripped over a body. She stopped to look over the crewman and saw they were limp, lifeless. Blood smeared over their face. She cursed, knowing they were dead, having either hitting their head on the terminal or been struck by some blunt object, as debris was scattered over the ground. She stepped over them for the pod and smacked her hand on the button to one side, freeing the door.

Something shattered behind her, and a sharp pain cut across her back. She yelped as she pulled herself inside the pod. Glass spilled over her shoulders onto the seats. The burning pod's doors had blown out nearby. There were four seats in total, and she dumped her bag and kit at her feet as she strapped into one. As she secured herself inside, she hesitated on hitting the controls to seal the door shut. Someone else might come. Any second.

But as the fire grew and the wind picked up, she knew she couldn't wait. No one else was coming. And she had no more time. She hit the button beside the door, and it slid shut, locking in place. There was a jolt and hiss of pressure as the pod detached. Fire licked at the windows of her pod until it separated from the ship and shot off into the storm.

CHAPTER ELEVEN

CHARLOTTE

It was dark except for the slow blink of a red light above her. A dull hum buzzed in her ear. Charlotte groaned, her head throbbing just like her hand and back. Her eyes fluttered open, and she saw nothing but hazy, blackened glass in front of her. She shut her eyes tight, then opened them again slowly. The glass became less fuzzy. She even noticed a hairline crack to one side.

The pod was no longer moving. And through the ashen window, she could see the sky above, a swirling darkness with the mist of rain and the spark of lightning. It took her a moment to realize she was no longer within that storm but below it now. On the ground. On Fargis itself.

She took in a slow breath at that realization, then another to keep the panic at bay. Carefully, she righted herself into the seat, then groped around until she found the clasp to her seatbelt and released it, letting it slide from her. She felt dizzy, as the pod had thrown her around in its flight through the storm, toward the ground.

When it had landed, it had jolted her nearly out of her seat, only the seatbelt keeping her from tumbling around inside. As she leaned forward to press the door button, she felt a searing pain along her back, across her right shoulder. She winced, falling back, and stifled a cry. She felt a sticky wetness clinging to her shirt and onto the seat. She reached around to feel for the wound. She might not be able to see it, but by the way the pain cut sharply, she gauged she had a deep gash, her skin sliced by a piece of glass. She looked down at herself and touched at her chest, her stomach, her thighs, then winced again. She had a cut on her leg too, though she wasn't sure how that one happened. The rest of her, miraculously, seemed intact.

She moved her limbs and concluded there were no fractures or broken bones. Preparing herself this time, she tried again for the door button and reached, fighting the pain. She smacked at it a few times until there was a click and hiss, and the door slid open.

Cold air whipped at her like an icy, wet hand. She sucked in the cold air as she pulled herself out of the pod.

The first thing she saw was the orange and red blaze of fires. Dozens of them surrounded her in the darkness, some only a few dozen yards away, others for miles. She could see the plumes of black smoke billowing into the sky. She dropped her gaze to where she had landed. It looked like an open section of land, perhaps what had once been a courtyard or a small park, except the grass was burned and the small trees barren. The buildings nearby were broken and crumbling, the metal frames and concrete blocks scattered along the ground. She was within the city sector, she was certain, as she could see abandoned vehicles and storefronts and a giant, broken wall. Charlotte took in the devastation, at first confused. The ship couldn't have possibly done all this. She couldn't even see it at all, though she could hear the roar of something large burning nearby.

As she took a step, her mind reeled. She thought of all those on board, prisoners, soldiers, crewmen. She wondered how many could have escaped in time, if any had survived the crash. And if they had gotten to safety. If any needed her help. She should go, find them. They would need her aid.

She turned back for the pod and took out her bag and kit. As she threw the bag back over her shoulder, another thought came to her. The prisoners. Were they stuck inside their cells, or had they gotten out?

Then she remembered. Something had attacked the ship and had brought it down. It had been an ambush. Whoever had attacked the ship had done all this, had destroyed the city base.

She recalled the ship she had seen out her window. A dark shape, sharp and ominous. She'd seen that type of ship before.

She turned toward the fires, her eyes searching the sky. Nothing, just the rainless storm. She dropped her eyes back to the ground, and her hands tightened on the strap of her bag.

She needed to find their ship. She needed to see how bad the wreckage was. Even if her panicked brain wanted her to flee and find a way out of the city, she had to pull forward. There were people who might need her.

She started to walk when a sound made her pause and look around. She waited, then heard it again, and a chill ran through her. She turned to her right and started for one of the buildings close by, this time running. She slipped inside and hid herself in the shadows, waiting. She watched the pod, then stiffened as she saw something move toward it. No, there were several things. Men. Alien men. She had heard their jitters and yelps close by. One was a corax, with a wide shark mouth and black eyes, and the other was a grex, with greenish-brown scales and venom dripping from its mouth. They each wore simple gray and blue uniforms. Prisoner attire.

"Smell her. I can smell her," said the grex. He placed his hands on the pod doors and stuck his face inside. "Blood. She's injured." He was speaking in xolian, which she understood. The corax responded in the same tongue.

"Can't be far." The corax jumped on the pod and hit his fist against the top. He pulled at one side of the ship and ripped a hole.

He looked around, tilting his face up. "There are others. Alive. I saw the pods like this one in the distance."

The grex growled. He slunk passed the pod and—to her relief—started the opposite way. The corax followed behind.

Thankfully, neither race had a good sense of smell, and she was downwind. They must have seen her pod fall and went for it. When they disappeared, she hunkered down and opened her kit. She rifled through and found a bottle of antiseptic. With shaking hands, she unscrewed the bottle. She took off her shirt and poured a little across her back, hissing in pain. She couldn't mend the cut without proper help, but she could stifle infection for now. She pulled down her pants and poured some on her thigh as well, then quickly wrapped it with some spare gauze before putting her clothing back on.

Those prisoners had to have come from the actual prison. They didn't look injured at all or dirtied by debris and smoke. Which meant the prison was compromised. Someone had attacked the city and freed the prisoners. The same someone who had attacked *Tarus*.

She thought of the dark ship in the storm again and shuddered. If that ship belonged to who she thought, then whatever was happening was very bad. She wanted to find others and give help, but she also understood she was in great danger with the prisoners roaming the city and perhaps beyond. And the attackers were still out there in their ships, watching from above.

She put away the antiseptic and took out a dark blue jacket from her bag, quickly pulling it over her dirtied light blue uniform. Then she took out the transmitter Grayson had given to her and turned it on.

"Grayson. Grayson, can you hear me?" she said in a low voice, worried about others who might hear. They might not be able to smell very well, but some could hear better. "Grayson, we need help."

There was nothing but static on the other end and a dull whining noise. Charlotte checked the device over and saw the crack in its side, some of the wires poking out. *Damn.*

She couldn't be sure if it was fully broken or only partially. Either way, it must have broken when she'd been fleeing the ship, possibly when she had slammed into the wall with the bag. Cursing, she made a call one more time, but there was no response in return. She dropped the transmitter back in her bag and straightened. She looked at her wristpad. There was no signal either, all networks down. She was alone.

She peered through the dark building and saw a stairwell nearby. Without another thought, she went for it and started to climb. When she got to the top, she walked along the roof to one side and searched the city. A couple miles away, she could see part of the ship to the south. It was burning on its left side, having crashed near one of the great walls of the city. It looked to be the top half. It had broken apart sometime in its fall. The bottom half was closer, near to the dock where they were originally supposed to land. She stared at it, seeing smoke seeping out of the windows. That was where the prisoners were held. Where Axrel was.

She wasn't sure how to feel about that. She wasn't sure whether she wanted to see him coming out of the wreckage or not. He might be dead inside with the others already. Or not. If he was dead, she knew it would affect her whether she wanted it to or not. But if he wasn't...

If he wasn't, he would also be a danger to her. Now more than ever. She didn't want to think of him at that moment. Didn't want to think about either scenario. But it couldn't be helped.

A shadow moved in the clouds, and Charlotte immediately crouched down to hide herself. Heart hammering, she watched as the dark ship moved toward the wreckage of the upper half of *Tarus*. Then another appeared and another. There was a burst of light from the wreckage, then several. Aiming at the ships. She heard gunfire and saw the blast of missiles as they flew into the sky, toward the dark ships. There were men fighting back. Somehow, some had survived.

The ships steered back, then lowered themselves, disappearing past the buildings to land somewhere in the city. It made sense for them to do so.

Because the vrisha fought better on the ground.

She knew it had to be them. She had seen their ships before on Terra Centra and images from the web. Only these ships did not carry the alliance symbol on them. They were rogue vrisha, the Blood Guard. They had gotten to Fargis and somehow broken through the defenses. And they had tricked them. The voice from the tower telling them it was safe to land had sounded off, and she knew now it had been one of them. Imitating a human voice. Most likely, all the control men and prison guards had already been slaughtered.

Charlotte covered her mouth at the realization. Why? Why were they doing this?

She looked over the edge and watched as bursts of man-made fire and lightning brightened the city. She had to make a decision. Go toward the wreckage and aid in any way she could with hope she wouldn't be caught and killed in the crossfire. Or start for the edge of the city. Get out and head as far away as possible.

She knew the logical answer. She might not get a chance to help anyone if she died trying to get to them. Better to just go, head for safety. But the side of her that wanted to save lives was hesitant about fleeing when there could be those alive and in need of medical attention.

She scanned over the city and stopped on a building not far from the dock where the bottom half of *Tarus* lay. A symbol on top of the building caught her eye. A medical cross. It was a medical center.

She hunkered down again and started to form a plan. She would go toward the medical building. See if she could find anything. Maybe there were doctors there trying to treat survivors. The building was close enough to the wreckage that she could see it better. She could get a read from there if anyone was still alive. She had a better chance on that end than she did where the fighting took place. If there was no one, then she would continue on past the dock to the edge of the city and get out from there. She could see the wall in the distance, a shadowy barricade.

She knew she'd be going into danger regardless of which way she went. The prisoners would be coming from there if any had survived, but there could be others lurking who'd escaped the prison. And she felt a pull to go toward the wreckage. To at least see for herself if it was hopeless. She could hide if she had to.

It was all she could think to do with the little time she had. Quickly, she got up and rushed for the roof door, racing down the stairs. She just hoped she'd get there without running into the monsters that now dominated the city.

CHAPTER TWELVE

Axrel

He had felt himself falling. Even in his deep sleep, he could feel the heat of fire, could hear the groan of metal collapsing. The screams and roars of otherkin and men alike around him. Even through it all, he did not wake. Not even when there was a crash of glass and the hiss of vapor slowing then stopping and a cold rush of air taking its place. He felt himself being shaken violently, but the restraints held him firm, a curse and a blessing, they had kept him from spilling from the pod.

It wasn't until everything went still and silent that he felt himself beginning to rise from the deep slumber. A bright light filled his vision—a deep red—and for a moment, he thought he was back on Tryth with the sun coming up to start a new day. But Tryth was never this cold except maybe on the higher peaks.

He slowly opened his eyes and looked up at the red light. It was just artificial light coming from the floors now opened up above him, a gaping hole where the ceiling had once been. He was in a ship, but it was broken apart and not moving. They were on the ground.

There was movement at the corner of his eye, and he turned to see one of the other inmates that had been stuck in the pods rise out from where theirs had fallen. It was the fyrien. He had heard of their kind—an elusive breed much like vrisha. This one took a good look around, their long white hair falling across their back. Their skin, a dark purple, was covered by white stripes, hardly shining in the light. They turned and saw him, blinking at him with orange eyes. They started for him, but before he could let out a growl in warning, there was a crash, and glass spilled over the floor. The drogin tumbled out of his pod and jumped up, teeth bared. The lygin nearby was caught in its pod but had also awakened. It yowled at the drogin which leapt over and covered the lygin with his body, sinking his teeth into the lygin's flesh. The fyrien watched, unmoving. It glanced at Axrel, then turned and slunk away, disappearing. The corax beside him freed himself next and, as he came out of his pod, the drogin turned, mouth bloody, to glare at him.

There were others moving now too. Those caged inside cells were escaping. He could hear them. Hear doors being torn away and the sounds of fights as they attacked each other. It would be a blood-bath before long.

Axrel looked down at his restraints and saw the clasps on his left arm were bent aside, but the right ones were not. The ones on his legs were still secure. It seemed the emergency mechanism for loosening the clasps had not worked on his pod but had for some of the others.

The drogin lunged for the corax, and they began to fight. Axrel freed his left arm and reached for the clasp on the right. With all his strength, he bent the one on his arm, turning it upward. He was still weak from the drugs and from his injuries in general, but vrisha always had some power stored for dire need, and he had been saving his for such a circumstance. Granted he had expected to find himself in a lab not still on the ship which he now knew had crashed. He didn't allow himself to think too much about it yet, only to free himself.

The drogin was winning the fight, and when he was done with the corax, he'd start on Axrel. He wasn't afraid of the drogin, but he didn't like having such a disadvantage. He bent the second clasp and freed his right arm, slipping it through. He started on his legs when the drogin got the last blow and the corax fell to the ground. The furry beast turned on him, and Axrel paused to fix the prisoner with his own glare. He hissed, and the scent of his anger released in the air as a warning. *Come and try it*, he thought. *And see what happens.*

He tugged his tail out from underneath him and waited. The drogin bared his teeth, but he didn't come closer. He started to back off and, at the roar of some other prisoner nearby, he broke away. Smart of him.

Axrel freed his right leg and started working on the next when a band of inmates clambered out from the wreck onto the ground before him. They were confident at first until they saw him and got a whiff of the scent of his fury. Still, they moved around him, trying to gauge if it was worth the risk. Axrel tried to bare his fangs at them and discovered a metal device covering his mouth. The aliens saw the disadvantage as an opportunity. They started for him, and as the first reached him, he swung out his tail like a whip, hitting them across the face, making them fall back. As the others halted, he gripped the final clasp and bent it. He dropped from the pod, then righted himself. His legs were stiff and weak, but he kept standing, waiting for the aliens to move.

When they did, he moved too. Most fled, while the few brave stood their ground. He cut through them, frustrated that it didn't come with the usual ease because of his weakened state. That would have to be remedied. Still, he moved faster than them and struck one after the other till they lay around him in a heap.

He looked around at the empty pods, save for two where the lygin now stood dead and the grex as well, not having survived the crash.

He heard the cries of others close by. More would come. He reached behind his head to try and unclasp the metal device from his face, but it wouldn't budge. Likely it was locked, so the user couldn't get out of it on their own. He would need a human hand to do so.

As soon as he thought that, Charlotte popped into his mind. He could tell by the wreckage it was bad. The humans might not have had a chance. The thought of her small body, crushed or lying somewhere, filled him with such rage, it shocked him. He felt it for her more than he could understand. In that moment, he had a sudden, deep urge to start looking through the wreckage for her. To know for sure.

He tilted his head up but sensed no trace of her, of her scent. Only the smell of blood and ash. From what he could tell, this was only a piece of the spacecraft, where the prisoners were held. Where was the other?

He looked up toward the hole and moved to one wall, then began to climb.

When he made it to the top, he saw a city before him, small, with wide buildings surrounded by a wall. Fires consumed a large portion of it, and to the south, he could see the other part of the ship burning as well. Even under the dark sky, he could make out the smaller ships that floated nearby. His people's ships.

He knew who they were. His rogue brothers and sisters. The Blood Guard. His fury burned brighter at the sight of them.

Traitors.

He had a memory of lying in the snow and a band of them surrounding him.

You'll learn, Axrel. You'll see. This is for your own good. But don't worry, brother, when the humans are done with you, you'll come to understand. You'll find us again. Or we will find you.

He growled deep and low. Yes, they had found each other again. The Blood Guard had come here, but not for him. They had come for some other purpose, though his need for revenge was still great.

The other half of the craft was nothing more than flames and smoke, but there was gunfire along one side where the ships hovered. If Charlotte had been anywhere, it was there. What humans had survived were losing the fight.

His brothers had caused this. They had caused the crash. And they had killed the only person he had felt anything for. Now he had someone to avenge.

He started across the top, bounding over broken metal. He saw nothing else but the ships and the fire. He knew he would die, but he would die fighting. He'd kill as many as he could before they broke him. He would kill them for...

He froze before taking another step, his eyes widening. The wind had picked up, driving back some of the smoke, and in the air, he caught it.

A dark, flowery scent.

His nostrils flared, thinking maybe it had just been his imagination, but, as he twisted around and tilted his head up, he caught it again.

There. To the north.

It was real.

He found he was unable to move. He was torn between two paths. He could still see the Blood Guard as they fought near their ships. He could go in and take his revenge just as he had wanted. But the scent told him Charlotte was alive, and she would be in danger from those scattered throughout the city and beyond. No matter how powerful his need was to fight, somehow the drive to find her was greater.

Go. You will have your chance another time, a voice deep within said. *She needs you.*

Those last words drove through him like a knife. He couldn't escape them. She would die, he knew, if he ignored his instincts and moved forward.

He took two slow breaths and watched the ships a second longer before he moved again. This time away from the wreckage, northward.

CHAPTER THIRTEEN

CHARLOTTE

The storm, which had consisted mostly of lightning, had now turned into a torrent of rain once outside the city. It had grown darker now too, with the sundown and night approaching.

The only light came from bright blue and white street lamps that stretched along a narrow road, likely used for small cargo vehicles and transporting workers. Charlotte stuck close to the road but did not move along it for fear others did the same.

She was glad that she had made it this far. But she wondered how long her luck would last. She tugged her jacket around her, the hood covering her head and face from the rain. It was getting colder, and if she didn't find somewhere dry and warm soon, she could get hypothermia. Mud caked her shoes as she slunk through tall grass parallel to the road.

The medical facility had been empty, but she had found a few supplies that might aid her. She didn't stay long to search. She had seen prisoners moving about, attacking each other, and she knew it wouldn't be safe to linger. She stopped only one other time to check the ship from one of the upper levels to scan for any survivors. She had seen none. Only bodies and prisoners who didn't look injured or friendly enough to approach. She veered away then, hiding when she had to, then crossed the wall, through a narrow tunnelway. That had been the scariest part, not knowing if she would run into anyone along the way.

Once she made it through, she started east a little ways, but her plan was to veer north, to walk parallel to the city. She had a clear memory of the map of Fargis in her mind. The one she had studied on the bridge when speaking to Officer Leslie. She remembered seeing several guard stations scattered around the massive island, each of which could be possible safe points. It was one in particular that made her want to go north, a tradeport and communications station called The Lightpost. The map it had clearly labeled it as such. There, she knew she would find ships—as tradeports were hubs for transport of supplies—and, hopefully, a working transmitter. She didn't know how to drive a ship, true, but maybe there would be people who would. And if there wasn't, then maybe she could send for help.

She knew if she stuck to the roads, they would lead her past many of the stations and take her to The Lightpost.

Up ahead, she could see the lights of one station already. It looked empty, and she could see the trail of dirt from vehicles leading away. Whoever had been posted there was gone.

She paused briefly a few yards away to assess whether the area was clear before she approached with caution. There were four buildings along either side of the road, each simple metal warehouses save for one at the end that looked more like a two-story office. She slipped past the other buildings and into the last. Inside, it looked like another kind of storm had blown through. Chairs and tables were overthrown, papers and boxes were scattered everywhere. It was dark, almost pitch black. Only the light from outside through the windows allowed her to see anything at all. She stepped over the debris and into a hall. There were rooms upon rooms but nothing of any value. It wasn't until she found a storage closet at the back that she paused to search. She found a working torchlight and a matchbox, but the rest was either cleaning supplies or tools. She put the matchbox in her bag and the torchlight in one of her pockets, then turned to leave the closet.

Out in the hall, she heard voices. She froze, her heart skipping, and realized they came from outside. She crept over to a nearby window and looked and saw a group, or pack, of inmates lurking in between the buildings.

"I saw her. I saw her pass here," one said in xolian. A grex. The same from before when she had fled the pod. He and the corax were now with several others, a lygin, another grex, and—

She stiffened, her heart leaping in her throat. The drogin–Prisoner One–was with them too. He had survived the crash and somehow made it out of the city.

He tilted his head and bared his crooked fangs in a tight snarl. He was mangy looking, even more now than before. "If you're wrong, I'll cut your head off," he growled.

That seemed to scare the grex enough to start searching one of the buildings opposite.

Her blood ran cold under her skin. They were looking for her. She could have sworn she had been careful, making sure to check her surroundings every so often. Through the rain and the dark, she must have missed them. And hadn't noticed them stalking her.

They would find her if she stayed. She needed to run or hide.

She heard the front door of the building open, and she forced her feet to move. She started for an emergency stair nearby and paused only for a moment to consider which way to go, up to the second floor or down where there looked to be a lower level. Hearing them behind, coming down the hall, she took the steps two at a time, going down. As silent as she could, she passed through a door into a yellow lit tunnel. She rushed down it, glancing behind her every so often. She didn't know where it led or where she was going, but she didn't think too hard about it. She just needed to flee.

She turned one way, then another, down a long passage until it ended with stairs. She took them up to a door and snuck out. The tunnel had taken her out onto the road again. The door was hidden under a large rocky mound, covered by leaves. Some sort of emergency escape.

From there, she ran. She ran blindly into the night, until her lungs were burning, and her legs were straining. She didn't know how long she ran, but eventually, she had to slow to catch her breath. She took small breaks, then continued on. She kept her distance from the road, knowing now it wasn't safe. She passed a small creek and climbed up a rolling hill before she saw lights again.

Exhausted, she stumbled down the hillside toward the next station. This one was smaller—just a cabin—and had a garage connected to it. She wondered if there were people. She slipped into the cabin and found it empty like the rest, only it was in less disarray. By one desk, she saw a phone and a local transmitter with a call monitor. She checked the phone first and found the connection dead. She tried the transmitter, turning on the monitor. All frequencies and communication towers seemed unresponsive. There was only one channel with a voice coming from a recording. A voice filled with a low hum.

"Come to The Flame. Come and join us."

The voice made her stomach twist. It was talking in xolian like the others. It was alien. What the hell was going on?

There was a crash somewhere outside, and she jumped. She backed away and searched around, noticing a door at the back and going for it. As she stepped through, she found herself in the garage. A truck sat by an empty lot. She searched around for keys, hearing a low howl come in the distance. She found a set on the wall and began pressing the buttons, aiming toward the vehicle. It lit up, and she rushed for it. As she threw her bag and kit inside, the door behind her crashed open. She yelped as she fell onto the driver seat and a pair of clawed hands reached for her. She kicked at her attacker, one of the grex. As he tried to grip her ankle, she struck with her other leg, kicking him in the face. He stumbled back and hissed in annoyance. He lunged for her again as she shut the door. His fist struck the window, shattering glass, shards falling on her lap. He reached again for her, and Charlotte kicked again until he caught her by the hair and tried to pull her out of the window. She cried out, one hand searching, until she grabbed a larger piece of glass and stabbed him in the face. This time, he shrieked and pulled away. With no time to waste, she started the car and put it into drive. She slammed her palm onto the garage button on the ceiling of the car and the garage door slowly began to open.

Outside, the others waited there for her, stalking back and forth, their eyes glowing yellow and black in the light.

Charlotte stomped on the gas to drive through them. But they didn't move out of the way like she thought they would. They jumped on the roof and hood of her car, blocking her view. One of them punched the front window, shattering it just as easily as the driver side. Charlotte threw up her arms as glass flew into her face, and the car swerved, driving into the darkness, then crashing into a fence, sending her flying.

"She's coming to," said a voice.

Rain splattered on her face dripping into her eyes and down her neck. Her body felt cold and sore, like she had slammed into a brick wall. She could hardly move.

A foot nudged her, and her eyes fluttered open, a groan slipping from her mouth. Her vision was blurring, but she could make out figures standing over her, studying her. She groaned again as a pain shot through her bones. She turned onto her side and saw another pair of blurry figures rifling through her bag, throwing things on the wet ground. Her kit had been kicked to the side.

A foot nudged her again, and she began to remember what happened and where she was. She tried to crawl away, but the foot dropped onto her back, keeping her in place.

"She's a tough one," one of them said. The corax, she thought. "I wonder if that makes her flesh tough too."

There was a brief tussle, then, "No one touches her. She's mine," Prisoner One said. "She's my doctor."

One of them snorted. "What does that matter?"

If she had it in her to wonder how the drogin knew it was her who had fixed him, she would, but she had other worries.

"It matters to me. Only I say what happens to her."

"We should give her to the devils instead," said a grex, not the one she had stabbed. "They'll reward us, I'll bet."

"More like spare our lives. You saw they attacked us," said the corax

"Not us," said the grex. "The humans. They were only killing them."

They seemed to discuss, or rather argue about it, while she lay there, trying to see around her. Her vision started to come around, and she could see she was still at the small station. The garage was nearby, as was the wrecked car which they had pulled and dragged her from. Her bag was ripped open, items spilling everywhere or thrown about by the aliens.

Suddenly, they went silent.

"You smell that?" said the corax.

There was a low hiss among the group as they stepped away from her to circle around her. She lifted her head up and could see they appeared on edge as they stared into the dark.

"It's one of them," the grex replied, fear growing in his voice.

Charlotte took in their words one at a time. Then a smell hit her too. Like spiced, nearly burnt coffee. She gasped, her body frozen.

"The vrisha are hunting her too?" the lygin said, claws out.

"It's just one," Prisoner One growled. "I know which one." He went back to her and lifted her over his shoulder. She muffled a cry as a pain burned in her side. "We need to move."

As they ran into the dark wilderness Charlotte wondered what was worse: being carried off by these aliens or being stalked by another. One much more lethal. One she feared even more. She hardly felt the relief of knowing Axrel was alive because ever since she saw the vrisha ships, she was certain he was involved. Somehow, some way, he must have known. And even if he didn't, they must have come to free him. To save one of their own. He was one of them, he said so himself. Now that he lived, he was coming for her. For whatever crazed, obsessed reason, he wanted her. Perhaps as some sick thank you for keeping him alive. Or maybe he felt her life belonged to him.

He would eat you before becoming your friend. And he'd enjoy it.

She felt dread consume her. She was a fool to think she could make anything work between them, friendship or otherwise.

They broke into a small wood of twisted trees, green and black moss hanging from the branches. The rain slowed, turning into a fine mist as they trudged onward, beginning to ascend up a wide slope.

They didn't falter or stop to rest, but no matter how fast they ran or how far, the scent of pheromones only grew stronger.

She could feel the drogin growl low. As they broke through the trees and into a wide field, he halted and threw her to the ground.

"What are you doing? We can't stop," said one of the grex.

"He's going to catch up to us regardless." The drogin crouched over her, then gripped her arms tight, forcing her onto her back. "But I won't give him the satisfaction of having her." He lowered himself, mouth opening wide, aiming for her throat. Hot, putrid breath touched her face, drool dripping from his mouth. Charlotte writhed and twisted under him, his body too heavy for her to lift. She tried to knee him, but he wouldn't let off. He leaned down and bit her shoulder, and Charlotte screamed.

Her cry set off the others, and in their eyes was a sort of frenzy. They lunged for Prisoner One, some striking at him, trying to rip him off her, others trying to drag her away, tearing her jacket and shirt, pulling her arms and hair, tugging her around like she was a rag doll, a toy they didn't want to share.

She could see nothing but bodies around her, legs and arms, teeth and claws. She tried to cover her face with her arms from their attacks. They fought around her, then a howl broke from one of the assailants, and he went flying. Hands that held her suddenly freed her, and she fell back onto wet grass. There were shrieks and growls around her as the fighting continued, fur and scales flying. Charlotte began to crawl away, desperately hoping they didn't catch her attempt to escape. She crawled on her belly, making for a rocky hillside nearby.

Something large hit the ground next to her, making her jump. It was the body of one of the grex, its throat and chest slashed. From his uniform pocket, she could see a blade sticking out. She grabbed for it, then fumbled to her knees. With the knife now in hand, she twisted around and saw the others splayed out in the grass. Only the drogin was on his feet still, and before him was the shadow of a demon, with eyes made of fire.

The demon stalked the alien then, with one mighty swoop, struck Prisoner One in the face with his taloned hand. Blood gushed and the drogin reared back, roaring in anger.

As the demon started for the alien once more, Charlotte forced herself onto her feet. She took one step, then nearly fell. Her ankle throbbed as sharp pain shot up her leg. She must have injured her ankle when she crashed the car. Still, she didn't stop moving. She limped her way toward the rocky hill, thinking beyond it might be something that could save her. Save her from the monsters that had come to eat her. She hobbled past boulders, gripping the blade tight in one hand and steadying herself on the rocks with the other.

She heard a howling cry behind her, and when she glanced back, she saw Prisoner One running, fleeing into the brush. The demon did not go after him. Instead, he turned toward her. Charlotte let out a whimper and continued on, not wanting to give up yet. Not yet.

But as Prisoner One had said before, he was going to catch her. She knew. When she made it up to the hilltop and saw nothing but more rocky hills beyond, she slowed. She knew he was behind her. She turned and faced him and, with a shaky hand, raised her blade. The demon watched her. He took a step toward her, and she stumbled back, hitting a large boulder behind her.

"Don't," she breathed. "Don't come any closer, Axrel."

The demon stopped. He bowed his head.

"*Sifa shas ricar griss,*" he hissed back.

Charlotte's eyes widened, her hand lowering an inch.

Have no fear of me.

It wasn't so much a demand as a request. Heart racing still, her throat tightening, the fear wouldn't leave her. It might be a trick.

He took a small step closer, then, to her shock, he lowered himself to his knees. Now he no longer towered above her. He kept his head bent, his eyes still watching her. He didn't move, as if waiting.

Her first instinct was to bolt. But what good would that do? He would only catch her again. She waited too, wondering if he was going to strike. But he never did. His tail remained unmoving behind him, and his hands lay flat on his thighs. His mouth—her eyes narrowed, trying to see in the dark. He was still wearing the muzzle Officer Leslie had put on him before transferring him to the pod. He clearly wasn't able to unlatch it himself as the mechanism was programmed to only be taken off by a human hand. She stared at it, then locked eyes with his. If she removed the device, he could attack her. Tear her flesh like he warned he could. If she didn't, he could still kill her if he really liked.

Still, he didn't move or draw closer to her. She realized he was waiting for her to come to him. To trust him.

"If you try anything," her voice shook, "I will be forced to use this." She pointed her knife at his throat.

Axrel remained still, unmoved. "*Erisa lis na fisa...Eslis nefisa ricara.*"

If you try anything to harm me...I will do nothing.

Charlotte frowned, her weapon lowering again. He looked deadly serious.

They could be stuck in this situation for a long time if neither of them did anything. And she had a feeling he could go a much longer time sitting there than she could.

It was there in his eyes, however, that made her reconsider his motives.

Then he said something she thought she had misheard. It was not a common word used in vrishan.

"Please."

Her weapon lowered farther, struck dumb by his honesty. The fact he was asking was insane. She knew she had no chance against him. And he knew it too. Yet he was asking her to trust him.

Her hand tightened around the knife, and she took a step, then another, toward him. Still he did not move. Even when the knife point was an inch from his throat, he did not strike. She watched him for a moment longer, for one last sign of deception, then she cursed softly and let the knife fall from her hand.

The air between them was electric even as she moved around him and began to fumble with the locking mechanism. When it unlocked at her touch and unlatched from his face, slipping to the ground, Charlotte backed away as he slowly rose and turned back to her.

"For your aid, I am grateful," he said in the same tone as she remembered. In the same way that made her believe from the beginning that he might not be the demon everyone feared.

She stared up at him and nodded, her throat too tight and her mouth too dry to speak. The adrenaline that had pumped through her since being chased was finally starting to diminish, making her feel lightheaded. Her energy was seeping from her, and the pain now took a front seat to all her thoughts. She let out a soft groan and hunched over, a sharp ache in her shoulder where the drogin had bitten her. The pain seemed to be all over, and a dark cloud started to slip over her vision. She was shutting down.

Hands came around her and a pang of fear still hit her as she saw his clawed, bloody fingers keeping her on her feet.

She heard her name on his tongue. A gentle caress. "Tell me how to help you."

She almost wanted to laugh as the relief that hit her was so great. He really wasn't going to hurt her.

"My kit...they left it back at the station...past the woods." She pointed in the direction they had just come.

Suddenly, she was being lifted up. She gasped as Axrel placed one hand under her legs and another at her back, cradling her. She stiffened, at first surprised and a little wary. "What are you...?"

"I won't leave you here," he answered. "But we need to make haste. You are very cold. Did you know that, Charlotte?"

She did. She knew she was weak and injured, blood still trickling down her arm from the bite. She had a great urge to take a nap, and she knew that was a very bad sign.

He started to move, carefully returning down the hill toward the woods. Even as he held her tight, she clung to his neck, in fear of falling. He moved so quickly, with such ease, it was like she floated. He leapt off one rock and hit the ground at a run, gaining more speed as he returned to the woods and ran back toward the station.

CHAPTER FOURTEEN

CHARLOTTE

They made it back to the station cabin in half the time, Axrel making use of his swift, agile hunter instincts to move effortlessly through the underbrush. The garage was open, the car crushed into the side of a fence. He set her down by it and checked the perimeter for signs of others. As he did, Charlotte found her kit, thrown to one side of the garage, still miraculously intact. The bag, however, was torn to shreds, and most of the contents were scattered about, clothes torn and dirtied, her ISpad screen cracked. She found Grayson's receiver in a small puddle and feared it was more broken than before. Still, she took it, just in case, placing it in her kit.

Axrel came back a minute later, claiming it safe. He took her through the garage and inside the cabin, into a back room with twin bunk beds. Judging by what she could tell, the cabin was a ranger hideout. If a prisoner escaped or got too far off their work path, the rangers took the vehicles out to find them, or if those from the city got lost in the wilderness, they would form a rescue. Now, the rangers were all gone.

Axrel placed her down one of the beds, then took one of the sheets from another and handed it to her so she could dry. She laughed a little, thinking there was probably a bathroom and towels somewhere but the vrisha saw a dry cloth as it was—dry. She took it without complaint and wiped off her wet face and some of her hair. Blood and dirt smeared on the white. They stared at it, then Charlotte looked to her shoulder. She bundled up the sheet and placed pressure to stop the bleeding.

"What can I do?" Axrel asked.

Charlotte looked up at him, shocked at first. He appeared sincere, his eyes bright with concern as they glanced at her shoulder. "There should be more dry cloth in one of the rooms, thicker ones, if you look," she said. "The rest, I can take care of with my own supplies."

Axrel watched her a moment longer, then he quickly disappeared. She didn't tell him that her supplies were nearly dried up and that what she really needed was a surgical machine to help seal the wounds, but she doubted she'd find either of those nearby. She rifled through her kit and took out a small tool she'd found at the medical center—a meldpen. It would have to do for now, though her cuts were probably deep, and she would need to be careful. She would have used the tool earlier, but it took some time to heat up and to seal a wound, and it was relatively unpleasant if not painful. If she had made a noise, she feared she would have been heard and found. Now that she felt relatively safe—at least where Axrel was concerned—she could put it to use. But the pen wasn't fit for deeper injuries, so she would still need to be cautious of tearing the skin.

She clicked the tool on and set it to its highest setting to let it heat up. Her body shook as the cold set into her bones. She took off her jacket and then her shirt, as they were damp, and wrapped the sheet partly around her.

Axrel came back with a set of towels. She took one gladly, wiping away the blood. By then, the meldpen was ready. She took it up and held the tip to the bite, then pressed it close to the skin. The burning sensation grew from an unpleasant tingling to feeling like she was being burned by the end of a cigarette. She hissed in pain but forced herself to remain still. She was so focused on her job she didn't notice right away that Axrel was watching her still, tail beginning to weave back and forth, hands clenching and unclenching into fists as if the sight of her fixing herself but clearly in pain made him uncomfortable. She felt a little strange herself, as the big alien watched, his eyes drifting over her shoulder, neck, then down to her covered breasts then stomach. But the irritation of the melding made her worry little of how bare she was before him.

When she had sealed it entirely, she sighed in relief but knew she wasn't done. She still had her leg and back to deal with. She glanced up at him and cleared her throat.

"I will need to do my leg next and will have to take off the rest of my uniform."

He stood there staring at her. "Yes."

She stared back at him, wondering if he understood, but it seemed he didn't or he just didn't care. Her lips curled a little. Nakedness meant little to them.

She could tell him to go, but she somehow felt safer with him close where she could see him. She unclasped her uniform pants and let them slide off, leaving her in only her underwear. She unwrapped the gauze and threw it to the floor, then, shifting back on the bed, she spread her leg, aiming the pen over the gash at her thigh, trying to keep her shaking hand steady.

Axrel sat down on the bed next to her, hardly fitting on it, the bed groaning underneath him, his back arched forward so he didn't hit his horns against the top bunk. He watched again for a moment, then said, "We won't be able to stay here long. There are others that will come."

Charlotte hissed again in pain. "Yes, I imagine so...there is a station some miles north. I think it will have ships and communication there. That's where I was heading before..."

Axrel bowed his head. "Before I found you."

She paused, then nodded. Even beyond the pain, her mind began to race. Why did he come for her? Why was he here now? She had decided to trust him but at what cost?

She continued to seal the skin, pretending to focus. "I would still like to go there."

"I will take you. Make sure it is safe."

His response shocked her. He was going to help her? Why? The prospect of having a big scary alien bodyguard, however, didn't sound so bad at all, especially with others running around and the danger they presented. But his motives still made her a tad suspicious.

She remained quiet until her leg was finished. She then dabbed some of what was left of her salve on each wound and wrapped them with the last bit of gauze she had left. She carefully stood, then forced herself to meet Axrel's gaze.

"I have one last cut, but I can't get to it. I was hoping maybe you could..."

Axrel rose and took the tool she offered without question. She turned, placing her hair over her shoulder. She heard Axrel growl softly.

"That bad huh?"

"There is..."

Charlotte turned her head. "What?"

"Glass."

Charlotte felt her gut twist, but it wasn't like she hadn't encountered worse even if it was her own body. "In that case, you'll have to get it out first."

That would be very painful, but she would manage. Axrel didn't move at first, as if he didn't want to hurt her. "Hold still." His hand, heavy and warm, gripped her unwounded shoulder to steady her. A few seconds later, she felt him pull the glass out, the sharp, agonizing sting made her eyes water, and she clamped her mouth shut to stifle a cry. Her back throbbed, and she nearly doubled over, but Axrel's hand kept her up.

With the glass out, Charlotte exhaled a shaky breath. Her vision was going in and out again. She felt a wetness trickle down her back and knew the cut must be bleeding more now with the glass gone. She straightened and gave Axrel a towel to wipe it off. She stiffened as she felt his breath along her back and neck and felt her heart do a little flip.

How sweet it would be...

But he wouldn't dare, would he? Then she remembered reading from one of Dr. Hart's journals on vrishan healing treatments. Their saliva carried healing and anti-infection properties. It was why they had little need for tools and machines unless it was very dire.

She turned her head again to gaze up at him, wondering if he would dare. And if she would stop him. Before she concluded she wouldn't, he lifted his head then wiped the blood off with the towel. She was more surprised by her disappointment than she was of the idea that he might have almost licked the cut like an animal licked its wounds. It was both a jarring and curious thought.

He took the meldpen and sealed her wound, and Charlotte hardly noticed the pain this time, now feeling numb.

"Thank you," she whispered once he finished. His hand, still on her shoulder, squeezed it before he released her. Charlotte turned and took the tool and towel from him, then stood there as their eyes locked on each other. They seemed to remain in that moment for a long time before Charlotte finally said, "Why did you go looking for me?"

Axrel's head rose slightly. He seemed to think on his words then decided on, "I had a debt to pay."

Charlotte blinked up at him. "You crawled your way out of the wreckage of a ship, traveled through wild unknown territory, and fought a bunch of alien thugs all so you could find me to pay a debt?"

Axrel bowed his head. "Yes." But something in his eyes made her unconvinced. Still, he said, "You treated me, saved my life. I felt compelled to repay the favor." He turned to move her kit off the bed onto a table. "I had promised, didn't I? Save another for my own. A life for a life. And I have chosen yours."

Charlotte stood there, nearly speechless. So that was it. He had gone through all the trouble all to honor her favor.

But that couldn't be it. She had asked him to spare a life, not go looking for one to save out of some dire situation and then to protect them through their ordeal. But he was willing to do this for her. With everything that was happening, he had chosen to come and be with her instead. And all for a favor? No, that was impossible.

So why then?

He threw back the covers of the bed and seemed to wait for her to come and lie down. "You should rest for as long as you can. As soon as I sense others, we will need to go."

Charlotte refused to move. "You know who attacked our ship. Axrel, you saw who it was, didn't you?"

He let the covers drop. "You needn't worry of it. I won't let them find you."

That was all well and fine but not the point. "I don't think it's me they are after." She hugged the towel a little closer. "Why didn't you go to them? Why are you here with me instead of with them fighting and killing the others? They are your pack, aren't they?"

His eyes flashed with fire at that. "Yes," he hissed softly. "And no."

"What aren't you telling me?" she asked firmly.

He tugged at one of his horns, as if frustrated. "I am one of them. But I disobeyed orders, and they in turn betrayed me. They left me for dead. That is how the humans found me and then how you came to find me in the state I was in."

She covered her mouth. "Are you saying they did all that to you?"

His eyes turned to the ground. "They thought it would teach me a lesson. And it did. It taught me to seek vengeance."

She slid her hand to her throat. "What are you going to do?"

Gently, he placed a hand on her arm to direct her to the bed where this time she allowed herself to return. "I'm going to get you out of here. Then I'm going to kill them."

CHAPTER FIFTEEN

AXREL

He let her sleep, making little noise as he stalked the rooms and the outside, watching and waiting. He had no desire to rest. On the ship, he had slept long enough. His energy was finally beginning to return, his strength increasing.

He checked on Charlotte many times, making sure she hadn't somehow started to grow worse in her injured state. He knew little of humans' survival capabilities, but they seemed fragile enough to warrant concern. Thankfully, she seemed fine, she slept peacefully, and at times, he found himself watching for longer than he cared to admit.

It was so utterly strange to him. He had never felt any sort of tender feelings toward a human before, nor any otherkin. He had always been of the kind that deemed others untrustworthy, especially humans. Especially after the kind of tricks pulled by them and the alliance allowing for unsavory acts to go unpunished. He had started to feel animosity along with the mistrust which led him to being found and persuaded by the Blood Guard. He was considered a worthy warrior in itself, having been offered several positions among different queens. But his anger made him seek a place among a rogue queen. Queen Theda had offered him a place among her warriors, had whispered promises of power and of justice served. Of vrisha rule. Conquering what they wanted and taking what they deserved. It was all very tempting. He hated the idea that nothing could be questioned in regards to the alliance, that there was corruption there as well, no matter how they tried to hide it. He didn't want to be a part of it, but he had few other options. The majority of vrisha queens had sworn themselves to the alliance. And their say was final. He didn't want the choice taken from him. And he wanted others to pay for their misdeeds.

But he realized his mistake on Obilis Zero. And now he wanted the Blood Guard to pay. He still hated the humans for taking him, imprisoning them as he did. He still hated them for many things. They were conniving, selfish creatures for all he believed.

He had thought this of all of them. But he found he could not see such things in Charlotte no matter how hard he tried. She made him question his own thoughts and feelings every time they were near each other, every time they talked.

He watched her still now, unable to turn away, feeling a strange sort of need. It frightened him a little. It was something new, yet something old at the same time. A deep instinctual need to protect.

At some point—he wasn't sure when, perhaps when he had gone searching for her or when he had found her and was chasing her up the hill—he decided he was going to make sure she lived. Make sure she was never frightened of him again.

He moved to back out of the room, to force his eyes away, when a sound made him grow still.

There were cries in the distance. And the sound of weapons firing. He could smell blood. Others were coming.

A deep growl escaped him. He wouldn't let them take her.

He stepped over to Charlotte's bedside and hesitated, wondering how best to wake her, not wanting to startle her. He reached down and gently shook her arm. She groaned softly and turned on her side.

He was about to call her name when the firing of weapons grew closer, the cries and shouts louder. No time to wait. Without another thought, he picked her up, holding her against his chest. She made another groan of protest, her lids half opening to fix him with a sleepy gaze.

"What's going on?" she said slowly.

"We need to go." He wrapped her in the sheet, swaddling her. With one arm still wrapped around her, he picked up her kit, then moved for the door.

"My clothes," she murmured.

"I will find you better ones," he promised. Her old clothes lay about the floor, wet and dirty and torn.

She seemed about to protest when there was a crash just outside. Her eyes flew open with fear. "Okay, let's just go."

She clung tightly to him, her body snug against his chest as he flew from the room down a passage. Just as they passed a window, the glass shattered behind them. Charlotte jumped, but Axrel hardly flinched. He swept through to the back of the building, the way they had first come in, then rushed off into the trees beyond. The rain had stopped, and now a thick mist seeped across the ground. The air was chill and wet, nipping at his scales. The dark was heavy, but he could see several feet beyond.

"We should head north," Charlotte said, her warm breath at his neck. She shivered, and he held her a little tighter. He tilted his head, gazing upward, but there were no stars, only the twisted branches of trees and beyond that a blanket of gray and black.

Axrel returned his focus in front of him. "We will need to find our bearings. We will look for a safe place first. Wait for daylight. Then we will start north if we aren't already."

Charlotte bobbed her head. She didn't say another word, and he wondered if she fell asleep again. It was just as well. He focused harder on his surroundings. Taking in every scent, every sound. He didn't slow or stop even as the terrain grew rockier and the land began to rise at an angle. Only when they came to a cliff wall was he forced to stop. He looked up, knowing he wouldn't be able to climb it with her in his arms. It seemed the land was very rocky and hilly in parts, which made things more difficult. If he thought she could handle it, he would have her on his back, but she was too tired, he knew, to hang on long enough. Instead, he began to run parallel to the cliffside, hoping for an opening.

Eventually, he found one and took off up another hill until he came to a dirt path. He knew other prisoners might consider following similar paths as they made it easier than walking through the terrain. But surrounding the path were more cliff sides and mountainous rock that would need to be climbed. For now, he would have to follow it. If he encountered anyone and they grew hostile, they would be sorry.

The path went on for many miles. Long enough for the dark to begin to fade. The path wound through the rocky hills, but the light breaking along the horizon told him which way was east. He considered beginning to turn northward, but he knew he would need to stop soon. Not for his sake but for Charlotte's. Even keeping her from jostling around as much as he could, trying to rest in such a position couldn't be pleasant. Eventually, she needed down anyway, to relieve herself. As she did, he decided to climb up a short way onto a set of boulders. As the light pierced the sky, turning everything gray, he searched around, wondering if the path led onward or ended.

Then, as he turned his gaze toward a higher outcrop, he saw it. Just a little ways northeast. A building.

He climbed back down to find Charlotte waiting for him. She was wrapped tight in her sheet, looking at him wearily, her kit at her feet. He wondered for a moment if she still feared his motives, but he couldn't blame her for that. She didn't run at least. And any fear he did sense in her was small. And maybe he could believe it wasn't for him.

"There is a place not far ahead. We are almost there."

She nodded her head. She took a step and another, limping still. She cursed. She looked at him, uncertain, maybe worried he would be tired of carrying her. He wasn't. But he wondered if she was becoming uncomfortable with being carried herself. "My leg," she started. "It's still sprained but I might be able to walk."

He picked up her kit and offered it to her. "Not much longer." She took it, then looked up at him, searching his face as if to find something hidden, some trick still. He couldn't blame her. She was still cautious of him, even now. Even if he wished otherwise, he knew he couldn't expect her to trust right away. And really it was smart of her. She still thought him a killer. That he was only sparing her. He was still an enemy of her people. She would still doubt him, maybe for some time, unless he could prove to her otherwise.

He reached out and carefully lifted her back up. She stiffened this time, he noticed, now that she was more awake and aware of what was happening. He let it go and continued on down the path.

By the time they reached the building seen in the distance, the sky was growing brighter, showing off the dull gray clouds above. The building sat on the edge of a cliff with a tower to one side. Axrel placed Charlotte between a large rock and head of tall grass. "I'm going to make sure there is no one inside. I will be back." He turned to leave when she reached out and gripped his arm. He froze and looked back at her.

"If there are people, human or otherwise, please...don't hurt them. If you can. If they aren't hostile, it isn't necessary." She squeezed his arm. "Please say you won't."

He stared down at her hand on his arm, transfixed. It was as soft as he remembered back on the ship. "I won't," he promised, his voice rough. "If they are not hostile."

She seemed to relax, relief spreading over her features. She let go of his arm, and he could still feel the warmth there, tingling along his skin. He turned again and headed up the steps, two at a time. The building appeared dark, but that didn't mean there weren't others hiding inside. Still, he didn't hesitate as he slipped past the door and crept inside. He didn't smell or hear anything unusual. He searched each area and found nothing. When he was moving toward the last unchecked room, he heard the clatter of many things falling. He approached the open doorway of some kind of storage room. There was someone or something inside, their back turned, rummaging through cans and bags, pulling or biting them apart, then stuffing the contents inside into their mouth.

He let out a soft hiss, and the creature turned with a yelp. He didn't know what it was, just some strange furry creature with large ears. It was small and seemingly harmless. It looked up at him with big eyes, then shot between his legs and bolted out one of the open windows.

So, the planet had life of some sort, if not of the more intelligent type. He could hunt if they couldn't find food.

The storage unit, despite the mess the creature had made, was still stocked with some provisions. It would help.

When he returned, he found Charlotte huddled close to the rock, her knees bent to her stomach. She was so small compared to him, her light hair falling across her shoulder, clinging to her slender neck. She seemed alert but not frightened. She didn't cower or whimper. For a human, he was impressed by how collected she seemed, considering the state she was in. Undaunted by her situation.

Except maybe for him. When she saw him, her eyes widened, then dropped, falling across his body. Looking for fresh blood on his scales, no doubt.

"Nothing. Just a small scavenger. It's safe."

She nodded, then rose, keeping the sheet around her with one hand, so as not to expose herself as the wind picked up.

He stepped toward her, ready to carry her again up the steps, only this time she backed away.

"It's all right. I think I can manage." She turned away before he could say anything. He watched her limp her way up the steps, not liking the way she struggled but not wanting to fight her. He followed her up, keeping close lest she were to fall and he would need to catch her. When they made it to the door, she stopped to peer inside. It wasn't a large building by any means, with just one level not including the tower. Past the door was a room with a set of tables, some kind of machine placed atop each of them. Maps aligned the walls, and there was a large monitor between them. Charlotte moved slowly inside, studying them first before walking on down a short passage. There were two bedrooms connected to a washroom to one side. The room with the storage closet stood opposite. Charlotte entered and looked around as he stayed by the doorway, watching her. She approached a tall rectangular box with a set of doors and opened it. Inside looked to be more food. Cold air seeped out from the box, then dissolved away when she closed it. It was some kind of cold storage.

Charlotte looked in the storage closet next. "That creature made a mess, but there's at least something to be salvaged." She moved out of the room and into the last which was the base of the tower. Within was just some kind of lift to take one up to the top. A set of winding stairs stood beside it.

Charlotte tilted her head back to gaze up at the roof above. "Anything up there?" she asked.

"Just some kind of control and observation room," he answered.

She nodded her head and turned back to him. "Do you think this place is safe?"

He looked around, then said, "For now. I will keep watch. But I believe few would travel this far. They will stick to the main paths near the city. Or to other larger stationways."

"And to the working towns, if they aren't completely destroyed also by the Blood Guard," she said.

"Yes, that too."

She stood there before him, her gaze locked with his for a

moment before falling. "I think, if you're keeping watch, I'd like to take a shower. Clean up, I mean."

His eyes raked her body. The sheet clung to her damp skin, her hands stained with dry mud and dirt, her shoulder and arm cakes in dry blood. He bowed his head and stepped aside to let her pass. She moved cautiously by him, returning to the passage.

As she shut herself in the washroom, Axrel took to walking the grounds. Behind the building, which he decided to name the Tower, he found a small shed. Inside there were tools of various sizes, knives and other sharp weapons, ropes, nets, and pulleys along with supplies for what he could only assume was to keep the tower in good condition or if in need of repairs. There were no long-range weapons like shooters, all having been swiped when the occupants had fled. He thought at some point they might need one. He would dominate any fight up close, but even he couldn't dodge some of the more advanced long-range shooters. And he couldn't risk Charlotte getting hit. He would need something to defend with eventually.

There wasn't much use for anything in the shed, however there were a pair of what looked to be thick scraps of durable material made to be worn like a protective vest. Those could be useful.

After some time stalking around the tower and the area surrounding, he returned inside to check on Charlotte. When he made it to the washroom, he caught movement at the corner of his eye and stopped at the doorway of the first bedroom. The door was open slightly, and he could see, from within, Charlotte standing by a small closet , sifting through some of the spare clothes within. She was naked, clean of blood and dirt, her damp hair falling down her back, her last pair of clothing on the floor at her feet.

He felt a sort of twisting warmth in his gut at the sight of her, his muscles tensing. She was so different from him, soft-skinned, scaleless. But he found her strangely alluring despite her odd features. She was not repulsive to him like he considered some of the others, but he could not deny they were strikingly unalike in so many ways. Their forms opposed each other in every way. Yet there was something that drew him to her, pulling him, wanting to connect, to embrace. To claim.

His heart pattered a little faster than normal, and he backed away with a soft hiss. No, he shouldn't think like that. Not with a human.

He hesitated near the door before he forced himself away. He would need to keep control of himself. To not forget what she was despite who she was. He couldn't feel such things for a human. It wasn't possible.

He returned to the entrance room, watching out one of the windows, trying to clear his thoughts. As the light outside slowly sunk closer to the horizon, he heard the soft shuffling of feet behind him and looked around.

Charlotte stood now, fully clothed, the gray and green military uniform baggy in some places, especially at the waist and arms. She wore a belt to keep things more snug, and she had found a pair of boots.

"It's all a little big, I know." She pulled at the extra material at her sides. "The boots are a little loose too, but they were the smallest I could find."

He looked her up and down, not caring for the prison guard uniform because of what it reminded him of, but it was better than nothing in terms of protection and warmth. "It's good there were clothes left for you."

She smiled, agreeing, and the expression warmed him. He looked back out the window, not looking at anything in particular when she came up beside him.

"I'd say you could try some on too, but I can already tell they would be too small," she said. "I know you don't have a need for a lot of clothes, but this place is pretty cold and rainy. It must be pretty uncomfortable for you wearing only kelva leggings."

"It is, but I will manage. I would rather not wear human clothes and stink of them."

She gave him a surprised look, and he realized his folly.

"Ah, I mean of the men who wore them."

She looked away, back out at the dark, windy landscape. She was quiet for a long time before she spoke again. "Will you tell me what happened on Obilis Zero?"

He glanced back at her. Her face was almost expressionless except for paling a little in color. She didn't look at him, as if she didn't want him to see her true feelings. He could imagine what they were regardless. She had to know what had happened and what she suspected of him.

He turned back to the scene, thinking, remembering. Recalling the event in great detail. "I traveled with the Blood Guard in a stealth ship," he started. "We made it to Obilis Zero and to the trade base by nightfall. We had been given information that the place was actively creating weapons made for attacking vrisha specifically, being hidden amongst the usual trade supplies." He clenched his fists, leaning forward on the window sill. "We were to breach the walls, then kill whoever we encountered, human or otherwise, that guarded nearby. Then to destroy the place entirely, set it afire," His voice grew low. "I followed them to the gates. There were guardsmen at the borders. They aimed to shoot at us—at me—and I took one out. Then another. I hardly slowed as we broke inside. I heard screams and gunfire and knew others had already gotten in farther. Fire grew quickly as I searched for the containers of weapons." He paused for a moment, letting his breath catch in his lungs. "Then I saw them. It was a group of humans hiding behind a set of crates. My first thought was to do as ordered. Search and destroy. But then I looked closer and saw it wasn't a set of witless guards who'd run and hid. It was a family. Two humans with three small fledglings. Their children. Their faces...held nothing but terror. They didn't try to attack. They didn't even scream. They merely cowered and cried quietly, as if accepting their fate. My rage was so great. And yet I hesitated. I don't know why I did in that moment, but I did. I distrusted, hated all humans. But it felt...senseless to kill those who clearly couldn't defend themselves. The vrisha were fighters. We had always been warriors. We fought enemies on fair ground, as equals. We were not killers. Not slaughterers, unless we had no choice. But we did have a choice then. I had a choice. In my mind, I didn't see the harm of letting them go. They had no weapons. The building would be destroyed regardless. I wasn't afraid of retaliation. I let them flee." A soft growl slipped from his throat, and he clenched his teeth at the next words. "But one of my brothers saw me. He took out the family before they could get far. I grew angry and struck him. We fought out in the snow. I had him on the ground when others stopped me. My brother told them what had happened, and I didn't deny it. That's when they attacked me. With one, I could hold my own, but with eight, it wasn't so easy. They beat me even when I lay motionless on the ground. They left me there and told me they'd let the humans find me and take me. And that if I lived, I could return, once my lesson was learned. Once my so-called punishment for letting the humans go was paid. They left me. And for a pack to leave one of their own was the ultimate betrayal. I could never forgive them. And since then, I have sought to find them."

There was no response, and it was just as well. He could understand if she had nothing to say. But he was glad that she knew, even if the memory pained him. Made the seething anger and bitterness return. He'd find them once Charlotte was safe.

A hand dropped on his arm, and he looked back at her. She gazed up at him with her striking blue eyes, forcing a chill to run down his spine.

"Thank you for letting that family go," she said softly, squeezing his arm. "For giving them a chance even if it was in vain. I'm sorry for what your pack did to you, Axrel. I really am. But what you did...it can't be forgotten."

His eyes narrowed as he studied her face. "I still killed those guards. I still felt hate for them and others."

Her hand slipped from his arm, her eyes dropping from his. "I know."

"If you can't trust me, I'll understand. But I will never hurt you, Charlotte. I swear to that."

She looked back at him, and there was no longer uncertainty in her gaze. "I know."

She looked relieved and inside, so did he. Perhaps she would warm up to him. But he wouldn't allow himself to hope too much. He would do for her what he couldn't for that family. She deserved that at least. And if she couldn't stand to be around him through it all, he would understand. No matter what he felt, he would keep his distance if she asked. And in the end, he could feel he at least did the right thing.

She stayed beside him, looking out the window again, up to the darkening sky. "Why do you think they are here? The Blood Guard?"

He took a deep breath and let it out slowly. "It's hard to say. Whatever plan it is, they made it after I was captured. I had no knowledge of it."

"Back when I was in the cabin running from the drogin and his friends, I tried to use the local transmitter. I got an odd message on one of the channels," she said. "It was in xolian. It said to come to the Flame. To come join us. Whoever us is, I don't know for sure. But I think it might have been them."

Axrel dipped his head. He thought about when he had seen them from the wreckage of the ship. They had been attacking the humans. But no one else. They had never come near his part of the ship, and the prisoners that survived were escaping quickly. "I think they are trying to recruit the inmates," he confessed. "They want them on their side."

She looked at him, stunned. "You think they want to increase their numbers?"

He grunted. "Only so many vrisha are a part of the Blood Guard. They are strong, highly capable of doing incredible damage. But it is still not enough. Queen Theda doesn't just want a group of rebels. She wants an army."

Charlotte shook her head, eyes wide with fear at the realization. "And who better to try to bring into her fold than those wronged by the governing systems. By the human militia."

"Exactly."

Her face turned a shade paler. "We have to warn others. We have to tell someone. Even if the military knows what's happening here, by the time they get to Fargis, it might be too late."

"Maybe one of the stations has a communicator?"

"One strong enough, I can't say," she said. "So far, I've only found local transmitters. The prison would have had one, and inside the city. The main docks. Outside of that, the station I was heading for might be the only other place. If it's like any tradeport station mainly running supplies, they would have had to communicate to outer systems. Even if there are no ships there now, I'm confident there would be a way to get help."

"Assuming the Blood Guard hasn't found it already."

"Judging by the map I saw, it looked well-hidden and far enough north it might have gone undetected," she said, then rolled her shoulder in a shrug. "But yes, there is still a chance. It's all I can think besides going back into the city."

"And by now, it's in ruins and infested with inmates. We can't risk it," he said. He tapped his tail on the ground, thinking. "We continue north."

She smiled, and then there was a strange growling that came from inside her which nearly startled him. She placed a hand over her stomach.

"Ah, I guess I need to eat something." She laughed softly. "It's been several hours. I've been too stressed to think about it."

His eyes drifted over her. "Let's find you something." He turned away from the window.

"And you too," she said.

He looked back at her, confused.

"You need to eat too. You might be my guide now through this place, but I am still your doctor," she said, a smile still playing on her lips. "It's been too long since I gave you that jerky, don't you think?"

He blinked at her, then bowed his head. "It has."

"Good." She started down the passage. "We find something for both of us."

CHAPTER SIXTEEN

CHARLOTTE

They ate together, watching as the dull light from outside began to fade into darkness. Night was coming quickly again and with it, her fear. Fear of what was out there and what might find them in the night.

But she felt safer at least. Less terrified now that she was no longer alone. Knowing Axrel would be there to protect her. Her doubts about him were lessened considerably though she still watched him, waiting to see if something in his gaze or manner would slip and reveal some dark nature. But he never did. She had been wary of him before they had come to the Tower, afraid he might be deceiving her somehow. She didn't want to be afraid of him. But it was hard after seeing the Blood Guard and learning he had been searching for her. At the time, she'd thought it more like hunting. Hunting his prey.

But now, after what he had told her about Obilis Zero, she no longer believed him capable of harming her. He had sworn. And she had believed him. She still wondered about his motives, but she no longer worried whether they were sinister or not. She knew they weren't.

To have a vrisha helping her was beyond lucky, she knew, considering their situation. And, in truth, she was beginning to feel content being near him like they were, with him no longer chained. She had been right about him at least in some small part. There was some good in him. He wasn't completely innocent of course. He had admitted to killing her own as she feared. But his confession about the family made her feel there was a chance for him. And maybe she could still get through to him.

When they finished eating—she with her canned vegetables and chicken and he with some dried turkey—Axrel did another quick perimeter check and deemed the area still safe.

"There was a light in the distance. A fire. But it was miles away. I caught no scent of anything, but we should keep the lights off just in case."

She agreed. Those with the fire would distract others in that direction. Even if it was cold, a fire was a good way to gain unwanted attention. She felt sorry for whoever might get attacked in the night.

"I want to go up to the tower before the last light falls," she told him after. "Just to check it out."

Together, they headed to the tower, both deciding to take the stairs in case the elevator was faulty or loud enough to be heard. This meant Axrel had to carry her up, but he didn't seem to mind. At the top, he let her down, and she took in the sight. It was just a room with a terminal, but the view beyond was impressive. From the windows, she could see out a great distance in every direction. To the west and the setting sun, she could see the fire Axrel mentioned. It flickered along the side of a low hill. To the south were patches of woodland and fields, and she thought she saw the station cabin and its winding road. To the east, way on the horizon, were the lights of the city, still burning, no doubt. To the north, she turned her gaze, and her heart dropped a little. It was vast wilderness and rocky hills.

"Looks like we have quite a walk ahead of us." She glanced over at him. "What do you think?"

He stepped closer to the window, his eyes scanning over the land. "There's a bridge down to the northeast." He pointed. "But it's barricaded, and I see movement. It's likely been taken."

Charlotte followed his gaze and was astounded he could see it let alone enough to notice people walking. It was miles away. "You vrisha really have pristine senses, don't you? I hardly see it in this light. Can you tell who is moving along it?"

"I don't see military uniforms or humans. It's prisoners. They are hunkering down. Some have weapons."

Charlotte sighed, placing her hands on her hips. "Great, so much for the easy way."

"There is another trail, however, that passes through the mountains," he said, pointing again to the rock hills.

She stared down below but saw nothing. "Are you sure?"

"It's narrow but I am certain. There is a small stream that follows it. There."

She followed his hand and saw the sliver of a stream going through the trees and the rocks. Just barely.

"I think we will have to take that route," he said. "It might be a little rough—"

"A little?"

"—but we should encounter few others."

"Maybe it won't be too rough for you, but I think you forgot you have a human with you who can't leap up or climb rocks like it's nothing," she reminded him. "I can hardly walk on regular ground as it is."

He scratched at his neck. "I will think on it. But that is likely our best way."

It probably was. But with the harsh terrain and the weather, it was going to be a challenge. And that was even if they didn't encounter anyone or anything. There weren't just the inmates. Who knew what other beasts called this place their home?

Deciding to worry about it later, she moved back to the terminal and turned on the main machine, watching the monitors flicker to life. A map appeared, hovering over the window before them. It was similar to the map she had seen on the ship.

"Here's where we are." She pointed to the Tower, several miles east of the city. "And you were right, there is a route. It's a ranger's trail. It winds through the hills, going past a working town to the main road. Not far from the Lightpost. We could make it there...in a few days maybe, if we don't stop much."

"Faster than that, I think," Axrel said from beside her. She looked over at him curiously, and he caught her gaze. "I can carry you, and I can run far longer and faster."

"I'd hate to make you do that. And, besides, you can't carry me and climb." She shook her head. "We might have to find another way, or I'll have to manage on foot. My leg isn't as bad as it seems despite the limp. It'll swell pretty bad, but I think I can manage."

He seemed to be thinking of something, but he said no more. He'd tell her if he thought of anything, she was sure.

Something flashed at the corner of her eye, and Charlotte looked down at one of the monitors. There was an unread message. She clicked on it and read it quickly. It was from prison officers telling those at the stations to evacuate. Clearly, those at the tower had already figured that out before seeing the message.

There was another message that caught her eye, and she clicked on it. It was a video. It floated over the map before them and showed a man. She recognized him at once. It was the warden.

"Who is that?" Axrel growled.

"The warden of the prison. This message only came through several hours ago, just before the ship crashed." She played the video, and the warden began to speak.

"Everything is under control. Do not attempt to get off world. Stay in your stations and wait. If your station is compromised, go to the Flame, station 5603. Others will be waiting."

"The Flame," Charlotte repeated softly. "The same I had heard through the local transmitter. But why would he..." Then she saw it and quickly, she paused the video, her heart pounding, breath stopping in her lungs. "Do you see...?"

Axrel hardly moved beside her. "Yes," he hissed. "I see him."

In the shadows beyond the warden's light, a vrisha moved, his tail up, ready to strike.

"They had been here all along. Back when I was on the bridge of the ship, the warden looked the same, gaunt and pale, like he was sick. But he wasn't ill, just terrified," she said in a rush of breath. "The Blood Guard had directed the ship to land near the city so they could take it out with ease. They had planned it even then. They wanted the prisoners on the ship too. They wanted..." She looked over at him. "Did they know you were on the ship, Axrel?"

His eyes stared at the video, then shifted over to her, glowing with red flames. "Maybe."

"They must've thought you would survive. They might come for you too."

His eyes brightened. "Or expect me to come to them." His hands clenched at his sides. "Even they would not let a vrisha be taken by others for long. If they knew I had been taken, they might have learned of where and therefore planned to free me themselves. Free one of their own along with the rest, let those who are stronger cull out the weak. Tell them to come to a specific place to be deemed worthy. Any humans would be killed immediately or taken hostage if they considered them useful. The survivors would be offered a place in the Guard. If they refused..."

She looked back at him, already knowing. If they refused, then it was death. There were no other choices. When those who were left gathered, they would go, leaving the planet to burn.

"We should leave by daybreak tomorrow," she said. "They might start looking for you, and we are running out of time."

Axrel looked back at the video of his brother lurking in the shadows beyond. "I agree."

Charlotte went over the map one more time before shutting down the terminal. She had it memorized now in her head. They watched the last layer of light slip past the horizon before they decided to return below. Charlotte grabbed some water from the kitchen before bed. Axrel waited in the hall beside the door of the second bedroom.

"Will you sleep?" she asked, curious.

He turned his head to the other bedroom, his tail flicking beside him. "Likely not. I have slept for too long, and I am restless."

She nodded, understanding completely. "I'm restless too. But exhausted."

His eyes drifted over her. "Rightly so. Rest. I will be near."

She smiled softly, her hand resting on the door. "Thank you, Axrel."

His eyes lifted to hers, and he bowed his head. There was something in his gaze, a flicker that was gone in an instant, too quick for her to recognize. She watched him for a second longer, her heart skipping at his stare. It was nothing, she was sure. She went into her room and closed the door. She waited to hear his footsteps tread down the hall and disappear. She stood there for a minute longer, unable to unlatch her thoughts from him, from his burning gaze. She found herself trying to decipher what it meant. Vrishan expressions were known to be very difficult to read. She didn't think he was angry, but the way he looked at her was intense. Perhaps it was only an expression she was unfamiliar with.

Her pulse quickened, but it didn't feel like fear. She could really use those little red pills right about now, but they were gone, tossed away when the drogin and his gang had rifled through her bag. She went to her kit now and opened it. There were painkillers and anti-inflammatories. But nothing to dull her growing anxiety and help her sleep. She took one of the painkillers as her leg was throbbing and her injuries, despite being sealed, still held an uncomfortable ache. She tossed off her clothes after and went into bed. She lay there for a long while, her body exhausted but her mind awake.

Her thoughts raced, mostly concerning her situation and the dangers that lay ahead. If they did get to the Lightpost, would there be anything there like she hoped? And if there was, what would happen to Axrel? He said he wanted revenge. Would he really stay in hopes of gaining vengeance on his brothers? He might die if he did, and that bothered Charlotte more than she cared to admit.

Eventually all she could think about was him, still trying to understand what drove him. Now that she knew he wasn't out to kill her or her kind, she had come to terms that she was glad he survived the crash. Glad he wasn't going off to his death to fight his brothers and sisters. Not yet. Maybe there was still time to save him from such a fate...

Charlotte sat up, opened her kit, and took out the broken transmitter. It still had a long crack on one side which water now likely seeped into. Still, she clicked it on, and there was static that followed.

"Grayson," she spoke softly, mouth close to the speaker. "Grayson, if you can hear me, we need help. Fargis is compromised. The vrisha are here. They are trying to take prisoners." She waited, but only static answered her. "Grayson. Please tell the others. Tell them the Blood Guard is here. The city and prison have been taken. Many are dead. More will follow. Bring help."

More static. But Charlotte didn't want to give up hope. Not yet. It would be a long night, and she wouldn't find much sleep, so she would keep calling until exhaustion took her.

CHAPTER SEVENTEEN

Charlotte

The morning was as bright and gray as the last. Charlotte sat by the steps of the Tower, looking out at the path and the hills beyond. A light breeze caught in her hair, the dampness of a thin fog touching at her skin. She tightened her green coat around, her bag cinched tight around her shoulders. It carried her kit, a pair of clothes, provisions, and a flashlight. She found the bag collecting dust in one of the storage closets. The coat too had been hanging in the second bedroom. She felt she was as prepared as humanly possible for the journey to come. She wished Axrel could have worn some of the extra clothes, but they had been too small for him, and he claimed to be fine anyway, despite having nothing but his kelva pants for protection. She had to remind herself he wasn't fragile-skinned like a human. His scales were thick enough and warm enough against the chill air. Still, it was hard not to feel uncomfortable for him, even if he didn't complain.

She heard the soft rustling of grass behind her, and she turned her head to see Axrel coming down to meet her from behind the building. He wore something across his shoulders and back that looked like a bulletproof vest but had been cut in places and re-tied with rope to fit his size. Tied along the shoulders of the vest was a set of straps cut from some bag which were then tied to the ends of a thick, long strip of cloth that might have once been a net.

Charlotte rose and turned to face him. "What is...?"

"Once you are on top of my back, I will wrap the other half around you and tie it to me." He lifted another strip of the net in his hand.

Charlotte stared at it and him until she understood it was meant to be a sling. "You honestly want to carry me? Like that?" She almost sounded mortified. The idea of being carried around like a baby on the back of this towering vrisha was—in the words of one her nurses on Larth—"Mad stupid crazy'".

"There's no way that will hold me," she argued.

"I've secured it well enough and made sure it won't break," he countered.

"Your spikes will tear holes in my clothes and probably my skin."

"That is what the vest is for."

"It will be too much weight after a while, I could hurt your back."

He looked at her, amused and annoyed. "I doubt that."

"You could aggravate the wounds on your back."

"Charlotte."

She looked at him, heat beginning to rise in her face. He knew as well as she it wasn't about his comfort or really even hers. It was about the most efficient way possible for them to travel on foot with her injured leg through rocky hills where one would need to climb. And with no vehicle in sight, there were few other options.

"I can walk. I can—"

"You barely can walk," he pointed out. "And you certainly can't climb. You wouldn't be able to run if need be either. Unless you wish to stay another day and night to think of some other plan, this is the best I could see."

Charlotte bit her lip. She definitely didn't want to stay. They couldn't. They needed to gain as much time as possible. And they were wasting it arguing all because she was...embarrassed really by the idea.

She sighed and crossed her arms. "Fine. But as soon as my leg is better, I want to walk."

His eyes brightened, his amusement growing. "If you wish." He stepped up to her and crouched down beside her, waiting for her to hop on. She hesitated, and he glanced over his shoulder at her, waiting.

She mumbled a curse under her breath, then took off her bag. She pulled the net tied to his vest over her, letting it settle across her middle back just under her arms before grabbing his shoulders and hopping up, wrapping her arms around his neck as he rose carefully. He swung the other half of the net around her ass and under her thighs then across his chest, tying it at the front.

"How do you feel?" he asked as she moved into a comfortable position, pressed snuggly against him, with just the vest between them.

"Crazy. But secure," she admitted.

He grunted. "I'll go slow at first. If anything feels off, let me know." He picked up her bag and handed it to her.

She swung the bag onto her shoulders and secured it. She then gripped the straps across his own shoulders and wrapped her legs around him. "You'll know."

He started down the steps, first at a slow gait, then a light jog as they slipped onto the road which eventually ended and had them going down the hillside through the underbrush. Her body bumped against his, bobbing up and down with every stride, but once she got the hang of his rhythm, she felt less afraid that she might tumble off him. He never faltered. His large size coupled with his unnatural strength kept her firmly in position, the sling tight enough she didn't slip. As they came to the bottom of the hill, they quickly started up another rise. Axrel pushed on, his pace quickening. Charlotte looked back, and the tower stood lonely on its hill, then the woods began to thicken around them, and she saw nothing but the twisting branches that closed in.

* * *

They made decent ground, despite the challenging terrain. The hills, which had been mostly covered in thick woods, began to grow steeper and rockier. At one point, they stopped walking up them and had to actually climb them, up high cliffs. Charlotte found herself holding tighter, her muscles growing sore just from clinging on to Axrel for dear life, refusing to look down. Axrel, however, never complained, never slowed. Only a few times did they stop so that she could rest and eat something. She had to coax him to eat and drink something several times, and he did, though it seemed only for her benefit. The breaks were short, and they were off again in no time.

The thin fog of the morning quickly turned to misty rain as they made their way through a patch of forest now along the ranger's trail which was nothing more than a sliver of dirt hardly wide enough for Axrel to move along. Down a slope to their right was the stream, as he had said, slowly moving the other direction to the south. They saw very little life, but what they did see filled Charlotte with wonder. Several species of bird with gray and black stripes flew above them, making a sort of whirring noise as they went. Axrel almost stepped on some kind of armored mammal that looked like a cross between a woodchuck and an armadillo with little tusks sticking out of its mouth. In the distance, she thought she caught the figure of a slender gray and white creature like a greyhound or a fox with tall legs as it slunk silently into the shadows. None, so far, were threatening, though she wished she had considered looking into the wildlife of Fargis while on the ship to know what else might call it home.

As they came to the edge of a small rise, she noticed Axrel slow. "Do you need to stop?" she asked.

"No." He slowed to a walking pace, his footfalls hardly making a sound. "There are people up ahead."

Charlotte stiffened behind him, her hands tightening at his shoulders, knuckles turning white. "Should we move around them?"

"They already know I am near. They are afraid."

She gave him a confused look, even though he couldn't see it. "How? How can they...Oh." He was giving off warning pheromones. She could smell the coffee-like scent coming from him, pleasant to her somehow but not so much to those who were a threat.

Axrel carefully crept up the rise. "They already caught my scent a few spans back. That's when I smelled them. I thought maybe they would have fled, but they are curious."

Charlotte kept her head down near his neck, the hood of her coat covering part of her face. "Are you going to try to pass them?"

"I would rather pass through than try to find a way around that will take longer. If they threaten us, they will regret it." Axrel continued onward.

She didn't want to ask, but she had to know. "Are they human?"

A pause and then, "No."

Charlotte wasn't sure whether to be relieved or not. She turned silent as they passed over the rise into a small open patch of grass. There, a group lingered, all in inmate uniforms. It was two lygin and a corax. They turned their heads toward them, their eyes wide with wonder and then fear as they saw Axrel coming closer.

Axrel slowed and then stopped and gave off a low, warning growl. The inmates did not bare their teeth or growl back. They only stared in astonishment, the hairs on the lygins' neck and head standing on end, the corax taking a step away, its fins trembling.

There was a standstill for a long moment, until Charlotte lifted her head for them to see. The prisoners looked at her, wide-eyed and curious.

"Hello, we are just trying to pass through," she said in xolian, assuming they could understand. "We are not interested in a fight."

Axrel mumbled something, and Charlotte tapped his shoulder, giving him a warning glare.

The group looked at each other, then back at them. The corax, with more bluish skin than gray and beady eyes, spoke first. "We are just trying to pass through too. There are others blocking the bridge to the main road. They aren't letting any pass. Tirin" —he gestured to the smaller lygin of the group with faded graying fur—"saw the path, and we thought it might take us around."

"If you keep on it, there is a way past the bridge a little north," Charlotte said. Axrel's tail began to move behind her as he watched them, ready in case they moved to attack, but she thought it unnecessary. They seemed harmless. Just afraid.

"We had hoped that would be the case," the corax said. "But the trail beyond has been blocked by fallen rocks. We were resting here in order to consider our options."

Charlotte looked to Axrel, who glanced down the path. A blockade was going to be an annoyance, but Axrel would find a way, she was sure.

"If you just follow the stream up, there might be a way around."

"We thought that," he said. "I swam up a ways. It seemed clear, but..." He looked to his comrades, then back at her. "Something wasn't right. Caught a bad scent."

"Ah, afraid that was us." She patted Axrel's shoulder.

The corax shook his head. "We caught your scent when we were going back. That is why we stopped. Danger one way and another. Weren't sure what to do."

Charlotte frowned at him, confused. "You smelled another? Like us?"

The corax shook his head again. "No. But the same bad feeling from both."

Charlotte squeezed Axrel's shoulder, who had hardly moved. "I'm sorry we can't be of much help then. But if you are considering traveling the opposite way, there is a tower on the hills to the south."

"We want to go north and then east, around the city," growled the lygin Tirin, his golden eyes locked on hers. "We are trying to get to the Flame. That is where we heard others going."

A soft rumble started in Axrel's chest. Charlotte patted him again, this time to calm. "You shouldn't go. Those waiting there might kill you, and they will make you fight others to survive."

The lygin's eyes narrowed, glancing between her and Axrel. "Is that really true?"

"It is."

"It's your kind, isn't it?" the corax said to Axrel. "I saw the ships above. What do they want?"

Axrel shifted. "They want to recruit you, but they will only take the strongest. She is right that they will make you fight to prove it," he said in broken xolian. Some of the words, Charlotte had to retranslate. "If you refuse, then they will kill you. If you value your lives, don't go."

"Then where?" the corax asked. "Where else can we go?"

"Somewhere as far away as you can," Charlotte answered. "Wait and hide if you have to. I'm going to try and bring help."

"Why should we believe you?" Tirin said, crossing his arms. "A human. Your kind put us here. You're just going to bring more military to gather us all up and lock us away again."

"I can't say when the military will come, but it won't be by my doing. I'm going to try to contact Grayhart to help aid those in need."

"Grayhart...they would take us?"

"Maybe. They will bring ships. They won't take sides where the military is concerned, but they can try to save your life."

They seemed skeptical, but they must know of Grayhart and the organization's cause. The people who ran it weren't experimenters or jailers.

"We will go, then, to this tower, and wait," said the corax. "Thank you." He looked at Axrel too and bowed his head, and the lygins followed suit, showing respect to the higher predator in their wake, and gratefulness he spared them. The group began to pass by them, and they watched each other, still cautious. The corax stopped to look back at them.

"You really shouldn't go that way either," he said. "Something waits that way. I don't know what. But it's bad."

"I can manage," said Axrel with confidence.

"Maybe. But she won't." He pointed to Charlotte. "Whatever it is, it'll go for her first. Easy prey."

The group disappeared. Charlotte looked to Axrel, who stood still on the path. "What do you think?"

"If I were alone, I wouldn't even worry of it," he said honestly.

"But you are stuck with me," she said. "And I complicate things."

She thought she felt him shiver. A hiss of breath escaped him. "You certainly do," he whispered.

She wasn't sure what he meant, but she didn't have time to pry. "If it's too dangerous, maybe we can go around another way."

"There are few options, and any other way we take will be long—several days if not weeks out of the way. But I would not put you in danger if it can be avoided."

She thought for a moment, deciding their best option. "We don't know what it is. And there could be many of it all over this land. We knew there would be things lurking. We might not be able to avoid it either way. And there is no better path."

"Are you trying to say you trust me to protect you?"

"I am."

He grunted. "Then we proceed."

They started again on the path, the sky darkening ahead, threatening rain. She meant what she said—she trusted him. There was no one better to get her across. She firmly believed that. Yet still, she clutched to his back with a tight grip, her eyes searching the dark-wood wildly as they tread onward. She knew they wouldn't stop this time, not for anything. She pressed closer to him, hoping whatever the corax sensed was gone or they would pass it by without a problem.

Eventually, they did come to the blockade the prisoner had warned about. Axrel didn't hesitate. He climbed over, letting rocks spill down behind him. As he dropped to the other side, he paused, smelling the air.

He hissed softly, then took off, moving fast. He must have caught the scent. He flew down the path, and the rain started falling heavier. Charlotte clung to him, her muscles burning, aching, but she dared not ask to stop.

The terrain rose again, and Axrel was forced to climb where the stairs were too narrow and the path too muddy to stay on. As they reached the top of one outcrop, Charlotte looked down and could see a set of caves on the opposite side of the stream. Something moved inside. Heart thumping, she willed Axrel to go faster.

When they climbed another rock and reached the next landing, they found a bridge going across the stream. It was a simple swing bridge made of thick steel cords and narrow metal planks.

"Axrel" she whispered in warning as the stream, frothing and bubbling from small waterfalls, flowed underneath them, beginning to rise and foam with the rain and mud that slid down from the cliffs.

Axrel started carefully onto the bridge. It hardly swayed as he went, though it shook a little as he reached for one cord and then the next.

There was a low rumble like thunder. Axrel made it to the other side, then was forced to slip them through a narrow passage between two rocks. Charlotte could feel her bag bumping and scraping against the earth as they went. When they came out the other end, he froze, and Charlotte gasped.

A large furry body lay near them. It rose and fell slowly, like it was asleep. But it wasn't asleep. It was waiting. It turned its head, and two large, hollow sockets for eyes stared back at them with a long set of sharp teeth. It looked like a bear, with arms like a sloth that reached for them, hooked claws ready to strike. It roared at them, a long booming shriek. It swiped at them, and Axrel dodged.

Charlotte yelped as the beast came at them, and Axrel was forced to move in such a way that she swung around on his back. He leapt away, whipping his tail around to strike, cutting into the beast's arm. It roared again and lunged for them. Axrel flung them away as the giant clawed hand struck a large set of rocks, shattering them into dust, pieces flying.

"Axrel!" Charlotte cried as he backed away, and the beast turned. Suddenly, she was falling off of him as he undid the net around her and ripped off the vest. She dropped to the ground, and he picked her up, pulling her out of the way of the charging slothbear.

"Go. Hide," he snapped at her. "I will distract it. Then I will find you. Go!" He shoved her away just as the beast swung another paw around, this time catching Axrel in the side, throwing him against another large rock.

Charlotte cried out, and the beast turned to her. She backed away, nearly falling as it started for her. It opened its jaws wide to snap her up, then faltered back with a shriek, as if in pain. Axrel was on top of it now, sinking his teeth and claws into its back.

She wanted to stay, not wanting to leave Axrel, but she might kill them both if she did. She turned and ran, her limp still making it difficult to do so. She ran down the path through the hillside, passing towering black trees. She didn't know how long she ran, but eventually, her leg began to ache with a sharp pain, and she could no longer run. She walked a little longer, moving around the hillside until she could no longer walk either. She stumbled into a small marshy field and slipped down into the grassy underbrush and rested. Her heart hammered in her chest and her lungs burned. She stared wild-eyed back at the direction she came, waiting for Axrel to appear. He had to come. He had to be all right.

She shivered, waiting in the rain. She was cold and wet and sore, but she cared little. Axrel was out there fighting. He might be hurt. Maybe she should...

No. She had to stay. She had to believe he would come.

The light was beginning to fade. Being in the open at dark felt like a death sentence. She forced herself up and kept going. She hated having to put more distance between them, but she knew he would find her again. He had to.

"Please, Axrel, please be okay," she pleaded softly. Her foot hurt something awful, but she was able to walk steadier, which meant it had healed some at least before she had aggravated it. She would try to wrap it when she had the chance.

She took her time, checking her surroundings, making sure there was nothing else she might run into unexpectedly.

She hit the woods and trekked her way up a low hill. Rocky cliffs stretched around to her right, and she followed them. Caves began to spring up more and more, but she dared not peek inside. It wasn't until she found another station, hidden in the entrance of a short cave in the rock, that she finally stopped. It wasn't really a station but more of a hub, used for whatever purpose the rangers might need—hunting, camping, exploration, who knew. She was just glad it was there, even if it looked run down in some places, clearly not having been used for many months. Its metal siding dented in some parts, and the roof rusted at the edges. A cracked window stared back at her, dark and stained with mud.

She crept up to the door and opened it slowly, sticking her head in. It was dark and quiet. She moved inside and searched around for a switch, finding it next to the door. The lights flickered on, and she stared around her. It was one large room with a table and chairs in the middle. There was a computer in one corner, collecting dust, and shelving along the walls filled with various things left behind: tools, hiking boots, cans, even books. A bunk bed was placed snug into an alcove on the left, and to the right was a small wood burner. At the back was another small room which looked to be a kitchen. It was tiny compared to the Tower, but it was shelter, and that's what mattered. She looked out the one window and could see hardly anything. She closed it with a metal sheet to keep out the light and shut the door behind her before exploring deeper inside.

The kitchen wasn't stocked with food, no surprise. She did, however, find various cooking pots under a cabinet, including a large metal tub. The water even worked in the faucet connected to a set of tanks underneath the sink. There was a small showerless bathroom to one side of the kitchen and a closet opposite. She rifled through the closet and found a small medkit with spare gauze. She was nearly out of her own. She took a seat at the table, dropping her bag at her feet. She wrapped her leg and checked for any other injuries. She sat there for a while after, staring at the door, waiting.

Axrel was still out there somewhere, and she felt the pull to leave and find him. She knew he could hold his own, and yet she worried all the same. What if the slothbear had gotten the better of him somehow? What if he had fallen and hit his head? She knew vrisha were incredibly tough, but the caretaker in her still fretted. She couldn't help him when she had to hide.

She got up and looked around, knowing the smartest thing to do still was to wait. If she went back out, she put herself in danger. But damned if she wouldn't at least do something. She looked back at the kitchen and the wood burner. She could at least prepare. He would find her. She knew he had to. And when he did, she would be ready.

CHAPTER EIGHTEEN

CHARLOTTE

The hub was warm, almost too warm, as the burner heated the small space quickly. The room looked different now with the orange glow and a few things rearranged. She'd moved the table to the front wall, making room for the mattresses she slid off the bunks. Together with a blanket, they made a sizable bed in the center, though she suspected it would be too short, but it would have to do. There was a basin of hot water ready with wash towels she'd found in the closet and a bar of soap. She had some canned meat stew from her provisions, heating on the stove and a kettle she had also found stashed away, ready for tea that she'd also brought with her from the Tower. She didn't know if he'd like it, but she would drink it if he didn't. She had changed into dry prison guard clothes since getting everything ready, her wet ones on a chair by the burner. She had her kit out where she sat on the floor, organizing what she had and what she might need, taking a few things from the medkit as well.

There was little left she could do, and once more, she found herself waiting, dark thoughts returning. Was he dead? Was he too injured to find her? Maybe he couldn't sense her in this rain? She had gone out briefly and set one of her wet socks on a tree nearby in hopes he would see it and know she was there. She thought about pulling away the metal sheet from the window so that he might find the light in the dark but in the end, knew it was too risky.

Her eyes shifted down to a slender black box at her side. She opened it and stared down at the gun within. She'd found the box on one of the high shelves. She'd learned how to use a gun before when she was younger. Her father—strange man that he was—thought it would be of use to her despite the many defenses around their home and his lab. Maybe he thought in case one of the alien bodies he'd gotten wasn't dead, they'd need to use a weapon. She shuddered at the thought, hating the memory. Hating him too.

She didn't want to have to use the gun, but if someone else besides Axrel showed up, she didn't think she would have a choice. Night was in full swing now, and who knew what hunted in the dark.

She closed the box up but kept it close. There was a hunting knife on the table as well. She really hoped she wouldn't need them.

She got up from the floor and moved to the window, pulling the sheet back a crack in order to peek outside. Nothing. Just rain and darkness. She pulled the sheet back and sighed. Anxiety creeped and creeped over her, and she forced herself not to pace.

She could take the gun and the knife and go, just search nearby, see if there were any signs.

She closed her eyes and rubbed them gently. She hated waiting, hated not knowing. She didn't like being alone, but even more, she realized she didn't like being without him. That realization hit her hard, but, as she stood there thinking more about it, she didn't feel afraid. She trusted Axrel. Maybe he didn't feel the same. Still, he had come for her. He was helping her. That had to mean something.

Without another thought, she took up the gun and then moved to the table, placing the knife in her pants pocket. She put on her coat and threw up her hood before opening the door enough to slip through, shutting it firmly behind her. The cave entrance stuck out a little from the hub, allowing her to stand dry underneath the rock. She looked out through the water that poured down from the top of the cave to the forest beyond. Her heart dropped as she thought that he was out there somewhere alone. He could take care of himself, but he had to be miserable.

She stepped through the water and into the rain. She could hardly see anything except the shapes of twisting trees and large mounds of rocks. She stared wide-eyed at each rock she passed, fearing one of them would move. She thought about going back and getting a flashlight, but the glow might catch unwanted attention. She slipped down the rocky side, passing several trees. She stood in the middle of a bare patch of land and lifted her head. Maybe she'd catch that unmistakable scent of coffee and know he was near.

There was a snap nearby, and she jumped. The gun instinctively went up, aimed in the direction of the noise. She stared into the woods, unmoving. Her breath caught in her lungs as something moved toward her. The huge shape was bent forward, watching her. It moved again, and she backed up a step.

"Don't come any closer or—" She froze. The shape turned its head, and she caught the set of horns on its head. A tail weaved from behind. Her heart leaped at the sight. "Axrel?"

He stepped closer, and this time, she didn't back away. When he was only a few feet from her, he stopped. "I thought I told you to hide, woman," he said in a low, husky voice. "What are you doing out here?"

She lowered her gun and blinked back tears of relief. She closed the distance between them. Her free hand reached up to the side of his face, needing to touch and make sure it was really him and not an illusion. He went still at her touch but didn't pull back. His eyes, glowing faintly in the dark, stared back at her quietly. Feeling a little embarrassed and fearing she might have crossed a line, she let her hand fall and cleared her throat. "I was worried. I wasn't going to go far," she said carefully. "I was waiting for you and was afraid something might have happened."

He grunted, his head bowing toward hers. He watched her still, his eyes moving over her body. "You're all right?" he asked.

She nodded. "Come on. Let's get out of the rain. I've found a place." She smiled, then took his arm, leading him back up the rocky incline. He followed, letting her pull him. She noticed he held the vest and nets still in his hands, somehow not losing them in the fight.

When they made it to the hub, she felt Axrel pause to look at it before allowing her to lead him the rest of the way. She opened the door and found it as it was before. She made room for him to enter as she slipped off her coat.

"It's small, I know, and you might be too tall, but it's better than any cave I've found while I was—" She turned and gasped sharply. Axrel stood by the door, but for a moment, she thought it wasn't him. His violet scales were nearly black in some places, and the scales along one arm were nearly gone, leaving purplish black skin. His face, already scarred, was cut in several places, and his torso was swelling and blackening on one side.

"Oh, my god, Axrel, what—" She took the vest and nets from him and threw them on the table before dragging him around to a chair by the burner. He sat down, the chair groaning under him. Or was that him groaning? She wasn't sure. She was gathering her kit up from the floor and dropping it on the bed. She rushed to the kitchen and carried the basin of hot water over, setting it by his feet. "What happened?" she demanded to know as she dunked a washcloth into the water and squeezed out the excess.

He glanced down at her, his chest rising and falling slowly. "The beast threw me from its back. I landed against the rocks." His eyes glazed over as he stared past her. "It charged again, swinging its great claws, tearing into my arm. I grabbed on to it and ripped into its flesh. We fought for a long time. I got on its back again and bit my way into its spine. It still went on. I was impressed."

Charlotte stopped to study him. He didn't look angered. Not at all. He looked almost calm. Content even, his eyes bright with excitement.

"It threw me again, then pinned me," he continued. "I swung my tail up toward its open maw and stabbed it, piercing the top of its mouth into the brain."

Charlotte's stomach twisted. She didn't exactly want those sort of details. "You killed it?" she said, shocked.

He dipped his head once. "It was a valiant opponent. It fought well. A victory I will remember proudly."

Charlotte blinked, then looked at his torn arm and the scars that would appear even after she mended it. "Axrel...are you saying you enjoyed that fight?"

He gazed back at her, and his expression told her enough. He had. A lot. Perhaps it had briefly quelled the anger stirring within him. She turned back to rinsing out the cloth, uncertain how to feel. She remembered learning that vrisha considered fights like games to be won more than a need for survival, and they were proud to fight those who equaled them. Still, irritation stirred in her.

"You could have been killed."

He huffed. "I wasn't afraid."

"I was!"

He stared back at her in surprise. She turned to her kit, took out a clear bottle of liquid healing agent, and put a few drops into the water. She then took a dollop of salve and dropped it in as well, letting it dissolve. She dunked the cloth again and rinsed, then took his arm and began to wipe at his blackened skin. "I was," she repeated, more calmly. "I didn't know if you were dead or injured or lost."

She felt him go rigid and knew he still watched her as she worked to clean his arm. "You worried?" he asked softly.

"Of course I did. Why wouldn't I?"

"I told you I would find you. Did you not believe me?"

She frowned. "I did believe. I just... You've hurt yourself again. This time for my sake. I'm sure the fight was magnificent and you with your ridiculous stamina would find a way. But I still didn't know."

He leaned in, putting his hand on hers, stopping her from cleaning his arm raw. "I wouldn't have allowed myself to be killed. Not when I knew you were waiting for me. If there had been any thought I wouldn't win, I would have stopped."

"But your ego told you you would win," she said sharply.

"I suppose it did. But I swore to you, and that was more important. I couldn't allow the beast to live and hunt us. I was confident, maybe too much so. But I am here now. I'm sorry that I made you worry. I would not have let you go on alone."

She bit her lip, her eyes dropping from his to stare at his hand on hers. "I'm glad you are alive." She let out a shaky breath, unable to meet his gaze again. She focused instead on her work. "Sit still then, and let me fix you up again." She felt her throat tighten as she saw his beautiful scales disappearing more and more. She hoped maybe someday they would grow back.

Axrel let out a soft noise of relief as she patted and rubbed his skin with the hot cloth. After, she used the meldpen on his deeper cuts, sealing them as best she could. The blackened skin, she learned, was from bruising. From his body being thrown against the rocks.

"Is it okay if I check?" she asked, remembering how he had stiffened when she'd touched him in the woods. Though she'd touched him many times before, she wasn't sure if he was still accustomed to it or if it made him uncomfortable.

When he said she could, she gently pressed against the skin along his side. His skin was drying quickly, so very warm. The black bruises were swollen a bit, but she felt no other deeper injuries. Of course it would be easier with an x-ray machine, but they didn't have any lying around. She used one of her portable scanners instead to check for any internal bleeding which—to her relief—there was none.

"The bruising should go down, but it will be tender for a while," she said, pressing on the skin. "Nothing seems broken though you've likely aggravated your previous injuries." She examined his arms, then his legs, touching the back of them. She rose and let her fingers brush along his skull and across his horns, making sure there were no fractures along the head or signs of a concussion. His eyes followed her, half-lidded but aware. She caught his gaze as she pressed her fingers against his temple, heat rising up her neck. "Do you feel dizzy? Light-headed?"

"No," he mumbled. He shifted slightly in his chair, and she caught him wincing.

"What pain are you feeling?"

"Just sore. My body hasn't been in use for a while. It's why vrisha don't go resting very often."

Yes, on the ship while he was sedated, his body had plenty of time to lose a little muscle and weaken.

She let her fingers trail down to his face to examine the cuts along his nose and across his brow. They were shallow and would seal up before morning, given the speed of his healing. She took the hot cloth and wiped at them gently, trying to ignore his eyes on her, dim red orbs making her skin tingle.

"I wish I could make you promise to not do that again, but I know it's futile. Next time, I hope we can avoid something like that."

He grunted softly though she wasn't sure if it was to agree. She felt something drift over her ankle and across her leg, making her almost jump. His tail brushed against her. She stiffened a little but continued to dab at his face. "Feeling better?"

"Mm. Much."

She couldn't help smiling a little. "I'm glad I can do my part."

"You do it well," he said, and she could see he meant it.

"At least I could make use of my skills. Since you seem to be very good at injuring yourself."

"It's good I have you then."

Her eyes finally locked with his. Her hand slowed, and she found it nearly impossible to turn her gaze from him. She froze as his hand came up, reaching toward her. He touched a lock of her hair that had fallen over her shoulder, letting it trail through his fingers. Her heart sprang, making her inhale sharply. Heat crawled up her neck and down her back.

A whistling started in the kitchen and grew louder, breaking the spell he seemed to hold on her. Flushed, Charlotte dropped her hands from his face and straightened. She dropped the cloth in the basin and headed for the kitchen. Heart racing, she turned off the kettle and checked the stew. Trying to keep herself busy, she grabbed two bowls and cups, fumbling around the kitchen as her thoughts whirled, but she refused to focus on a single one or wonder about how she was still flushed, sweat breaking on her nape. The room really was too warm, but she knew he must like it. She would try to manage.

She brought a bowl of the stew and cup of tea over to where Axrel still sat and offered them over. "They're hot so be..." She realized what she was saying and stopped. A spark of amusement flashed in Axrel's eyes as he took them and bowed his head. She wiped her hands on her pants and returned to the kitchen. Making herself a bowl and some tea, she took a seat on a chair opposite him. "If you don't like your drink, it's okay."

"Anything hot will do," he replied, setting his bowl and cup on his lap. His eyes drifted down to the bed on the floor between them.

"I imagine it's even hotter than this on Tryth," she said, also eyeing the bed.

His eyes rose to hers. "In the day, yes. At night, about this, I would say. Though near the mountains and in the seas, it is a little cooler."

"I've always wanted to see it."

He tilted his head. "Really?"

She nodded, taking a sip of tea. The flavor was bitter, but she didn't mind. "When I was studying vrisha. From Dr. Hart's journals, she describes it."

There was a sudden howling cry outside from far away, and

Charlotte froze, listening. It died down quickly until there was only the sound of rain again.

Axrel looked over at the door, his eyes brightening. Tail flicking to one side, like a cat ready to spring up, wanting to follow the call of the hunt.

"Did you fight many things on Tryth too, like the slothbear?" Charlotte asked, curious.

"Yes, there were things we hunted, fought," he answered. "There was Sitra's Festival I liked the most. We hunted against each other and whoever brought back the largest or most cunning prey would be crowned headhunter. I won it three years in a row when I was in my youth and a smattering of times after." He stared out, as if recalling the memory. Then he blinked it away, lifting his bowl and taking a slow drag of the stew.

"Do you miss Tryth?"

He placed the bowl back on his lap. "Sometimes. Many vrisha are fond of our home world. Some of us only miss the heat. These other worlds are too damn cold."

Charlotte laughed softly. "Yes. And this isn't even the worst. There's no snow at least."

"Obilis Zero was a hellscape," he confessed. "I will take rain over snow any day."

Charlotte smiled in agreement, taking a small bite of stew. It was a little too salty, but it was filling. "Do you think you could ever go back? To Tryth?"

He thought that over, then said, "Likely not. I'd be imprisoned, then stuck on a working world before long. The queens and predomis don't take lightly to traitors."

Charlotte's smile dropped. "Because you are a member of the Blood Guard."

"And against the alliance," he said.

"So, if you hadn't joined them and only just disagreed with the alliance pact, would they imprison you?"

"No, but they would put me to work somewhere else, and I would not be given my full rights as a warrior."

Her frown deepened. "That's absurd. Just because you disagree. You can't think for yourself?"

"Warriors under a queen's command are expected to follow her rules. If the queens deal in alliance issues, then one cannot follow if they don't agree with them."

"I'm sorry," she said and took another sip of tea. "I didn't know they were so strict about it."

He dipped his head. "They took a vote, and the majority decided to agree to the alliance. Those who didn't were forced to remain silent." He looked over to her. "I might have been more open to the pact if not for..."

She gazed back at him surprised. "For what?"

He was quiet for a moment, his eyes turning toward the fiery glow of the burner. "When I was in training, I was put on one of my last missions before taking my rank as warrior. My team and I had been called to a small desert world where a nasty insect race was terrorizing a small port city. Several tradeships were stuck there, becoming infested." His voice grew low, his eyes burning red like the fire before him. "We took the insects out with ease. Within a night, they were destroyed. We searched the ships over, making sure there were none left. One ship belonged to the governing systems. A small research vessel." He looked back to her, the shadows of his face making his expression sinister. "We found no insects onboard. What we did find were the remains of bodies."

Charlotte went still, gripping her cup tight. "Bodies?" she said, her stomach twisting.

His eyes darkened. "Vrisha."

She closed her eyes, her throat tightening. "I'm so sorry. How?"

"The men claimed to have found them. They were dirra, non-warrior class vrisha. A ship had been found with them inside, already dead, they said. We don't know how. Either way, they had told no one of it. They had planned to take the bodies and examine them without the council's consent. It was unspeakable to take them, to disrespect the vrisha in such a way." He hissed softly, his anger rising. "One of my team was so angered by it they moved to take the bodies by force. One of the men got in his way, tried to stop him, and my teammate struck him down. The man survived but was badly injured. Eventually, the council was finally called to the situation. The bodies were given back to us, and the men who had them, who were planning to use them for whatever nefarious means, were let go without punishment. My teammate who had struck one down was stripped of his warrior rank. For trying to defend vrisha honor and the bodies of our own. The rest of us were to just let it go, to forgive and forget. But I couldn't. The council claimed it was to protect the alliance, but I couldn't see how. They wanted to keep the peace but in turn, we had to be punished because we were the bad ones, the ones who others feared, and so we had to remain silent."

Charlotte watched him carefully, her heart sinking. A chill ran through her, and ugly memories began to surface. "You had every right to be angry, Axrel. What happened wasn't fair."

His tail swayed by his feet. "It was then I knew how I truly felt. Not long after, when I was soon to be assigned to a queen, I turned to the Blood Guard instead, my anger too great to stay silent, to let such offenses slip by. But with my allegiance changed yet again...I suppose I am a *soltari* now."

She didn't recognize that word. "What is that?" she asked.

His expression turned somber despite the spark in his gaze. "A lone warrior. Shunned by all to live a life of solitude."

She fixed him with a despairing look. *No, not alone*, she thought suddenly.

She rose from her seat and turned away, setting her bowl and cup on the table. "I want to tell you something...I think you deserve to know before taking me any farther." She glanced back at him and caught him watching curiously. She looked away, not able to meet his eyes. "When I was younger, I was a lab assistant to my father. He was a very prestigious researcher in biomedical and gene enhancement. Some of the things he studied...were of non-human origin."

She looked down at her bowl as Axrel remained silent behind her. "I had been strictly told that all alien and otherkin bodies were one hundred percent donations. Freely given by the individual before they passed. I had...worked on such donations to further my studies, in hopes of having a leg up in school while helping my father." She shook her head, closing her eyes to the painful memories. "I never knew," she whispered. "Never knew he had lied. He'd paid for them through some black market trade. His awful experiments eventually came to light. I learned of them and told him I refused to help anymore. I assisted the authorities when he was caught. He was thrown in prison and his facility shut down. I was called in to question. Some didn't believe me, but those who did cleared my record in thanks for helping to stop him and those making the trades." She opened her eyes and, taking a deep breath, turned back to Axrel. He stared back at her, unmoving. "We never got a vrisha. It was the more commons ones—lygin, gyda—but since then, I have tried to put it behind me. Since then, I have tried to make up for my past. To help those in need." She took a careful step closer, standing before him. "But what I did was wrong. I'm guilty of my ignorance. I am sorry for it. If you wish to break from my favor and leave, I won't stop you."

He sat there quietly, his eyes never leaving hers. She couldn't tell if he was angry or not, but she dared not turn from him. "You swear you didn't know?" he asked softly.

Her gaze didn't drop from his as she answered, "I swear."

He let out a slow hiss and bowed his head. "Then I believe you. I don't have the authority to forgive it, but I will not leave you."

Her body relaxed, breath spilling from her lungs in a sigh of relief. "I understand. Someday, I'll have to come out to my peers. And to those I care for. I know it wasn't my fault, but I feel the guilt all the same. Maybe when I tell everyone what they were planning to do here, I'll confess."

"What were they planning?" he asked.

She crossed her arms, shaking her head. "Experiments. On you, specifically. I told them I was going to tell everyone. I didn't care what happened to me. I couldn't let them..." She dropped her gaze. "I couldn't let them do that to you," she said softly.

Axrel didn't respond, but she knew he studied her closely. Without warning, he rose from his seat. He took a small drag of his tea and winced.

"It's bad, huh?" she said, not blaming him.

"It's fine." He set his bowl and cup down next to hers. She turned to him as he faced her. He rolled his shoulder and touched the side of his chest. "I am just not used to being this sore. It's annoying."

Charlotte's eyes dragged over him, over the bruised skin. "I might be able to help with that, if you let me."

He tilted his head. "What do you have in mind?"

She took his arm and moved him over to the bed. "Lie down."

He looked at her curiously, only hesitating for a moment before doing as she asked. He crouched down to sit, then slowly allowed himself to lie on his back against the mats. As he started to relax, Charlotte went to her kit and took out a bottle of muscle relaxer. She dipped some of the balm onto her fingers, then rubbed it along her palms before turning to Axrel and crouching down beside him.

"I'll have to touch you again," she said, raising her hands for him to see. He eyed them before meeting her gaze, then dipping his head in a single nod. Shifting closer, she carefully placed her hands atop his bare torso. It was incredibly warm, almost hot against her palms. His scales were smooth, almost like a snake but not quite. They were harder in places but softer in others, like his stomach. She traced her fingertips along him, careful not to aggravate the still healing bruises and cuts. She pressed against his arms, moving up his shoulder, then across his chest. He breathed deep, chest rising, and closed his eyes.

"Move on to your stomach," she said, removing her hands. Axrel didn't hesitate this time. He rolled over and showed her his back. When he was settled yet again, she hovered over him, staring at the hard-cut muscles across his back. Tenderly, she brushed her fingers along him before beginning to knead below his shoulder, making her way downward, being sure to not get cut by the short spikes along his spine. His back rose and fell with his breath. He was very quiet, but he didn't protest, so she assumed he wasn't uncomfortable. He was very tense, but slowly, surely, he began to relax with the pressure of her hand.

A low growl slipped from him, and she paused. But it wasn't a growl, she realized, it was a groan. Cautiously, she started again, and she heard another. He arched his back, his tail curling. His legs and arms trembled, and the scales along his shoulders stood up straighter.

Charlotte couldn't help the smile growing on her face. "Like that, huh?"

A grunt in answer.

She caressed and petted, moving farther down to his thighs, then his shins. She returned to his back and moved across his shoulders, and he trembled once more as she pressed against the muscle along his spine. Another sound slipped from him, like a hum. He might have been snoring or perhaps even purring. She wasn't entirely sure, but as she continued to massage him, she wondered if at one point he had fallen asleep. Only when she finally stopped did he move again, this time to slowly roll onto his side. He looked up at her with half-lidded eyes, looking almost drunk or near sleep.

"Thank you," he said in a hiss of breath. "That felt...I didn't know that could feel so good."

Softly, she patted his side, her smile widening. "You're welcome. I think as a species, we humans have a sort of gift with our hands."

He snorted softly. "Is that so?"

She shrugged. "Many others have reacted the same." She petted his arm, letting it trail up to his neck. She found a spot along the side of his skull behind his horns and began to rub gently. Axrel's eyes closed, and he moved against her hand. He groaned again, letting his head fall against the mat. She thought he might have fallen asleep again until he spoke in a rough, sleepy whisper.

"It isn't that vrisha don't like to be touched. We just aren't nearly this...gentle," he said. "Though I suppose that might only be a matter of experience."

Her brow furrowed. "What do you mean?"

He looked back at her through a slitted gaze. "I have never been touched tenderly. By anyone. Caregivers, my den brothers and sisters, no one. Any touch that came was usually from fights. Fledglings were always rough with one another, to establish rank early. Caregivers could be attentive, but gentleness was uncommon. That is just the norm. For me, I was..." He turned quiet.

"Was what?" she asked, still rubbing.

He stared back at her, his breath coming slow and deep. "I was a runt of the den. Therefore, I was picked on more harshly. Got into more fights. Was given less attention. But I proved myself as I grew. In the hunts and fighting pits, I showed I was capable. Though much of it came through my anger. Made me rigid."

She gave him a sad look. "I'm sorry."

"But it's strange...ever since you came," he said softly. "My anger seems to slip. Your touch...it calms me."

She paused for a second to stare back at him. Her throat tightened, and her heart did a little flip. "I...I'm glad." She smiled sadly. "Axrel."

"It is so strange," he murmured, his eyes closing again. "I never would have believed..."

He said no more, and she stopped her hand, letting it fall. She watched him sleep for a long minute, thinking. Then she didn't think at all as she leaned down and brushed her lips against a scar along his mouth. She straightened, and her heart fluttered as his eyes opened again. They stared at each other in silence, and she waited to see if he would react. He didn't move or appear upset. Maybe because he didn't understand the intimate gesture. Charlotte went to stand, her face heating at his burning glare, when his hand reached out and took hers.

"Stay," he whispered.

She froze, watching him closely. She wondered what it would

feel like to be wrapped up against him, embraced in his warmth. She thought it over, then moved to lie beside him. Heart racing now, she curled up close, her back barely on the mat. But she didn't mind. She watched Axrel watching her, until his lids slipped over his eyes. He mumbled something again, this time inaudible, before she was sure he was fast asleep.

CHAPTER NINETEEN

Axrel

When he woke, he found himself lying alone. He became instantly alert until he heard the sound of something clattering behind him. Her scent touched at his nose, and he knew she was in the room at the back. Quietly, he sat up. He noticed his muscles were already less sore than they were last night. The balm she had used combined with the massage had greatly eased his tension. He had slept well though not the entire night. Mostly, he dozed on and off, and when he was not sleeping, he was thinking as he watched Charlotte resting beside him.

He was silent now as he sat on the mat, looking ahead at nothing while Charlotte moved around behind him. There was a stillness in his mind, like the calm before a storm. Somewhere deep was a stirring of thoughts that he kept at bay.

"Oh, you're up," came her voice. "I was just making some food. Are you hungry?"

He forced himself to look around at her and meet her blue-gem eyes. She was stirring something in a bowl he couldn't see. She smiled at him, her light hair brushing against her face.

He stared back at her before rising, trying to find the words to speak. "No," was all he could muster.

Her smile slipped. "Oh, all right. Well, I'll pack some away then." She turned from him as she placed the bowl down. "We should probably prepare to go...but I'll admit I'd like to utilize this hub a little more. I'd like to clean up since there's hot water and assess some of the items found here. Maybe replace some things in the bag. But whenever you're ready..." She looked back at him, waiting for a reply.

"I'm going out," he said after a pause.

Her brow furrowed. "Out?"

"I want to scout ahead a bit, get a lay of what's around. Make sure it is safe."

"Oh." Her face seemed to relax. "Right. That would be good."

"I'll stay close. Be back soon."

She smirked at him though her eyes read some other emotion. "I'll shout if anything happens."

He watched her for a few seconds longer before turning away and slipping out the door. He started down a hillside and into the forest. The day was gray and bright despite the darkened woods. The ground was wet with moss. The air was crisp and chill but not unbearable. He walked on, past dark rocks and thin, grassy underbrush, stopping every so often to check his surroundings. At one point, a breeze picked up, and he tilted his head back, checking for any odd scents in the air. He smelled earth and water and the odors of animals that did not cause any alarm. Creatures flew above him while others, he could feel burrowing in the ground underneath his feet. The forest was alive and thriving if one looked hard enough. As he scouted on, he had an intense urge to hunt, but he stilled himself from doing so, knowing he needed to be back to Charlotte, and he feared if he began to hunt, he wouldn't stop.

He hadn't planned on going far for very long anyway. He just needed to get away. Needed to get some distance from the hub so that he could be alone for just a moment. To meditate, to find a place to unleash his thoughts. He stalked the forest a little farther, finding a small cliffside with a thin waterfall to one end. Down below, he could see a small furry animal drinking at the pool. It seemed to sense him and looked up, freezing up before eventually scurrying away. He walked along the cliff, finding a way down till he came to the edge of the pool. He crouched and peered into the dark water, and, in seeing his reflection, he allowed the thoughts he had tried to shut out flood his mind.

He still resented those who had wronged him. He still distrusted the humans and hated his old pack. Those feelings hadn't changed. He still longed for revenge. But there was another longing in him now that couldn't be quelled. So strong and so deep that, more and more, it completely overshadowed his need for vengeance.

It was impossible and yet the longing—the need—was there all the same. He closed his eyes and remembered her touch, her caress, his skin tingling with the memory. A warmth had settled in his lower belly then and did so again as he recalled it. Before, he had fought to believe it meant anything. But now...

He opened his eyes. He looked back at the pool, and the realization hit him like a blade to the gut. The realization that he didn't care anymore how impossible or insane it was.

Because with every touch that filled his blood with a calming fire, he grew more and more hungry for it.

The warmth in his belly rose to his chest as he stood. He stepped back from the pool, thinking on how he would go about convincing her to understand when an uglier thought hit him.

What makes you think she would want you?

The thought stabbed at him just as the first, and he flinched.

What makes you think she'd ever let you that close when you've spent years hating her kind? What makes you think you deserve her?

A low growl slipped from his throat, surprising him. He stopped, hating how much truth was in those words. She was only kind because it was who she was. It had nothing to do with him. She was a healer, and she had healed him in more ways than one.

But that didn't mean she felt what he was feeling.

The warmth sank from him, and he grew cold. An animal howled in the distance, breaking his thoughts. He should return.

He made his way back through the forest, his thoughts growing blacker as he went, like the clouds he could see past the treeline in the distance. He felt like a fool until his thoughts turned again to last night, and he slowed his gait.

There was something...something different. The way she looked at him, the way her mouth turned up in that smile. And, perhaps he had imagined it in his near sleep-induced state, but she had touched him differently. Touched him with her lips instead of her hands. That surely wasn't normal. But he knew little of human affection. Maybe it was only a polite gesture, when she finally felt comfortable to consider him a friend.

It had been different, but it might mean nothing. He wished he understood humans better.

As he made his way up the hill toward the hub, he heard the sound of running water. As he reached the entrance of the shallow cave, he halted, growing still.

Beside the hub, Charlotte stood with her back to him. She was bare save for the slip of clothing covering her lower half. With a deep cup, she poured water over her head, wetting her hair, the water dripping down to pool at her feet. Beside her was a basin, steam hovering over the top. A single droplet trickled down the arch of her back, making a slow trail.

As if sensing him there, she turned to look back at him. She held the cup firmly in front of her, her face reddening.

"I didn't think you'd be back so soon," she said, her tone more timid than usual. "I didn't want to make a mess inside since there's no shower."

He stood there, his eyes not venturing away from hers. He'd already seen her naked, her body memorized in his brain, but now he knew if he looked again, he might not be able to hold himself together.

"It's fine," he said, his tone a little too short. The warmth was stirring in him again, quicker than before. He forced his eyes away. "I didn't find any threats on the trail. But there looks to be a storm coming from the west. If it passes quickly, we could leave after if you —" He stopped. Her face had gone from red to white, her eyes rounding in horror.

"Axrel," she whispered, and her fear knocked into his senses like a splash of cold water. Her hand shook. and she dropped her cup, taking a step back.

He noticed her eyes were not on him but behind him. "What is —?" He looked back and saw it. A violent snarl ripped from him, and he lunged forward. He shot for her, grabbing her arm before pulling her farther into the cave. He swept her firmly against the back side of the hub, his body against hers, shielding her.

"Don't make a sound," he hissed quietly, his arms to either side of her head, pressing close. They stood silent with only their breath between them. After a moment, Axrel dared to look around the wall over to the entrance.

It was closer now, hovering over the trees on the forest edge. The drone flew past, its single red eye scoping the ground below it. It was just one he noted, but he knew it belonged to his kind. The Blood Guard was searching. Either for him or for others, it was clear now they were looking, and if they found them, it wouldn't be long before a ship came. And when a ship came...

He watched the drone hover lower, flying only a few feet now from the ground. It flew closer, slowing as it noticed the hub. Its eye rounded, checking the front, studying the metal roofing and door. It swiveled around and saw the basin, creeping up to examine further. Axrel tensed, hardly moving. If the eye found them, he would have to take it out quickly, then they would need to run and hide, if they were lucky to get away in time. If not, he was going to be seeing a fight sooner than he expected. And if they found Charlotte, they would take her.

As the drone moved around the basin, he knew he'd kill them if they tried. He'd force her to flee, and then he would kill them. His upper lip curled from his teeth, knowing what he would have to do. Slowly, he moved his tail up, ready to strike as soon as the drone rounded the corner.

He could hear the quiet hum of it as it grew closer. As he lifted his tail higher, waiting for it to come into view, there was a high-pitched cry off in the distance followed by a low rumble. The drone seemed to stop. A few seconds later, the hum, which seemed to be right near his head, grew quieter.

He dared to look around and saw, to his immense relief, the drone leaving the cave, flying off in the direction of the sound.

There was another low rumble again and a flash. The storm was coming.

Charlotte trembled beneath him as he watched the drone disappear entirely. "What was that?" she asked.

He forced his eyes away from the entrance to look down at her. Her gaze locked with his, and it was in that moment he noticed how incredibly soft she was as he nearly crushed himself against her. He could feel the heat of her skin against his, damp still by the water. A lock of her wet hair clung to his shoulder.

Without thought, his face drew down close to hers. Her breath came in sharply as his mouth hovered over the curve of her neck. His heart hammered in his chest, his mouth salivating, craving to bite the soft flesh of her shoulder, wanting then to entangle his body with hers, to take and claim. To feel her darkest, deepest touch surrounding him. Oh, how lovely it would be.

His mouth widened, his teeth ready to pierce, when he felt her tense against him. Her flowery scent filled his senses like a drug, but in it also lingered another scent. One he hadn't expected to smell from her again, not after everything.

The fear mark was small, but it was there. And it was in reaction to him.

He lifted his face away and fixed his gaze with hers. She watched him closely, quietly, hardly moving. Her lips parted, and he could hear the fluttering of her heart. Was she afraid? Or was it something else? He couldn't be sure, but he knew he wouldn't take the risk if it was truly fear. He wouldn't break her trust now, even if it pained him to pull away.

The cold air that slipped between them as he broke the contact was nearly excruciating. He wanted that heat covering him. He wanted her soft body against him, under him. He stepped back, noticing her tension still, her breathless expression dazed as her face turned red again.

"It was a vrishan drone," he finally said, breaking whatever had come between them. "If it had found us, then my pack would have as well."

Her hand slipped to her throat as she tried to clear it. "Oh..." She exhaled a deep breath, her body shaking with it. A flicker of some emotion crossed her face, but he couldn't be certain what it was. She dropped her gaze as if she found it hard to look at him. "What should we do? Should we go?"

Unlike her, Axrel couldn't take his eyes away. Even if he thought he should, he couldn't. "With that drone out, it would be safer to stay than to go and risk getting caught in the wilds. The storm will draw it away regardless. We should stay another night. If we keep the place dark and the door locked, we shouldn't have to worry. I expect it won't come back, but we should take precaution."

She nodded. "All right. I'd rather stay." Her eyes rose to his. "I'm going to change. I'll see you inside."

He watched her return to the hub. There was another flash followed by a louder, longer rumble as the storm drew nearer. With the storm and the drone, he knew it was better to stay than to continue on. Yet, he felt uneasiness twist in his gut. They would need to be careful. If there were drones looking this far from the city, he had a feeling they weren't looking for just any prisoner.

He should return inside, but his restlessness grew. He still felt the fire in him as visions of her raked his mind, unable to shut them out. Now, feeling on edge, he moved back toward the entrance of the cave. He stopped and looked over at the door of the hub where he knew Charlotte now was.

The wind picked up, the crackle of electricity in the air. He turned his gaze to the sky and saw the clouds foaming and swirling. There was no sign of the drone or of any living thing. More than ever, he wanted to run down into the forest, to hunt until darkness came, to let the storm consume him, until he was exhausted and spent and the fire within was no longer burning.

And he'd do it every night if he had to.

He took a step as if unable to resist, then forced himself to stop. He took a deep breath, gritting his teeth, his hands turning to fists. The image of her against him, the tension in her body, the uncertainty in her eyes filled his mind.

He thought he heard his name on the wind, a soft whisper. When he twisted around, he saw Charlotte at the open door, now clothed, looking at him with concern.

"Are you coming in?" she asked.

He had no answer at first until lightning struck nearby. He would try to wait it out. He would try. He moved away from the entrance toward her and slipped back inside just as the clouds broke and the rain fell.

CHAPTER TWENTY

CHARLOTTE

The storm was impressive to say the least. Rain poured from the sky, the walls rattling as the wind shook the foundations, howling with anger. Every so often, something hit the sides of the hub, whether rocks or fallen debris from trees. With the building tucked into the shallow cave, she had no worries that it wouldn't hold. Still, she couldn't say she wasn't nervous every time something clattered against the roof or struck the wall, in fear it might rip a hole. She tried to occupy her mind by searching over the cabinets and closet one last time, considering what to bring with them and what to leave behind when they eventually left.

The storm wasn't the only thing making her uneasy. Axrel was unusually quiet. Most of the time, he sat on the mats as if meditating, and every so often, he paced as she sat by the table, looking over her supplies. She wanted to talk to him, but she feared he wasn't in the mood. Something seemed to be bothering him, and she highly doubted it was the storm. She thought maybe it was the drone they

had encountered. Maybe it had rekindled the anger in him and determination to get her to safety and seek his revenge. But his silence was
still odd, his restfulness worrying. He had never had a problem telling
her how he felt before, but now he seemed to close himself off. Eventually she asked him if he was worried about the drone, and in short
answer he said, "No". She didn't think he was lying.

She began to grow on edge as her mind turned over what it might
mean. If it wasn't the drone, then what? Was it something she had
done?

She thought back to the last few hours up until the morning. He
had been acting a little distant even then. Had it been because of the
night before? Did he wake up remembering he had allowed a human
to touch him, to lie by him, to kiss him? Had it filled him with regret?
With embarrassment? With disgust?

She truly hoped not, but what did she know? He was a vrisha
warrior, who loathed humans. It wouldn't be so hard to believe he
had begun to resent her. Perhaps he was restless to leave her. She
hated having those kinds of doubts in her head, but nothing could
make them go away.

And if she thought things would have been better when he
returned after scouting, she was wrong. When he had come across
her trying to bathe, his eyes had said enough. The fiery orbs seemed
to burn hotter than before, burning into her. His face had been
twisted almost into a scowl, like he was in pain at the sight of her. It
had made her shiver with the intensity.

And when he had pressed himself against her to hide her from
the drone, she thought she might melt into him. His powerful arms
beside her, his chest and stomach against hers. The drone had scared
her, yes, but when it had gone and only they remained, she was
frightened again by how incredibly—impossibly—hot he made her.
Her body's response to his was electric, like the lightning in the air. It
didn't matter that he wasn't—isn't—human, the heat he pulled from
her was astounding.

It had shocked her. Her mind had reeled, spinning to nothing, seeing only him. And when he had looked at her again with that fiery glare and had bared his teeth as if to sink them into her flesh, she feared for a split second she had lost him. That even after everything, he had changed his mind and that he was going to eat her after all. She hated the thought—absurd as it felt now—but it came to her all the same. Her heart had leapt in her chest, and her breath had caught, her body had tensed as his mouth came toward her.

But he had stopped. He had pulled away from her. And she had been both disappointed and relieved all at once.

She still wasn't sure what to make of it, what he had been thinking. But she knew she didn't want his coldness now. She wanted the Axrel she had the other night.

The storm was finally beginning to slow, though the rain didn't stop. Axrel, who had begun to pace again, finally stopped at the door.

"I'm going out," he said at last. "I'll be near."

She looked up at him from the table. His back was to her, waiting for her reply.

"You're scouting again?"

"I won't be gone long."

She let him go despite wondering what drew him out to the rain. She could have cornered him, convinced him to talk, but worried that would make things worse. She wanted to understand. But she didn't want to suffocate him.

She tried to set her mind on the days ahead. The computer to one corner was dead but there was an old map on the wall. A red tack showed where she believed the hub must be. Judging by the distance and location, they should be able to make it to the Lightpost within a day and a half. Assuming they didn't encounter anything else along the way.

And the way things were going, she would expect there'd be something. What with the Blood Guard searching around, and prisoners still wandering the area, and whatever animals roamed, maybe even worse than the bearsloth. If Axrel stayed with her, she had a good chance, but if he left...

She tried to set her mind at ease by continuing to gather and organize supplies. She'd found flashlights, lighters, flammable oil, hunting knives and rope, wire and batteries. She took bandage wraps from the medkit and some antiseptic gel. She took out older cans and replaced them with new, along with mealbars and two bottles of water. She thought it over and placed the gun in the bag as well.

By the time she was through with packing, Axrel returned but only briefly. She peeked out the window and saw him standing outside, some dead animal with matted gray fur dropped at his feet. He left it there and returned to the forest. He was hunting.

She cleaned after, even if it seemed unnecessary. It felt like a respectful thing to do for whoever else came next. When she wasn't tidying, she set to fixing Axrel's net, which had become tangled when she dropped from him, and his vest, which had ripped in his fight. Even with her limp improving, she still wouldn't be able to walk far, and they may have to use the carrying method again.

The day came and went as she kept herself busy. While trying to keep her mind focused on her work, she couldn't help noticing Axrel's absence more and more. Every time he returned with a new animal he'd caught, he went out again and was gone longer than the last.

The light was beginning to fade, and still, the rain didn't let up. The storm, though past its peak, kept on with no end in sight. Eventually, she could find little more to do than sit and drink bitter tea by the table while attempting more calls through the receiver, peeking out the window, waiting to see the large shape of a devilish alien stalking at the forest's edge. When night approached, her unease stirred yet again, and this time, she found herself pacing.

They couldn't go on like this. Whatever was bothering him, she had to know. It was ridiculous for him to stay out in this weather as if he'd rather be out there than near her. That, surprisingly, hurt more than she cared to admit. As if experiencing deja vu, she found herself zipping up her coat, ready to go out once again to look for him.

When she heard a thud outside, she peered out the window and saw Axrel's silhouette as a flash of lightning cut through the dark. With a sharp intake of breath, she went to the door and threw it open.

Just as Axrel stepped over another lifeless creature on the ground—this one with wide antlers and a silky hide—she rushed outside, walking toward him. He froze as he saw her.

"I don't think all this meat is going to fit in the bag," she said, standing a few feet from him.

He looked at her, confused, then glanced back down at the animals, understanding. "It is only for sport."

She crossed her arms, the cold spray of rain hitting her face. "Maybe we let the animals have a chance. If you keep up through the night, there might not be any left."

His tail weaved behind him as he dipped his head. "I'll be back before morning. Then we can go." He turned to leave, and she took a step toward him.

"Please stay, Axrel."

He stopped but didn't turn to look at her. She took another step closer, just on the edge of the cave where the rain fell like a wall between them. "You don't have to go back out there. Just...stay. Talk to me. Tell me what's wrong."

"It's nothing."

"No. It is something," she countered. "Whatever it is, you can tell me."

He appeared to shake his head. A bizarrely human gesture. He started to move away, and she broke out of the entrance, following him. "Fine, you don't have to talk, but I'm coming with you. Maybe you can teach me to hunt at the very least—"

As she was about to pass him, he threw out his arm to halt her. He turned, and the look he gave her made her freeze up. It was that fiery glare again, brighter and hotter than before.

"I want to protect you," he said, low, almost angrily.

She frowned, blinking away the water that fell on her lashes. "I know that. But that doesn't mean you have to stay out here all night guarding the place."

He scowled and turned away as if that wasn't the point. "You don't understand," he growled, walking some ways, then returning, almost circling her. "I want to protect you...from me."

She let her arms fall to her sides. She gaped at him, confused. "I don't understand."

He bared his teeth, refusing to look at her. "You're still afraid of me. I smelled it earlier. And, when we hid from the drone, I almost..."

She shook her head, her heart beating faster. "Almost what?"

He stopped. He glanced back at her, eyes almost glowing in the dark. His hands squeezed into tight fists, then released. He wasn't going to say it, but she remembered how he had nearly grazed her with his sharp teeth. Her hand instinctively went to her throat.

"I'm not afraid of you," she confessed. "Only of that moment. Because...I wasn't sure what you were going to do. But if there was any doubt, then I'm sorry. I still trust you, Axrel. You aren't dangerous to me."

He twisted around. "Not dangerous?" he said, in disbelief. He glared at her, then quickly closed the distance between them. "How can you say that?"

Before she could respond, he took hold of her hand and lifted it, palm facing up. In a flash of lightning, she saw the deep scar that was embedded there in the skin.

"Say that I am," he demanded.

She stared at the cut, then glanced back at him. "It was an accident," she said softly.

He glared back at her for a long moment, then turned her hand toward his face to examine the scar. "I am dangerous. Even now. Even to you. Nothing can change that. I will always be."

Her frown deepened as she watched him. It was like he was trying to convince himself, not just her. And maybe it really was true, even if he never purposely hurt her. But what did this have to do with anything? Why did this affect him now?

"Fine, maybe you are," she said. She felt her stomach twist at saying it. "And I was scared because I thought maybe it had somehow dawned on you that I'm still just a human. And protecting one, helping one, was insane to you." She tried to tug her hand away. "Because you finally see how crazy all this is." She couldn't help letting out a small laugh. "And you resent me now, don't you? You wonder how you got here. That's why I was afraid. I was afraid you were going to take back everything and let me go."

He was deathly silent, his expression darkening. He still held her hand close.

"If you can't stop yourself from hating me because of what I am, then don't bother to try to protect me," she said. "Because it won't work. You'll go on resenting and hating me more."

His hand gripped her a little tighter. "You honestly think I hate you?" he whispered.

"I don't think you're happy to be near me any longer, that's for certain. I think it dawned on you last night when I got too close. It was too much, and it was my fault."

His eyes narrowed. "You're wrong." He pulled her closer, bringing her almost against him. "What you are afraid of is wrong."

"Then what should I be afraid of?"

He stared at her as if willing her to see. She studied him for a long moment until the realization finally hit her. The spark in his gaze wasn't anger like she had thought. Far from it. It was a sort of hunger. A deep, excruciating hunger.

She watched as he brought her scarred palm to his mouth, almost crushing it to him. She let out a sharp intake of breath, her heart leaping in her throat as he kissed her hand.

He let her go and in doing so, she took a step back, not in fear but in full surprise. Before she could say a word, he was crouching down before her like he had the night he had caught her on the rocky hill, as if hoping not to scare her again.

"You calm the rage inside me." He tilted his head up, watching, waiting, maybe, for her to flee. "But there is a brighter fire burning inside me now, and I can't put it out. I've let it grow too big, and I fear it might consume me. Help me. Heal me."

She could see it nearly pained him to say it, as if he expected her to be appalled. He dropped the walls that he'd put up before and stood bare before her, and she knew it took everything he had not to put them up again.

The rain beat down on her head, trickling along her neck. She licked droplets from her mouth, tasting them, before taking a breath. "You want me to..."

He bowed his head, his hands curling again into fists. "Lie with me."

She knew he didn't mean like how they had laid together last night. Her body shook a little at the thought. "That goes against everything you stand for."

He looked up at her again with that pained expression. "I know. I don't care."

She gaped down at him. Rain fell off his horns and down his chin. He watched her, then slowly stood. He opened his mouth to say something else, but she beat him to it.

"Yes."

He froze. Heat rushed to her face from blurting it out so quickly. But she knew her decision before he even stood. He watched her for a moment before closing the distance between them. She could feel the heat coming off him, pulling her in.

"I will," she said. "Just stay with me."

His pain turned to relief. He cupped her face in his hands, his sharp nails brushing softly against her cheek. She closed her eyes to his warm touch, realizing how badly she had craved it. When she felt his mouth against hers, her breath caught in her lungs, his scent —like spiced coffee—filled her nose. He moved cautiously, allowing her to coax him deeper into the kiss. He didn't pull away or think it odd, as if he understood now the intimacy of the touch, unlike before when he hadn't responded like she imagined. But he was learning fast. She flicked her tongue out and felt his fangs graze her.

In a hiss of breath, his hands drew down to her waist and then along her thighs until he grabbed her and lifted her up. She clung to him as he moved quickly, taking her back into the hub.

The hub was still warm from the burner, now growing a little too warm. As he set her down, she hurriedly began to shrug off her wet clothes, letting her coat fall on the ground, peeling her uniform top off and throwing it on the table. She was surprised when Axrel helped her with the rest, tugging off her pants and undershirt until she was standing with nothing but her underwear. She backed into the wall by the door and Axrel moved with her, pressing himself into her like he had before, his body nearly crushing hers, his arms on either side of her steadying him.

A soft growl turned in his throat as his mouth moved down to her neck. Charlotte gasped as she felt his tongue flick against her skin, then felt his teeth pressing against her shoulder, almost breaking the flesh. So, this was what he wanted to do—what he had almost done. Things would have gone very differently that morning if she hadn't thought otherwise.

Her hands moved to his shoulders. She pushed at him so that he would look at her. "Are you sure?"

His fangs slipped from his upper lip, and his hips moved against hers. She could feel the hard length of him through his pants, out from its protective sheath and ready, rubbing against her belly.

"Oh."

"I will be gentle," he said, his hips moving slowly.

"You don't have to be."

That stilled him, and she felt his cock grow harder. Without warning, he pulled her from the wall, bringing them both down onto the set of mats on the floor. He lifted his hips and pressed against her again, groaning, wanting release. He pulled off his kelva pants with ease and hovered over her as if to prepare himself. She looked down and saw his curved red cock, swollen at the base. He raised his tail up out of the way, then dropped his head down.

"You're so soft," she heard him whisper, his warm breath brushing the nipple of her left breast. He squeezed it gently and took it into his mouth. His sharp teeth grazed her again, and she hissed, throwing her head back. With his other hand, he took her other breast and circled his thumb over the nipple. His long tongue swirled over her, then bit down, one fang breaking the skin. He lapped and sucked, teasing her as she gripped one of his horns, trying to stifle a moan. His mouth drew down, across her stomach, down to her center. His tongue teased around her underwear, brushing at her core.

"Axrel," she moaned softly, arching her back. Heat pooled in her center, the ache making her grit her teeth.

He stopped suddenly, locking eyes with her. "Tell me where. Tell me how to please you."

Breathless, she touched her center. "Do you want me to show you?"

His mouth widened. "I think I understand enough." He pulled off her underwear, nearly ripping it from her. She spread her legs, and his eyes dilated, his nostrils flaring.

He cursed something under his breath. "Your scent. It drives me crazy." He moved down and dropped his head once more. The tip of his tongue brushed against her core, making her tremble. He tasted her, and that seemed to break his will to hold. He growled low and shifted, moving on top of her. He dropped his hips, and she felt the head of him press against her center, sliding in with a slow ease.

Unable to stop himself, he thrust once, then twice, and Charlotte felt his heat spill into her. He let out a sharp hiss, gripping her thigh, bringing her legs around his waist. He wrapped an arm around her, lifting her, hugging her tight to him. His warmth spread through her, dissolving what chill there might have been left from the rain. Sweat now broke out along her back and neck. She thought he might free her from his grip now that he had found his release, but as she moved slightly, she could feel him hard still inside her.

His forehead pressed to hers. "Now I finally see," he said.

"See what?" she said, her voice almost breaking with another moan.

His hand came up to brush a sharp thumb across her neck. "Why some vrisha take a liking to humankind."

She laughed softly and saw him bare his teeth with a groan at the movement. Placing her hands on his shoulders, she lifted up, then back down, feeling him slide in her, slick and hot.

He let her move on her own first before he began to thrust upward to meet her. Pleasure coiled in her belly and in her center. He fell back on the mats, keeping her on top of him. She noticed his eyes on her, concentration hard, as he grabbed her waist and began to drive harder until she felt her pleasure peak, felt herself tighten around him, a wild cry ripping from her mouth.

She hardly noticed his release again, only by the twisting of his face and the shudder of his body. His legs trembled underneath her, and his tail curled and twisted as his nails dug into her skin.

When they disentangled, Charlotte slid off him. Axrel rolled to his side and brought her down to lie beside him, his arm around her waist.

"I think I'm going to need to bathe again," Charlotte said, unable to keep the smile from growing on her face.

Axrel's eyes moved across her body, and he grunted. "I should as well." His mouth thinned, and he bared his teeth at her. But it was different this time, and she realized, without a doubt, it was a smile. The first, she was sure, he had ever given her.

She reached out to him, placing her hand to the side of his face, and this time, he did not tense but laid his hand on top of hers. He kissed her scarred palm and nuzzled it gently.

"You don't regret it now do you?" she said, hoping it wasn't just lust that drove him. "Now that this happened?"

He looked back at her, and his eyes told her enough. "I regret nothing."

They stayed beside each other for a moment longer until she pulled him outside to wash. When they returned, they laid together again, closer now than the night before, Charlotte curled against him. She found sleep easily that night and slept better than she had in days.

CHAPTER TWENTY-ONE

Axrel

That morning, before the sun passed over the treeline, they left the hub for good. The rain continued though it had slowed considerably, enough for travel. As much as he wanted to spend another day in with her, continuing what they had started last night, he knew time was short, and they needed to keep going, on to this northern trade-port in hopes there would be what Charlotte believed to be there, whether ships or help that would bring her to safety. He was determined to get them there faster than the day and a half that she said it would take. And that was only if they didn't run into trouble.

He expected trouble. So, the faster they went, the better their chances.

He'd put on the vest with the net tied at the back and had her jump on before tying the second net around her. She complained a little, and he knew riding on his back was uncomfortable, but they both knew he could make the trip far quicker carrying her. Once she was settled and her bag was secured, they were off again, making their way through the forest. The hills became fewer which meant less climbing, and he was glad for that. The rain, however, had caused the earth to become soft, hills were now caked with mud, and fields were turned to marshland. It made running more difficult, forcing his muscles to work harder in order to keep the pace. Charlotte was quiet, clinging to him tightly. He could feel her breath along his neck where her head was buried. Unlike him, the rain caused her more discomfort as it sprayed her face, even with her head being covered by the hood of her coat.

They took short rests whenever they found a shallow cave or a thick stand of trees, to break from the rain and replenish their energy. They encountered no one on the trail nor any beasts in the woods though he sensed them every so often. Whenever they came upon an open field or meadow, he always paused to check the skies above or the surrounding forest edge for drones that might be hovering, searching still for any signs of those hiding or running. Once it was clear there were no drones, he continued on, racing faster than before to reach the shelter of the trees.

The next time they stopped was at a small lookout, nothing more than a one room dwelling on the top of a hill, its windows broken, the door gone. He let Charlotte down and guarded the entrance while she shook out the water from her coat and her hair, then dried her face. The rain was beginning to turn into a thick mist, the air growing colder. From the hill, they could see down into a patch of grass where a herd of the silky-skinned creatures roamed, their antlers sprouting from their head down their nose.

If they were on Tryth in the olden times, he would have crept down and caught one to bring back, gifting Charlotte the largest and strongest of the herd for their meal. Then they would cook the finest parts and together they would sit, with *sivas* to drink and a fire to warm them. They would talk into the night before returning to their den, as mates did.

He looked back into the room where Charlotte crouched, sifting through her bag. His heart thumped heavily in his chest.

As mates did.

He scanned the room and deemed it was too small to make her comfortable, and there was still too much daylight left to end their travel, but he couldn't help wondering if they could make time to lie together again. The urge was strong, but he wanted her safe first. Safe and warm. This wouldn't do.

She came back to him with a metal canister and held it out. He took it and drank a small serving of the water before returning it to her.

"If you're tired, we could stay here," she said before taking a drink.

He was tempted again, but not because he was tired. "No. I'm fine, and there's still too much daylight left. We should keep going."

She shook her head. "I don't know how you do it. All my studies and I'm still astounded by the stamina of vrisha. And you have been through so much. I can't help imagining just how far you could be pushed...but I guess I kinda know."

He glanced over at her and saw her shiver as she watched the herd beside him from the door. Instinctively, he wrapped his arm around her. She sighed, burrowing into him. "There's so much I could still learn."

"Whatever you want to know, I will tell you. Or show you if you desire," he said, tightening his hold around her.

She looked up at him with her wide blue eyes and smiled. "When we get off here."

He tensed at that. *When we get off...We.*

An ominous feeling twisted in his gut, but he said nothing, holding her close to give her some of his warmth, whatever he could give her.

When she was ready to continue on, he lifted her onto his back. An urgency pushed him to move faster. Before the light fell, he was determined to be near the end of the forest trail.

* * *

They were making good time, up until Axrel was forced to slow when he caught a certain odor in the air. It was something burning. And ash. He walked steadily up an incline, then halted at the edge of a shallow cliff. Down below was another stationway. Several buildings were blackened, smoke still rising from a few. At one end, some kind of transport vehicle was burning, singeing the ground around it.

He felt Charlotte's grip on him tighten. "What do you think happened?"

From the way the buildings were damaged and the large scorch marks on the ground, he could take a good guess. A vrisha ship or one of their more weaponized drones had spotted some hideaways. Or fighters. And so they'd destroyed what they found.

Cautiously, he made his way down to the scene. He stopped again at the edge of a few small trees and lifted his head. There was movement ahead, past the fire. Beyond the roaring of the flames, he heard a short burst of cries followed by several growls. He caught the slightest scent beyond the burning, one he was all too familiar with. The metallic scent of blood.

He loosened the net around him and crouched low, allowing Charlotte to safely drop from him. "I'm going to check ahead. Wait here and hide. I will be back."

Her hand caught his, and he looked back. Her eyes read concern. "Be careful."

He dipped his head. He slunk quickly out from the set of trees, into the open of several buildings, turned now to rubble. He weaved around them, jumping across a low wall before crouching low behind a large metal container with circuits on its side. He peered around and saw what caused the sounds. A wild pack of large beasts were making a meal of someone or something. The animals were furry across their back and scaly underneath and had serpentine eyes similar to his. One looked his way, its nostrils flaring. It let out a short burst of cries before the others turned in his direction. They snarled, and Axrel rose, lunging at them, snarling back.

The pack saw him in his entirety and deemed him more a threat than what was worth. They backed away and with another short burst of cries, disappeared back into the forest. Smart of them.

Tail weaving, Axrel stepped over to what the pack was scavenging and saw a pair of humans. So, there had been fighters. And they hadn't stood a chance. There seemed to be no others around and no signs of his kind either. They had moved on, likely looking for others.

Quickly, he started back for Charlotte, knowing even if the place was empty, they should get as far away as they could lest others notice the flames and come lurking.

As he rounded a building, he stopped in his tracks, then backed up a step. A low hiss escaped him as he heard voices. Human voices. He crept around one side and looked around to see. Near the upper end of the stationway, by a lone watchtower, he saw a group of humans sitting underneath a partially collapsed metal roof. They wore the guard uniforms he'd seen before. Among them, he caught the sight of bright brown-gold hair. Charlotte was there. They must have seen her from the forest edge.

A growl bubbled in his throat, his body tensing, ready to attack, when he froze. She was crouching down beside one, talking. Her lips curved up ever so slightly in that small smile as she placed her hand on his shoulder.

An odd sort of feeling came over him, something he'd never felt before. It hurt to see her touch another male, even of her own kind. He supposed it must be akin to his deep protectiveness over her. But something was different. He felt a great need to place himself between them and bring her to him. But the soldier—young that he seemed, was not harming her. Nor were the others. They were speaking low as she began to tend to the boy on the ground.

Carefully, he slipped around to the other side of the building so he could be closer. He knew as soon as he revealed himself, the men would become aggressive. As he moved in, he began to understand what they were saying.

"How long ago did it happen?" Charlotte asked.

"Early this morning," said one of the men. "Then the ship went east. We got in the basement just in time, but Hale got caught by one of the collapsed buildings."

"I don't see any major fractures. Just a few bad cuts on the ear and a bruised shoulder. Do you think you can stand?"

Axrel stopped behind a fallen piece of wall from one building and saw Charlotte help the boy up.

"He was under the rubble for a minute before we got him out."

"Are you dizzy?" she asked. She placed a gentle hand on the boy's temple, and Axrel made a point to appear.

One man, a tall lanky soldier with dark eyes and very little hair, saw him first. His face went pale, and his mouth gaped open as if to scream. He stumbled back and fell, crawling away. The others turned and saw him next. One went for a weapon at his side.

Axrel shot forward, then immediately halted as Charlotte got between them, throwing her hands out.

"No! Axrel, please!" she cried. He bared his teeth at the men who were beginning to flee. The soldier with the weapon fired it off, and Axrel felt a sharp pain in his shoulder. Charlotte jumped as he grabbed hold of her and pulled her back toward the wall.

The men fled, shouting and screaming into the woods. Axrel gripped Charlotte's arms, placing her back against the crumbling wall.

"I told you to stay put," he hissed.

She struggled in his grip, and he let her go. "I saw they were injured. I had to help!"

"Yes, good that you did."

Her jaw clenched, giving him a stern glare. "They were just scared."

He snorted. "Of course they were."

Her face turned from anger to regret. "I'm sorry, Axrel." She placed her hand on his chest, examining his shoulder. "It just grazed you. Let me fix—"

"Later. We need to leave here. Now." He crouched down, looking away, waiting for her to get on his back. She hesitated, then maneuvered herself on top of him. When she was secured again, he swiftly ran for the other end of the stationway, breaking into the darkness of the forest beyond.

"I am sorry," Charlotte said after a long moment of silence as they ran. "I didn't feel they were a threat. They were clearly hurt. Lost."

He felt a burning anger rise in him but knew it wasn't her fault. He felt that odd dark sort of feeling again too. "You shouldn't risk it just because you feel like it might be safe."

"I could have handled it. You should have waited for me to help the boy."

"Forgive me for caring more about your wellbeing than you seem to."

"That's not fair. I do care. But I'm also going to help someone in need, even with the risk. That's my job." He felt her breath on his neck. "They need me too, Axrel."

His hands curled into fists. Somehow, he had forgotten they were her kind. How could he expect her to ignore her own people? Still, he felt the annoyance of her actions.

"You could have gotten hurt," he said.

"I didn't. I knew you were near," she assured. "If they really had been a threat..."

"You would have allowed me to kill them?"

He felt her tense behind him. "I didn't say that. I think you would have let them be. And felt confident knowing that I wasn't in danger."

"Is that why you felt safe enough to approach? To touch the soldier?"

"To examine him, yes," she said firmly. "I would have tended to him just like any other."

"Just like me?" he said.

She turned quiet. "You think I wouldn't treat others? Only you?"

He felt an ache in his chest. "No. Of course not." And he meant it. "I know it's your purpose. But with those men...I didn't like it."

"Because you really dislike them."

"Yes. Seeing you help them when they are partially responsible for this hell—I didn't like it."

Her arms came around his neck as her head rested on his shoulder. "I understand how that might make you feel. And for the record, I don't treat anyone like how I treat you. And I don't think I ever will."

The ache in his chest lessened. "I won't harm them like you wish. But I don't want you going near them either. I know I can't stop you. But if they try to attack me, even in fear, I will defend myself. So, next time, you should give a warning."

She sighed, her warm breath tickling his ear. "I will. Hopefully, there won't be a next time."

CHAPTER TWENTY-TWO

CHARLOTTE

They found the road not long after. The light of day was waning, and the rain that had turned to mist was now no more than a light haze in the cool air. Axrel had slowed his pace as they came to the dirt path, checking the area, no doubt, for anything that might be up ahead. Cautiously, he made his way onto the road, and from there, they headed north. She knew the route would take them directly to the Lightpost, yet, the closer they got, the more on edge she became. Ever since seeing the devastation of that stationway, she feared when they reached their destination, it would already be up in smoke. She could only hold on to her hope that the Blood Guard had yet to veer that far north from the city. She could only hope.

Now with the path clear, Axrel quickened his pace. There were signs of tracks along the road from vehicles and at times even footprints but no signs of others. At least not right away. It wasn't until they curved around a cliffside and crossed a small one-way bridge that they started seeing more than just tracks.

First, it was only abandoned trucks and military explorers, sitting on the edge of the road, one having toppled over into a mudbank, a few sunk into the murky water where it had begun to flood. Charlotte peered over Axrel's shoulder at each car they passed, her pulse quickening, wondering if she would see anyone inside.

But they were all empty. Whatever convoy there had once been was now scattered along the road, stretching for miles. And by the looks of it, it might not have been the vrisha this time. There were no fires or scorch marks. Only dozens of footprints, both human and otherkin. Some of the top covers of trucks were slashed, as if cut through with a blade. There wasn't a car she didn't see that didn't have bullets stuck in their sides.

"What do you think happened?" she whispered, as if afraid to make too much noise. There was a stillness in the air that chilled her. "Was it the Blood Guard?"

With impressive stealthiness, Axrel moved along the road, hardly making a sound. "No," he said. "It was not them."

Prisoners then. Perhaps those who had been on the main bridge back before they had left the Tower. Maybe they had moved north on the convoy which looked to be going south judging from the direction of the cars. There had been a large fight. A deadly one. Where everyone had gone now was a mystery.

Axrel slowed almost to a halt. A soft rumble vibrated in his chest.

Charlotte's hold on him tightened. "What is it?"

Before he even answered, she caught the whiff of something awful in the air. She'd know that scent anywhere. And it was getting stronger.

"I think we've come to the end," he said roughly.

Charlotte didn't need to look to know there were bodies. First one, then several. Both prisoners and prison guards. She knew there was no hope in looking for those alive.

Not wanting to stare down at the ground where the dead lay, she gazed up ahead and saw the road led into a large tunnelway passing through a steep hillside. Only the tunnel was now blocked by several large military trucks covered in rocks where the tunnel had collapsed.

Charlotte cursed under her breath. "Looks like we'll have to find a way around."

They scanned the area until she saw over to the right a low barrier. "Over there." She pointed.

Axrel approached the barrier, and they peered down into an embankment. Below was a wide river cutting through thick woodland, moving through a set of tunnels underneath them.

"We could follow the river east until we can find a way around to keep north." She motioned. "What do you think?"

He was quiet, unmoving as he stared down at the river.

"Axrel?"

"It will have to do," he answered.

"If you don't think it's a good idea..."

"No, it's fine." He moved to climb the barrier. "It's just going to be damn cold."

"Unlike the rain you stalked through the last couple days?" she said, clinging closer to him as he hopped over the barrier and began to slide down the other side.

"I suspect so."

And he was right. As he dropped into the water, it rose to his chest and spilled around her legs in an icy grip. She inhaled sharply with gritted teeth as Axrel immediately started to move against the river.

It didn't take long for her legs to go numb. She worried for Axrel though he pushed forward with little effort. The river grew deeper in some parts, forcing him to swim. Nearly her whole body was submerged, but she held onto him, trusting he would keep them afloat even with the rushing water and the broken trees and rocks that got in their way.

Eventually, the woods around them turned to large rocky banks, then into steep cliffs on either side as the river weaved into a deep valley of canyons. The river began to narrow, and the canyons began to close them in, with little light streaming down from above. Still, Axrel kept on until the river swallowed again, and he was back to walking. It dropped to his waist and then his thighs, and she was no longer touching, the cool air sweeping through her wet clothes, making her teeth chatter.

The river cut two different ways, and Axrel took the northern route. Archways loomed above them until they were becoming more like tunnels, spilling light through openings like spotlights against the darkened path.

As the river began to open, and the rock walls between them widened, Axrel made an odd noise, as if suddenly taken by surprise.

Charlotte looked around. "What is it?"

"The water...it's warming."

She glanced at him, confused, before turning her gaze down to the dark water. It didn't look any different, and she worried he might be experiencing some form of numbness. But as the rock walls broke away, bringing them out into a large open enclosure surrounded by canyons on all sides, the river merged into a set of pools where she could see steam rising.

Axrel groaned as he entered one of the pools, his legs shaking. Around the edges of the pools were mossy banks followed by slates of dry rocks. He stepped out of the pool onto the rocks, then allowed Charlotte to slide off him, letting the vest and nets drop with her.

The air itself within the enclosure was warm from the steam. As she looked across one way, she could see low waterfalls spilling from openings in the rock, pouring into the pools. Walls of hanging vines reached down into the water from the tops of the canyons above. From what she could tell, they had discovered a set of hot springs.

Curious, she crouched down and placed a hand on the rock. It was warm as well. She looked at Axrel with surprise, who was peering out at the pools, dipping his tail in.

"I don't see another way out of here," Charlotte said, rising.

Axrel twisted his head around, tilting it up toward the top of the chamber. "I could probably find a way for us to climb up one of the sides." He glanced back at her with a spark in his gaze. "But the light is falling. And we don't yet know what lies on the other side."

She arched her brow at him. "You want to stay here?"

He grunted, stepping around the pool. "I think so. Just for a few hours rest. What do you say?"

She scanned around. It was no dry hub, but it was warm, and she didn't like the idea of going out into the chilly air with wet clothes. And she could see he greatly liked the heat.

She smirked at him. "All right. But just for a little while."

His tail swung around and for a second almost reminded her of a delighted puppy. She dropped her bag on the ground, knelt down, and opened it, searching for a thin towel she had stuffed at the bottom. As she took out her kit and a small pocket light, she saw Axrel move back to the pool's edge. He shrugged out of his kelva pants, then dipped his tail once more before slipping down into the water, not bothering to ease himself in. She heard him hiss with pleasure as he moved about the pool, gliding into the deeper end.

Giggling, Charlotte pulled out the towel and laid it next to the bag. Then, carefully, she began to shrug out of her clothes. She set her coat and uniform on the warm rock bed to dry and her undershirt and underwear on top of the towel before making her way over to the pool where Axrel swam.

"A warning—it is likely too hot where I am for you," he said, his head bobbing just above the water.

Charlotte tested the water with her foot. It was indeed hot, as much as a fresh bath, just bearable to her. She stepped down till the water reached her knees, and it was hot enough to turn her skin pink, but she didn't mind. It felt wonderful. She eased herself on the warm rock, letting the steam melt the chill away from her skin and bones. She watched Axrel circle around before tilting her head up to watch the last of the light above fade away. There was a starless sky above, the planet in endless cloud cover, the steam rising up into the top of the canyon. She missed the stars. She thought about home on Larth and how she could see the brightest stars, especially from the observatory. She hoped she'd be back soon to see it and could show Axrel.

That sudden thought made her chest tighten. The image of him there, looking up at the stars with her, made her feel a sudden painful longing. Could he even be there? Would they allow him to stay? She would try to make it work somehow. She could convince the heads, she was sure...

She tilted her head back down and stilled as she saw Axrel watching her. He watched her closely, and she stared back at him until he slowly began to move toward her. When he reached the shallow end, he floated over to her until he stopped at her feet, then rose partially out of the water to kneel before her. What scales he had glistened, what scars stood out, darkened. His eyes were bright with that hunger again, and she parted her legs invitingly. His eyes raked over her body, and his nostrils flared. He moved between her legs, and she was ready to let him do what he pleased when she noticed his shoulder, still open where the bullet had grazed him.

She clicked her tongue and placed her foot on his chest. "You almost made me forget."

He tilted his head in confusion, and she gave him a sly look before stepping out of the pool and reaching for her kit. She took out a healing salve she'd taken from the medkit in the hub and returned to the pool, sitting back in the same position as before. "Come here," she said, curling her finger.

With a devilish look, Axrel complied, settling himself between her legs. She took a scoop of the salve and lightly dabbed it on his shoulder, letting her fingers trial over his burning skin.

"There," she said coolly. She leaned in and blew lightly on the wound to make the salve dry quicker. "You'll have to wait to go in again till it dries."

Axrel's tail curled lazily along the water. She closed the salve bottle and went to put it back when he grabbed her ankle, stopping her. "I am in pain."

She froze, anxiety already creeping. "Where?" She placed a hand on his chest. If he was in pain, it must be a worse injury. Vrisha had an extremely high tolerance. "How bad?"

His eyes darkened. "Bad. The worst I've ever felt."

That got her going. Her brows furrowed, and she frowned. "Axrel, tell me where." Her hand fell down his stomach, pressing lightly, reading for any signs of discomfort.

Without tearing his eyes from her, he moved, forcing her onto her back. She hardly had time to react before he was on top of her. He pressed his hips against her, the apex of his thighs resting against her center. She felt nothing at first save the hard scales of his sheath. He pressed it firmly against her, then she felt his cock extending, stretching her, then filling her. She gasped and before a moan burst from her lips, he thrust several times. She felt him spill into her, but he didn't pause, his rhythm slow but deep.

He took hold of her hand and pressed it to his chest. "Here," he said. Then he moved her hand to his lower abdomen. "And here."

She arched against him, and his pace quickened. "I can...fix that too."

Heat tightened in her center as the slick length of him brought her release, shattering her. "Axrel," she cried softly, her mind spinning, his heat surrounding her. His face twisted with a pained pleasure, a snarl growing in his throat. As she writhed under him, he slid from her and quickly turned her over onto her hands and knees. As he entered again, thrusting wildly, her legs began to shake, her heart racing. She felt his chest against her back, felt his teeth on her neck, about to bite down. She tensed, then locked her arms, biting her lip to stifle her moans, her body trembling. The heat rose again in her belly, and she threw her head back, resting against his shoulder.

She let herself fall into the feral pleasure of the alien warrior on top of her. As she turned her head to give him more access to her neck and shoulder, where his teeth kept a hold, her gaze turned to the rockwall nearby, where a blanket of vines fell into one pool. Behind them, she caught a shadow.

Breathless, she focused in on the shadow, then stiffened as it moved. She saw a pair of eyes blinking back at her from the cover of vines.

"Axrel," she gasped, now afraid. He didn't halt, thinking her only crying out again for him, too lost in his need.

The shadow moved again, and this time, she saw a face to go with the eyes. It was an otherkin, their skin green and shiny like an amphibian. She recognized it now as a skra. It crouched at the edge of a rock hidden by the vines.

"Axrel!" she cried.

As he came, he finally lifted his head up, his eyes turned to where she looked, and when he saw the skra, a violent snarl ripped from his throat. He detached from her and shot to his feet, his rage so blinding he didn't notice his seed still spilling from him on the ground. Charlotte scrambled away, grabbing the towel to cover herself as he lunged for the skra which had quickly lurched back into the shade of the vines.

She watched as both disappeared behind the vines. She wrapped the towel around her and rose, listening to the scraping of claws against rock and the sounds of a scuffle before there was a short yelp of surprise or pain, echoing back into the chamber. A few seconds later, Axrel returned from behind the vines, the skra in his grasp. His cock was sheathed, and fury burned in his eyes. He dragged the skra by his prison suit over to the edge of a pool, holding him over the burning water.

"Who are you, and why are you spying on us?" he snapped, baring his fangs in warning.

The skra shook his head, his eyes wild with fear. He said something in xolian in response. He talked so fast and so quiet, Charlotte couldn't catch his words.

Axrel shook him. "Tell me," he hissed.

"Axrel, wait!" Charlotte approached them and turned to Axrel first. "He doesn't understand vrishan. Let me talk to him."

Axrel's burning eyes glared at her, then they softened as he dipped his head.

"Let him go. He won't hurt us with you standing over him."

Axrel hesitated, then he took a step back and dropped the skra at their feet. The skra scrambled up, keeping his head bowed and back bent in front of Axrel.

"Who are you?" Charlotte asked.

The skra turned to her. "Silf."

"Silf? Why were you watching us, Silf?"

He looked at her, embarrassed. "It was not my intention," he mumbled. "I come here to gather hot water. I didn't know you'd be here. I was as surprised as you. When I saw the vrisha, I thought to immediately warn the others—"

"Others?" Axrel growled.

"—but then I saw you, a human, with him, and I was too shocked to move," he said quickly.

"Where did you come from?" Charlotte asked.

"The tunnel ways." He pointed to the vines that lightly swayed.

Axrel took hold of him again. "What others?" he hissed.

There was a sound of scraping rock, and Axrel flung the skra away. Charlotte whirled around and saw all around, shadows moving, circling them.

Then the others appeared.

CHAPTER TWENTY-THREE

Axrel

He placed Charlotte behind him, keeping her close. He growled at the prisoners atop the rocks, at least a dozen by his count. If they tried to swarm them, he could cut them down quickly before they could even draw weapons. If they had any. He didn't see any shooters on them, only a few who were wielding blades, others short spears. Nothing he couldn't handle. And judging by their stance and how they moved, they weren't looking to get close. They knew what he was and what he could do to him.

But they didn't flee either. They weren't so afraid that they would run at the sight of him like the men before. They were curious too.

He felt Charlotte's hand on his arm, trembling a little. The men circled, and they waited. It seemed they were at a standstill. He contemplated attacking first, then asking questions later. Or rather getting Charlotte as far away as possible. He felt the heat of anger rising in him, ready to strike, when Charlotte suddenly spoke.

"We aren't looking for a fight," she called out.

"Neither are we," responded one of the prisoners.

"Doubtful," he said in xolian, knowing a little of the language. His hands curled to fists. The prisoners eyed him curiously if not warily. They were all different types of otherkin—grex, lygin, corax—and only a couple like the skra, Silf, with shiny green skin. The one who spoke was a lygin—female, with a slender face and long, narrow ears, and a scar across one green eye, her light gray, nearly white fur smudged with dirt.

Silf scrambled to his feet, backing away. The female lygin's sharp eyes narrowed on him, then glanced at Axrel. "But you are not in good company, vrisha, if you mean to harm us."

Axrel stared her down. " I could say the same."

"We aren't here to harm," Charlotte confirmed. Her arm squeezed his. He looked back at her, and her eyes told him to wait. She gazed back at the lygin. "We were just passing through."

Another prisoner, a corax with a few broken fins along its head, snorted. "He's a vrisha. He's one of them. When they pass through, they destroy whatever gets in their way."

"No. Not him," Charlotte said. "He's not here to hurt you. He's here to help me."

The prisoners looked between them, shocked.

"Why should we believe you?" the corax said, showing them his sharp, crooked teeth.

"Would I still be standing here? Would any of you?"

That got them quiet. Silf turned to them, his head still bowed. "It's true," he said softly. "She told him not to hurt me, and he obeyed. And I...saw them together."

The female lygin's eyes widened. The others murmured amongst themselves. "He's helping you, a human?" she said in surprise.

"Yes," Axrel spoke. "I am."

"And he won't attack any of you as long as you do the same." Charlotte gave him a firm glare.

Before the lygin or any of them could respond, there was a low hum in the air above. They each gazed up, the prisoners backing

away against the rock, Axrel bringing Charlotte to him as his eyes
scanned the skies.

"It's them!" a prisoner cried.

"To the tunnels!" the lygin woman hissed. The inmates started
disappearing behind the low hanging vines. The lygin turned back to
them before following. "You may come, but know you will be
outnumbered if you decide to attack us."

Charlotte faced Axrel, fear in her eyes. The humming was
growing louder, the wind picking up. "Axrel, please."

It was either risk the tunnels with the prisoners and hope they
told the truth or risk getting caught by his pack. Even if he still didn't
trust them, he knew following the prisoners was a better option.
Anything would be better than having her be taken by his kind.

He bowed his head once, and she turned, quickly snatching up
her kit and bag. As she did so, he grabbed his kelva pants by the pool-
side. He picked her up swiftly, cradling her to him. Kicking her wet
clothes, along with the vest and nets, into the pool, he bolted for the
hanging vines where a tunnel lay hidden. He slipped through, just as
a pair of lights passed by over the hot springs, engulfing the area
in red.

* * *

The tunnel was narrow and short for his height, forcing him to keep
his head bent. The tunnel curved one direction, then another, cutting
through the canyon. At one point, it broke off several ways, but he
followed the scent of the prisoners, keeping behind them. For those
who couldn't see well in the dark, the tunnels appeared pitch-black.
But for him, and likely the otherkin, he could make out the barest
light coming from narrow gaps above.

The passage seemed endless until it came to an erupt end, and
he found himself standing at the edge, looking out into an impres-
sively tall, almost circular chamber with several other entrances and
exits at various corners. There were small hanging lanterns above,

casting down on what could only be a hidden encampment of prisoners. He let Charlotte down so she could twist around and see for herself.

He heard her take a sharp breath at the sight. "What is this?"

The inmates looked over to them, several taking defensive positions. There were mats and blankets laying around in various alcoves where they found places to sleep. To one side was a set of tables and chairs. Next to them were several barrels and piles of food supplies stacked on top of each other. To another end was a giant machine embedded in the rock.

The female lygin approached them with a few others behind her, weapons drawn, watching for any signs he might strike.

Charlotte took a step forward, placing herself between them. "Thank you for letting us hide with you. My name is Charlotte Lockley. This is Axrel."

The female lygin glanced between them. "I am Kira. Of the Korrok line. I am the head of this camp. Imprisoned for two years and twelve days."

"You all escaped the prison?"

"Some. Others were in the working towns. Me and a few were working in these mines when the attacks happened." Her eyes narrowed, shining in the dark. "How is it you are here?"

"I am a doctor," Charlotte explained. "I was assigned to the ship *Tarus* which crashed with new inmates. Axrel among them. I was to help the injured on board before they made it to Fargis."

A few lowered their weapons though they stared at Axrel still with suspicion.

"You're a doctor?" Silf said excitedly, appearing behind the group.

Charlotte nodded. "I studied...otherkin medicine and treatment on Terra Centra."

Silf's eyes brightened. He turned to Kira. "She could help us."

"Why should we believe her?" said the corax with broken fins. "She might just be one of those from the city trying to keep hidden."

She turned back to Axrel, placing a gentle hand on his shoulder.

"Axrel was one of my patients on the ship. He was close to death. He wouldn't be with me now if I hadn't treated him in time."

"It is bizarre to see a vrisha with one of them," a grex beside Kira noted.

"She tells the truth," Axrel said.

They whispered amongst themselves until Kira put up a hand to quiet them. Silf approached Charlotte, giving Axrel a nervous glance.

"Please," he said, bowing his head. "If you truly are a doctor, my sister needs help."

"Silf," Kira hissed in warning. Silf cowered, backing away.

"No, wait." Charlotte put up her hand. "Let me take a look." She showed them her kit. "You can watch me."

They seemed to think it over, Silf looking at Kira, then to Charlotte with pleading eyes. "Please, Kira, she's needed attention for days. Let her try."

The lygin looked to the others who seemed uncertain but still waited for her command. She thought it over, then turned to the grex beside her. They talked quietly for a moment before turning back to them. "We let her try."

"Let me just put on some clothes, then you can show me where she is." Charlotte began to move toward them when Axrel reached out and caught her arm, stopping her. She looked back at him in surprise.

"She is with me," he said clearly. He looked down at Charlotte, speaking to her in his tongue. "My xolian is not perfect, so you will need to translate more."

Her brow furrowed, but she didn't argue. "All right."

"Tell them if they so much as look at you wrong, I will tear out their insides and feed it to them."

"Axrel!"

"Tell them. Tell them you are mine to guard, and they will answer to me if they harm you or scare you. They need to be told otherwise, or some might try to claim you. But you are mine...mine to protect." He was deadly serious as he said it. Even now, he could see a few looking at Charlotte in a way he didn't like. Their eyes lingered longer than he cared for them to linger. "Unless you would choose not to have me protect you here. I will respect your wishes. But if you want me still, then you must tell them."

"Axrel, of course I—" her words were silenced by his glare. Her jaw clenched though her gaze was soft. "All right."

She repeated his words, with a little more care. A few of their eyes fell, while others nodded in agreement, knowing not to cross him.

"She goes unharmed," Kira confirmed. "You have my word."

Charlotte turned to him, and he bowed his head, telling her it was safe, and he would be right near her should anything happen.

They dressed quickly—he into his one pair of clothing and Charlotte into a spare set in her bag—before Kira and Silf had them follow deeper into the cavernous chamber. They passed through a wide tunnel to one end, into a small room where several otherkin were lying on thin beds on the ground. Axrel could see they were all injured in some way, some worse off than others.

"What happened?" Charlotte asked as they passed by them.

"Different scenarios here and there," Kira explained. "Some got caught in the storms, the forests and beasts within weren't kind. Others encountered inmates who were not friendly and got into fights. A few had run ins with prison guards while fleeing."

They came to one end of the room where Silf crouched down next to another like him, only this one was more slender, and their skin was a paler green. Silf shook the figure gently, and they rolled over with a groan. It was a female of his kind. She had several strips of clothing wrapped over her left arm and around her torso. Her breath was shallow, eyes half-lidded with sleep.

"She was fleeing some of the guards when the attack happened," Silf said sadly. "She got shot in the chaos."

Charlotte crouched down to examine her. "I might be able to help her. Just give me time."

They gave her the space she needed as she opened her kit and went to work. Axrel stayed close, watching, noticing others studying her as well from a distance. They conversed quietly in the shadows but never drew near. They watched him too, and he glared back at them until they turned their gaze away. They were all on edge, and they feared him, some still suspicious, and rightly so. He just hoped they would keep their distance.

* * *

It was late into the night by the time Charlotte finished with the injured in the cave. She had become so focused on her work, determined to help all those who needed it, she appeared to have forgotten they were in the lair of possibly dangerous aliens. But even Axrel had begun to loosen his protective walls. The inmates here were not like some of the others. They were desperate to survive, yes, but they also knew there was a better chance in numbers and to keep the peace until they could find a way to safety.

They remained cautious of him but were willing to trust he wasn't going to harm them. And they grew quickly to like Charlotte. She had proved to them how capable of a healer she was, and their gratitude was insurmountable. Silf's sister was already in a better position to survive, and the others were healing quickly. Axrel's heart swelled with pride for Charlotte at her gift and knowledge of medicine. She really was extraordinary.

They praised her for her efforts, gifting her with food and supplies, and it seemed the uneasiness in the air was dispelling for a time.

"You should stay. Stay here with us," Silf said.

Charlotte gave him a sad look, then shook her head. "I can't, I'm sorry. I'm looking to find a way to get help though. Me and Axrel are trying to get to the Lightpost."

That got some others' attention.

"The Lightpost?" Gnar—a grex and Kira's second—asked.

"Yes. It should only be a half day's walk from here," Charlotte said. "Have you heard of it?"

They shook their heads.

"Check the map," Silf suggested.

He and Charlotte followed Silf and his leaders to the set of tables at one side of the chamber. On top of one shiny metal surface was a flat device with a screen. When Kira turned the device on, it showed a map in faint blue, displaying the land which they were imprisoned on.

"We are here." Kira pointed to a small set of canyons and the river webbing through them. Not far to the east of it was the main road. To the south was the city and a smattering of working towns along the main route. "Many of us came from this small mining base just a few miles from here. But to the north..." She tapped the map to focus on their location and the northern edge of the land. "There is nothing but small stationways and guard posts. Are you sure?"

Charlotte nodded. "I'm sure. I suspect some maps won't show it save for those with security clearance. I only know of it from a map I saw on the ship, used by the heads in command. Its coordinates were hidden, likely for safety reasons, but I saw it was a tradeport which means it has the potential to have ships and a communications tower."

They each looked at her skeptically, and Axrel couldn't blame them. Even he had some doubts, but he believed for her sake it was there.

"It could already be up in flames if the vrisha have found it," Kira said.

"Or swarming with other more violent inmates if not," Gnar said.

"Those are all possibilities, but if the communication tower is intact, I could try to make a distress signal. If I can somehow connect my receiver to the tower, I can get my people specifically."

"Your people?" Kira asked.

"I am part of the Grayhart organization."

"Ah. That explains how you know much about otherkin. I take it you will leave soon then?"

"We leave at first light," Axrel announced.

"After I've checked over your injured, of course," Charlotte mentioned.

The lygin female blinked slowly, nodding her head in gratitude. "We can't thank you enough."

Charlotte smiled, taking Axrel's hand in hers. He gripped her hand firmly. "I'm just glad I could help," she said with honesty.

* * *

They gave them a place to bed down after. A couple of spare mats tucked into a low alcove in the rock. Many of the others were lying out for the night, lowering the lights of the lamps around them. The cave was chilly but not unbearable, colder than the springs but warmer than the outside with the storms and rain. It felt well-hidden and therefore safe. Still, as Charlotte settled in next to him, he decided he wouldn't sleep. He was still too on edge, and he couldn't completely let down his defenses with the inmates even if they had been hospitable. Even if Charlotte trusted them.

They were very close now. Once seeing the map and where Charlotte had claimed the tradeport to be. He wouldn't risk falling asleep for the prisoners to attack them. Or for some other unknown force to find them. They were too close.

And once they arrived, he would stay with her until help came. If there were ships, however...

When we get off here.

The memory of her words caught at him, tightening his chest.

"You're unusually quiet," Charlotte said as she snuggled up against him. He felt her warm breath against his chest. Without thought, he wrapped an arm about her, bringing her closer. His mouth brushed along her head in a gentle caress.

"I was just thinking," he said in a hushed tone.

"About?"

He shifted to look down at her, meeting her eyes. "About the coming hours."

"I'm nervous too," she confessed. "If the place isn't there, or if it's destroyed, I fear what we will be able to do."

"We will find a way. I will find a way to get you out, I swear it."

Her eyes searched his, still filled with worry. "I know. We will keep going, but the longer we are out here, the bigger the chance of the Blood Guard finding us. And it's only a matter of time before they stop searching and they..." She couldn't finish the rest, but he understood well enough.

"They will destroy everything," he finished. "But they won't get the chance."

She stared at him, the worry growing. Her soft hand gripped his arm. "If it does work, if we can wait it out and my people make it in time, we could save some lives here. Some might still have to answer for their crimes, but others can be given a second chance." Her hand squeezed him. "You could have a chance. With me. If there are ships, we can get out first, return to my home base. They will listen to me."

His chest tightened more, making it hard to speak.

"They will listen," she said, as if seeing the uncertainty in his gaze.

He rubbed his hand across her back, feeling the small ridges of her spine, then brushed his mouth against her forehead. "Let us get to the Lightpost," he said. "Then we will know where our path lies."

CHAPTER TWENTY-FOUR

CHARLOTTE

She was given a few hours of restless sleep before it was time for them to gather their things in preparation for their departure. She ate a quick meal with Axrel before she checked on the injured prisoners. Silf's sister was awake when she returned and drinking and eating like normal from Silf's hand, who continued to speak his gratitude. The others were coming along nicely, broken arms mending, open wounds healing. For some, the injuries would only be temporary. Others wouldn't be so lucky. The care they needed was more extensive, but she did her best with what she had. They would survive at least and could heal with time.

"I can't thank you enough," Silf said, crouching beside his sister. "I wish you a safe journey."

"If all works out, I will tell my people you're here, waiting for help. Just stay strong, stay hidden."

"We will."

After she'd said her goodbyes to Silf and his sister and those who were awake, she slipped back into the main chamber to meet with Axrel, only to find him surrounded by the other inmates, including Kira and Gnar.

"What's going on?" she asked, rushing over to make sure they weren't picking a fight.

Axrel looked at her first. "They wish to come with us," he said, clearly annoyed.

She turned to Kira, surprised. "But you're safe here. Why would you—?"

"We want to see this tradeport for ourselves," replied Gnar, his lizardish eyes narrowing. "If there really are ships or a way to communicate to the outside, we want the chance to help."

"And we want to make sure you get there safely," Kira added.

"And I told them you had me for that," Axrel said, giving her a sharp glare.

Kira glared back. "Better chances with more numbers. We work together."

Axrel snorted. "Or better chances to be seen."

Charlotte looked between them, then grasped Axrel's arm. "Maybe it wouldn't be so bad? We could use allies."

"It would be too much attention."

"We are stealthier than you think," Kira interjected. "We can run fast too. Maybe not as fast as you, vrisha, but as you can see, we are good hiders."

"And fighters," Gnar said, a trickle of venom dripping from his mouth.

Charlotte looked back at Axrel. "You've gotten me this far, and I know you will get me the rest. They won't be in your way, and they could help. We could use some of that."

Axrel's scowl softened a little as he let out a slow breath. He looked at the inmates. "You do as I say. You follow and stay hidden. If you get seen or caught..."

"We understand," Kira said, and the others agreed.

"It will be a lot of us to keep an eye on, but I'm sure we can make it work," Charlotte said.

"We aren't all coming," Kira assured. "Just a few. We talked it over last night. I will join with a small band, and Gnar will stay with the others. We will keep in communication with this." She lifted her arm to show a wristpad. One clearly taken or found. Gnar had another on his arm as well. "They were fixed so others can't trace them, and they only work between each other. We didn't want any guards trying to find our call." She lowered her hand.

Charlotte looked down at her own wristpad. She had no one in range to call, all her contacts on Larth, and had little use for it while on Fargis. But now... "Can you link mine as well?"

They connected their bands without issue. Among Kira's group, there was the corax—Jemma—a pair of grex with grayish scales, and another lygin—a male named Naba who had sleek dark fur unlike Kira's lighter coat.

Kira's green cat eyes sparkled with anticipation as they readied their gear, all of them carrying some kind of weapon, from wicked looking blades to large mallets. Such weapons wouldn't get them far if their enemies had shooters, but Charlotte hoped they wouldn't have to use them regardless. They didn't offer her or Axrel any, and that was just fine. She carried enough with her kit and had the gun still tucked safely in her now fully stocked bag.

They followed Kira and her band out a separate exit from the one they had used, weaving through tunnels until they came out the other side of one canyon right into the thick of the forest.

The light was dim, and the clouds were black with the threat of rain, but they would go on, bad weather or no. Charlotte, however, stilled by the entrance as the others began making their way past the twisting trees.

"What's wrong?" Axrel said, beside her.

Charlotte glanced up at him, for once feeling ashamed of her weaker body. At least compared to the others. "I...I won't be able to keep up."

He looked back at her, concerned, his eyes falling down to her feet. "Is it your leg still?"

Charlotte rolled her ankle, then bent her knee and shook her head. "It's healed enough to walk fine, it's just that...I can't move as fast. Shorter legs and all."

Without hesitating, Axrel took hold of her bag, swung it over his shoulder, then picked her up, holding her to him. She shifted in his arms, protesting.

"Axrel, I can walk."

"I know. And if you wish to, at your pace, we will. But I can always carry you. It is your decision."

He waited for her reply. She looked at him annoyed. But she knew they would make better time if he did. Even with stung pride, she knew.

Her arms wrapped around his neck. "Only for a little while. When we get closer, I'll go on my own."

He dipped his head, then, with one quick leap they were off, catching up to the others in no time before taking the lead.

* * *

They were only a few spans away when she had Axrel let her down. She walked on her own, keeping up as best she could, and Axrel never left her side. It was better now for them to slow and check their surroundings for any unusual activity, whether drones, or vrisha ships, or other prisoners waiting in the shadows. The closer they got, the more they paused to scan, to listen, to sense anything.

But there was nothing. Just the sounds of the buzzing from birds and the soft rumble of thunder in the distance. There were no signs of convoys or of prison guards either. Even when they found the main road again and followed along it, there was nothing, and the road itself started to narrow.

She began to worry that they might not find anything after all. That maybe she had somehow read the map wrong back on the ship, her mind wanting her to believe she had seen something out of desperation. Her anxiety grew as they came upon more open land, the forest growing thinner the farther north they went, making it harder to hide. They had been going for a long time, and she was sure they should have come upon it already yet every patch of wood they broke from, there was no clear sign of any tradeport. They hadn't even discovered a stationway. Just wilderness.

Her anxiety began to choke her with fear until they started up a small hill through a small thicket of wood that opened out into tall grass as they climbed. Naba had gone up ahead to see, and as he made it to the top, he shouted out to them. Heart leaping, she walked faster, then started to run, practically bounding up the hill. At the top, she slowed, then froze.

Below, tucked into a small valley, was what looked to be a base surrounded on all sides by a metal fence. At one end was a tall tower —the communications tower. It was all there, intact, before them. There was no one to be seen, but there were lights in the main building and in the tower, meaning there might be others. And as she looked over to the hangar connected to the building, a soft whimper escaped her. Through large glass panes, she could see inside there were ships.

She turned to Axrel, and he in turn looked back at her, his face unreadable. But he must be in shock like her.

She started forward, and he caught her arm.

"Wait, Charlotte."

She gazed back at him. "We need to go. We don't know how long we have—"

"I know. But we should still be cautious. We don't know who might be lurking within."

She looked back at the tradeport. To the entrance gate on the east side was a sign and engraved on it was a symbol—a lightbulb atop a long pole enclosed in a circle. The gate wasn't ripped open, there were no signs of forced entry, nothing was burned or broken. The lights were still on, which meant there might be people, possibly hundreds, hunkering down inside, waiting for others to come, waiting to depart. Or they were up in the tower and had already been calling for help and they were just waiting now, waiting to be saved.

She wanted to believe it so badly that her feet started to move again without her. Axrel kept her in place.

"Charlotte," he said. "No."

He brought her down with him to crouch against a mound of rocks. The others followed, scanning the area with sharp intensity. They looked over the base in silence, searching.

"What are we waiting for?" Jemma called, his broken fins trembling. "The ships are right there, let's go!"

Kira put up her hand to have him wait. She turned back to them. "We should look inside first. Just to see."

"What is there to see?" Jemma said. "You can clearly see now. The human was right, everything is intact. We should just go."

Naba and the two grex looked just as ready to bolt. The ships gave them the same powerful desire to run in and jump on board. But their leader commanded them to stay.

Kira looked at each of them, stopping last on Axrel. "We make sure it is clear."

Axrel bowed his head. He forced Charlotte around to face him. "There could be others hiding, waiting for someone to take the ships. It won't take long for us to find them if they are there." He rose and she joined him. "If it's safe, I will get you on that ship."

Charlotte frowned. A rumble of thunder grew louder in the distance. Or maybe it was a roaring in her ears as her pulse thudded in her head. "We get on together."

The look he gave her pierced through her like a needle to the chest, making her stomach turn. "No." She shook her head. "No."

"I promised I would get you out."

"Not without you," she whispered.

"The Blood Guard will follow. They will always be a threat. But not if I can stop them, here and now." He cupped her face in his hands. "They will never find you."

Her face twisted. "You still want your revenge."

"Yes," he said, with pained honesty. "I do. But now I have something more than that. Something to protect. And when I've left them in pieces, I will come back, Charlotte, I swear it."

She reached up to grip his hands. "I can't. I can't go without you. I won't."

His gaze softened. "Charlotte..."

"I'm not going without you." Her words were final.

His eyes searched hers for a time until he let out a slow breath. "We will check the place. If it is clear... we will discuss our next move."

It was all he would give her. But if she had to fight him to get them both on that ship to safety, she would. Damn his revenge. She would do anything to keep him from risking his life to have it.

He dropped his hands from her face to grip her shoulders, squeezing them gently. "Wait here for me to return." He glanced over at the others. "Stay by her side."

Charlotte watched as he and Kira moved together, silently making their way down the hill toward the fence. The others stayed close as Axrel ordered, but she could see in them the restlessness of wanting to leave. The ships were right in their line of sight, just a fence over and a few dozen yards between them within the glass hangar. But Charlotte knew it was better to be safe than sorry.

The light was fading as the thick rain clouds rolled in yet again. She couldn't wait to get off this world with Axrel, away from this endless dark.

As the pair crept across the landing and disappeared into the main building, she opened her bag and took out the gun just in case. Gripping it tight in one hand, she took a deep breath, her pulse still hammering in her ears. The others had their weapons out as well, ready to fight if need be.

They waited. She wasn't sure how long, but the more time passed, the more restless the others became.

"Where the hell are they?" Jemma grumbled after a time.

"Maybe they found something after all," Naba said, beside her.

Charlotte kept her eyes on the entrance, her hand clenched on her lap where she now sat, finger on the safety of the gun. She waited to see Axrel step out, to see him jump the fence and come running up the hill...

"Screw this," Jemma hissed. He leaped up from where he sat and started toward the base.

"Jemma, stop!" Naba called. Jemma hardly slowed. Charlotte rose as both of the grex—looking suddenly panicked—followed after. "You idiots, Kira will have your head!" Naba yowled. He moved to go after them, and Charlotte quickly reached out to stop him.

"Don't," she said.

"They get on one of those ships, and it could alert others," Naba protested. "Jemma!" he called again.

Jemma looked back as he gripped the fence. "We gotta survive. And I'm done waiting for whether I live or die. You guys are on your—"

She didn't hear the rest of his words as a sudden loud buzzing vibrated in her ears. The air around them turned electric, like a switch had been flipped. The hairs on her arms stood on end, and her whole body tingled. Before she could take a breath to shout that something was wrong, a blinding flash turned everything white.

Her mind in a split second of time thought they were being struck by lightning, just as the flash dissolved and an explosive boom knocked her backward several feet, ripping the gun from her hand. Her body turned instantly hot as she fell onto her back into the underbrush, pain shooting up her spine. Her ears popped, and an awful ringing clouded over any noise.

The thunderous explosion made the earth tremble under her and made the very trees sway. She felt it in her bones. A sharp pain sliced across her back where she landed, her arms scraped up by rocks, her pant leg ripped. She lay there in shock, curling into herself as fire and smoke hurdled into the sky. The roar of flames and groan of metal jolted her senses.

No. Please, no.

She forced herself to her knees, her arms shaking, her breath coming in gasps. She fell twice before she could finally stand, stumbling first up the hill, then crawling. She hissed and groaned as the pain in her back amplified with her movement. Tears stung her eyes from the heat. Ash fell from the sky as she reached the top. She turned her gaze ahead to the tradeport, and a cry ripped from her throat.

The fence was bent from the explosive force. Jemma and the two grex were lying underneath. A few feet to her left, Naba was lying on his side, blood trickling down his head.

As she tried to crawl toward the now burning tradeport, there was another noise above the fire—a low hum. As the noise grew, a shadow covered what little light was left.

She didn't need to look up to know what it was. The wind whipped up, rocks and dust flying. She covered herself until the low hum quieted, and she heard the soft steps of feet approaching.

"A human female," came a low, grating voice, speaking in clear vrishan.

A foot pushed at her side, forcing her to roll over. Terrified as she was, she couldn't stop herself from peering upward at the tall, menacing figures around her.

A whimper escaped her lips, her hands curling tight. No, no, please not like this.

The foot nudged at her again, and when she didn't respond, the sharp end of one of their tails pressed against her neck, forcing her to her feet.

She lifted her hands as if that would save her. She looked at the vrisha, their appearance a lot like Axrel only different shades of red and orange. But they were nothing like Axrel, and they scared her more than anything. She knew if she didn't keep her composure, the tip of the closest vrisha's tail would end her.

She licked her lips, her throat dry, making it nearly impossible to speak. She coughed and breathed, forcing air through her lips.

The closet vrisha, a maroon colored one with narrow horns and fiery yellow pupils, inched his face closer to hers, his head tilting, nostrils flaring.

Charlotte licked her lips again and tried to speak. "I—I'm not a prison guard. I'm not a soldier." As if any of that mattered. Her mind could hardly form the words in their tongue. It was all she could say as her thoughts scattered.

"This one speaks our language," the maroon vrisha hissed.

They circled her. Their hands touched at her, claws in her hair, pinching her skin. "Who are you?"

The tip of the spiny tail, pressed harder to her throat, demanded an answer. She coughed to hide a whimper, keeping very still as if one wrong move might kill her.

"I'm...a doctor," she said in a shaking voice. Her knees felt like they might give out at any moment, but the tail held her.

"You are far from any of your own to save around here." The maroon vrisha bared his teeth, black and shiny as the others.

"I'm not a doctor of humans."

They looked back at her curiously. "You come from the prison then. An experimenter?"

She shook her head quickly. "The ship, *Tarus*. To help the prisoners arriving."

They turned to one vrisha standing a few feet away, watching her closely with shockingly red—almost pink—eyes and brownish-red skin. Along with the strips of black armor they wore across shoulders and stomach, she noticed he and a few others had black markings along their arms and torso, even some along their neck and on their shins or feet where they weren't covered by their scaly pants. This one had an X on the left side of his chest.

"Kill her?" they said.

The X-marked vrisha's eyes narrowed on her, his head tilting as if examining her. She stared back in wide-eyed fear, hardly breathing as the maroon vrisha's tail brushed against her throat, waiting to strike.

"No," the X-marked vrisha said. "We take her. Vraxa will want to question her. If she is truthful in her claim, she might be useful. If she lies, she'll meet her fate as the rest."

The tail dropped from her neck and incredibly strong hands gripped her, lifting her from the ground.

"What of this one?" Another vrisha kicked at Naba, still on the ground. "And those lying down the hill."

"Leave those down below. They're as good as dead," said the X-marked vrisha. "Take the lygin."

They picked Naba up and together, pulling Charlotte away, they made for their ship, leaving the Lightpost and everything around it to burn.

CHAPTER TWENTY-FIVE

Charlotte

The ship landed at the center of an industrial complex, what she could only assume was a fuel refinery source. Chemical reactors and petrol tanks made up most of the station with a few buildings for storage. Fires of various sizes burned along metal towers like giant torches, dispelling some of the gas. Steam billowed from pipes, mixing into the thick clouds above. This was the Flame station where the vrisha had made camp.

As she was pulled away from the ship, across the open lot serving as their dock, she saw other vrisha leading prisoners around from various sectors. Some prisoners were placing goods onto ships from the storage houses, others were organizing supplies. Some were huddled in groups, waiting around to be commanded or taking turns fighting each other. Some were injured badly from these fights, their faces scratched up or bruised. Charlotte tried not to look at them.

Their heads turned toward her as she passed, curious, she'd bet, as to why a human—one not yet dead—was walking among them.

She and Naba, who was hanging across one vrisha's shoulder still partially unconscious, were led underneath a large steel hangar where fuel trucks were stored. Workbots stood motionless beside barrels of chemicals and oil. The air stank of gas and iron.

Not far in, near the center of the hangar, several vrisha congregated. Four males and two females from what she could tell. Counting the five that had found her and those she'd seen so far around the station, there were almost two dozen vrisha. A small number, maybe, to some, considering how many more prisoners there were in comparison, but to those who understood their packs, it was a formidable size.

As they approached, the group's eyes shifted to her, glaring. She kept her head down, only glancing their way, not daring to stare back. Like the five before, these also had unique traits, different reds with oranges and purples in their skin, eyes the colors of blood and fire. Many had black markings along their scales, some more than others. She wondered if it was some form of ranking. One male with several markings including a large V at the center of his chest rose from where he sat on a crate. His amber and orange eyes narrowed on her.

"So, you found them?" he asked.

"Just this human and a lygin," answered the X-marked vrisha who held her arm tight.

"And the northern base?"

X-marked dipped his head. "Gone."

"And this is all you found, Xano? A wandering human and a lygin?"

"There were no others alive from what we could detect, Vraxa."

Vraxa swung his tail irritably. "No sign of our brother at all?"

"No. But this might be the human he was seen with."

Charlotte's heart pounded in her ears, her throat constricting. How...how did they know?

Vraxa moved closer. He reached out and took hold of her jaw, forcing her to lift her head. His mouth came down inches from her throat. She kept still even when her mind was on the verge of fight or flight.

"If you had bothered to smell her, you would have known." Vraxa lifted his head. "His scent is all over her." He took a fistful of her uniform and pulled her with him, making her nearly trip and stumble before he shoved her to the ground. He took a seat back on his crate. "So, little human, tell me who you are."

It took several tries for her to get the words out clearly. She repeated to them what she told the others. That she was a doctor of alien medicine.

"And how did you meet our brother?"

By brother, she knew he must mean Axrel. She told them how she was on the ship *Tarus* and was assigned to keep him alive then, after the crash, he had found her as she was fleeing out of the city.

"And what?" Vraxa said. "He just decided to take you north?"

"He..." She wasn't sure how much she wanted to tell him. She certainly didn't think it would go over well if she confessed they'd formed a bond. "He found me useful. He was still healing and...he wanted my medical abilities."

Vraxa watched her carefully. "And you were heading for the north base."

"Yes, to the Lightpost."

"Why?"

"To get off world."

He scratched his jaw thoughtfully. "And he disappeared inside, I take it. Leaving you behind?"

"Yes."

His head tilted. She tensed as she could feel his tail trailing slowly across her back. He looked over at a female vrisha with rose-colored eyes. "Bring back over the ones we spoke to before. And Roon."

The female vrisha slipped away and a moment later came back with several prisoners. All of which Charlotte recognized. They were the same ones she and Axrel had encountered in the forest who had warned them about the bearsloth. They were dirty and beaten, their hands tied, bodies thin from lack of food for possibly days. They clearly had declined being a part of the Blood Guard yet the vrisha had kept them alive.

"Is this the human you saw with a vrisha?" Vraxa asked.

They glanced at her, then looked quickly away, unable to meet her eyes. With heads bowed, they mumbled "yes" in xolian.

"And they told you they were heading north? And not to come here?"

"Yes."

"The vrisha you saw was carrying her?" Vraxa said, turning his eyes to her.

"Yes, he was."

He ordered them away. As they were dragged off, another prisoner, one she also knew, who wasn't tied or beaten, appeared. The sight of him made her heart sink.

Prisoner One came around and bowed his head to Vraxa. His prison uniform was stained with dark blood as was his wiry, matted fur.

"Getting into trouble, Roon?" Vraxa asked.

"Yes, sir," he said through a smile. His eyes shifted down to her, and his smile faded, eyes widening.

"This is the human you spoke of, Roon? The one my brother fought you for?"

"My doctor!" Prisoner One cried. He reached out and grabbed her hair, yanking it, and Charlotte cried out, struggling from him.

"Listen, Roon," Vraxa hissed. "Answer my question. Did he fight you?"

"Yes," Roon said. "He took her from me."

"Good. Now let her go, Roon."

"But—"

"That's an order."

Roon let her go.

"Now leave," Vraxa growled.

Roon reluctantly backed away, his eyes lingering on her, drool dripping down his jaw. He bared his teeth in annoyance, then disappeared back the way he came.

"It seems you're not telling me everything, Doctor," Vraxa said with a purr, his spines cutting into her uniform.

"I told you the truth," Charlotte argued.

"But there is more to this, I know it." Vraxa leaned in, his face inches from hers. "My brother wouldn't want to get off world. He wouldn't go looking to help some human. He'd want to come back to us. It wasn't he who wanted to go north, it was you, wasn't it? And somehow, you convinced him. I'd like to know how."

She pursed her lips, not willing to respond.

"It's just as well you won't tell me. You humans are always conniving, scheming little maggots. Maybe you offered him something he couldn't refuse, hm? Yet I find that hard to believe." He rose from his seat and forced her to her feet. "And now he's very well dead from setting off our trap. But if he couldn't learn the first time, it's his fault. As for you," His claw grazed her cheek, then pierced it lightly. She inhaled sharply as blood trickled down her face. "If you really were useful to him, maybe you aren't worthless like the rest of your kind. We are finished here anyway. I should kill you for the loss of our brother. But an army comprised of lesserkin needs healers." He gripped her hard, pain shooting up her arm as he started to drag her away. "Xano, take those prisoners who oppose us and get rid of them."

The other vrisha dispersed as Vraxa pulled her across the hangar, past a set of empty military-grade trucks. At the back corner of the hangar were mats placed down, many of which were occupied by otherkin. The vrisha carrying Naba threw him down on one of the mats beside them.

"These are still possible fighters," Vraxa explained. "Survivors still needing to prove their worth. Some have won their fights but not without sacrifices. We've decided to give them another chance, but they can't fight if they are defective." He released her, letting her stumble forward. "Prove yourself, and maybe we will keep you."

She scanned over them. Some already looked dead, others had horrible injuries even she couldn't fix without machines. And her kit was gone, left behind at the Lightpost. She had nothing.

"I--I need supplies. I have nothing to work with," she explained.

"Find some then."

She looked around. There were so many wounded, she couldn't possibly look over them all.

Her eyes fell over to a group farther back at the edge of the hangar, separate from the others, being watched by a pair of prisoners. She let out a small gasp as she noticed them. She rushed forward, past the injured, then halted as a grex inmate got in her way.

She looked around him and saw a few dozen men and women. Her people. Several she recognized from the ship. She saw Officer Leslie among them. Some were as badly injured as the inmates. They were forced to sit up with a cloth over their eyes, arms tied and backs hunched over.

"Let me pass. Let me help them!"

"No," Vraxa said, behind her. He grabbed her and flung her away. She hit the concrete floor with a thud. As she tried to sit up, he came hovering over her. He forced her onto her feet by her uniform, and she pulled away from his grip.

"Damn you," she whispered. "You told me to help."

"Not them," he sneered. "They are the true prisoners here. They get nothing."

"They'll die!"

He laughed. "That's the plan. They only needed to give us information. But they've served their purpose. They'll rot here."

Charlotte shook her head. "Please. I'll help those wounded if you just let me—"

He got real close, silencing her.

"Don't try to negotiate with me. You do as I say." His fangs slipped from his upper lip, curved and long like a cobra's. "If I find out you went against my orders, I'll split your skull."

She stared him down this time, knowing he meant every word. He stepped back from her and turned to leave.

"Get to work," he snapped as he walked away. "If one of these fighters dies on your watch, I'll kill one of your own in return. That's a promise."

* * *

She scrambled to find a medkit anywhere. When she did find one, it was inside the compartment of one of the fuel trucks. It was small, nothing compared to her kit which she missed now dearly. She found some spare rags in one of the vehicles and a bucket in a bathroom in one of the offices next to the hangar. She filled the bucket with warm water and set it down. She went by each inmate in a row, doing what she could. She washed away blood, fixed deep cuts with the small bottle of sealant from the medkit and wrapped broken bones with the torn rags. It wasn't enough, she knew, and she was already struggling by the second row. When those who were awake noticed her, they began to cry out and call to her, shouting and hissing, angry and desperate. A headache was beginning to form at the front of her skull, a sharp pounding. She tried to keep her mind focused, tried to do what she could, but her energy was waning and more so was her concentration. She kept thinking of Axrel, and at times, she had to pause in her work to stifle a sob from escaping her. He couldn't be dead, she couldn't believe it. But she'd seen the tradeport. It had been up in flames, the building a burning mass. The explosion had torn a massive hole the front and top, the windows shattered, pieces of steel and concrete flying.

She squeezed her eyes tight, taking deep breaths. No, she needed to concentrate. Her people needed her. She couldn't think of him now, couldn't accept he was gone. If she did, she would break completely. She forced herself onward, forcing her mind blank as she moved from one inmate to the next.

She didn't know how long she held on, working on those around her. Time ceased to exist in that place. The inmates' jeers and angry cries became white noise, their faces began to blur together.

Eventually, Naba came to, but he had no words of comfort for her. Besides a bruised side and small concussion, he was all right, but his eyes told her how defeated he felt.

As she pushed on, trying to keep the prisoners stable and their wounds sealed, some would tear their injuries open again in their hastiness to get back up. They clawed and bit at her as she struggled with them, all while her people were sitting nearby, withering away. And she could do nothing.

Eventually, night came. Some of the inmates had walked off when they became too impatient after she'd sealed their worst wounds. Some fell asleep, not noticing her. She curled up by the tire of one truck, staring at nothing, her hands curled into fists on her knees. She knew more would come eventually, and she would have to scramble to help them all over again. She was exhausted but couldn't sleep. Axrel was gone, and she wanted to scream, to weep till she passed out. She did cry but silently. No one was coming to save them. She was alone. And the nightmare was only beginning.

CHAPTER TWENTY-SIX

Axrel

Smoke drifted into the sky from the tradeport, now nothing more than a ruin, the building now a shell of twisted metal and broken stone, the ships' skeletal remains scattered across the hangar bay now gone. Rain had dispelled most of the flames save for those scattered underneath the collapsed roof to one side of the tower.

From under a fallen piece of thick metal walling, Axrel crawled out, clawing at the ground with one hand while his other pulled Kira's limp body. He dragged her out with him, rolling her onto her back as he knelt atop shards of glass and dust.

He glared around at the destruction, his body vibrating with fiery energy. Rain hit his backside, sizzling across his skin, steam rising. There was nothing left. Everything was broken, blackened, or turned to ash. His burning gaze shifted past the torn walls to where the ships had once been, now piles of steel and wires. He rose on shaky legs. Not because he was weak, no. He'd never felt stronger. Filled now with an unimaginable power, driven by fury alone.

Kira groaned beside him. He picked her up, throwing her over his shoulder. He took one more glance around, then began making his way out of the wreckage.

He knew something hadn't felt right as soon as they had stepped inside the place. There was a stinging odor in the air, metallic and sharp. The air alone was electrified by some unseen power. Still, unable to place it, they had looked for signs of life, but the place had been empty, not a person in sight. All the lights were on, all the machines too. Yet there was no one. Kira had thought they had run off and left everything, but there were no signs of anyone fleeing. Nor a sign of struggle.

They searched the place extensively, but the building was clear. When they made for the hangar, things changed. Once the doors opened, a soft humming started growing louder. That would have been enough for him to know what danger they were in. But the bodies piled by the entrance, unseen from the outside, put him into action. He knew they wouldn't make it out in time. It was only by the grace of his ancestors that they found the stairs leading down into an underground level. They slipped into a machine parts room with a thick sealed door just as the explosion went off. His body was able to take the heat. His lungs were able to absorb the last of the oxygen before it was dissolved by the smoke. Kira wasn't so lucky. She was singed badly, and it was a wonder she hadn't yet suffocated. But she was alive.

He trudged over debris, making his way out of the building, then across to the overturned fence. The bodies of the other inmates were there, but he hardly looked at them. He stepped over the fence and climbed up the hill which was empty.

He had no hope in him to think Charlotte would be there still. He knew once the bomb ignited, the Blood Guard would come, and they would find her. Still, his heart turned to ice as he saw her bag laying by the rock.

An awful darkness began to consume him. He had let them take her. He had failed her. She was with the pack now, and he didn't want to think what they were doing. Or if she was dead already. The image of her broken body surrounded by his kind filled his vision. A painful snarl tore from his throat, turning into a deep roar.

* * *

He covered many spans of forest in a short time, his rage driving him forward without a thought. In the half day it had taken them to make it to the Lightpost, he returned to the canyons in less time, with some daylight still left. There were inmates guarding the entrance, and when they saw him with their leader slung over his shoulder, they immediately let him pass. They guided him through the tunnels until they reached the main chamber.

It looked the same as before only Axrel noticed there were far more prisoners this time. Some shouted as they saw him, taking up defensive stances while those who knew him from before kept the others from attacking or fleeing at the sight of him. He hardly paid them attention as he placed Kira on one of the empty mats near one cave wall.

"What happened?" came Gnar's voice beside him as he straightened.

"The place was compromised. They had laid a trap, possibly expecting us or someone to come," Axrel said. "We were scouting the building when the bomb went off. We only found shelter in time but..." His hands curled into fists as his vision turned red. He slammed his fist into the rock wall beside him.

"The others are...?"

"Dead. Only Naba was missing and Charlotte...she was gone. They took her." He growled, unable to stop himself. He stepped back from the wall. "I have to go."

"Wait, vrisha," Gnar said.

"I have to find them," he hissed. He went over to the map now displayed over one table and scanned it. The Flame. That's where they said they would be. Where she would be. If she wasn't dead.

He'd kill them either way. He'd find them and tear them apart like he'd always wanted.

Silf appeared and let out a soft cry at the sight of their leader. He and others rushed over to aid her. Gnar joined him by the map. "I feared something might have happened when I did not hear back from Kira at our planned time," he said, then shook his head. "They might have Naba too. He is of Kira's line. We should discuss our plan."

He had a plan. Go for the Flame, take out anyone who attempted to challenge him. Find Charlotte.

"I know you are angry. But you can't possibly go on your own."

"I can and I will." His eyes traced over the land until he found the station he sought. It was to the east, near the ocean. Judging by the distance, he could be there by morning if he left now and didn't stop or rest.

"You are in no state to fight them all. There are dozens if not hundreds of prisoners with the vrisha. They outnumber you."

"You think I don't know that?" He turned to the old grex, annoyed.

The grex put up his hands. "There are more of us now. More prisoners came from the south. If it's true our way for help is gone, we should look to fight. Many here will."

"Most are too scared to even look at me," Axrel argued. "You honestly expect me to believe any would stand up to the others? None here have the guts to even face me, let alone a pack of my kind."

"I do," came a quiet voice from the shadows.

Axrel looked over and saw a pair of large orange eyes staring back at him. A growl started in his throat, then stilled as the figure stepped into the lamplight.

"You," Axrel hissed.

The fyrien cautiously moved around the table opposite him. It was the same one from the crash, who had escaped her pod. Her purple skin was scarred in some places including her face. Her long white hair was messily tied in braids. So, she had survived and somehow found her way here.

"Of all those from the crash, I thought you'd keep hidden."

The fyrien crossed her arms. Like the others, she wore a dark blue prisoner suit only she had found a belt which she had hooked a set of knives to. None were the trademark blades fyriens were said to carry as hers must have been taken by the humans.

"I did for a time," she said. "Then I moved south where I overheard there was a ship port." Her eyes drew to the map, narrowing. "But it was overrun and the ship already destroyed. At a gateway nearby, I found a map and saw there was another port to the north. But I take it that's no longer an option either."

"No, it's not."

"So, the only ships now are vrishan. Which is where I will go next."

He scoffed at her arrogance. "Even you would be caught by my kind. And I doubt you'd stand against one let alone several vrisha."

"That is why I will join you."

He snorted, looking away. But he could not deny having a fyrien on his side would be useful. They were said to be one of the few who could at least stand their ground against one of his kind though whether they could win a fight against a vrisha was debatable. They were also said to be impressive assassins and thieves who moved silently in the shadows.

"What do you go by?" Axrel asked.

"Zeti."

"Zeti...you can come if you can keep up." He started for the supplies, but Gnar got in his way.

"It's still too risky. You can't hope to get close without being caught. They have drones watching for miles across. You will be seen."

Axrel studied him. "How do you know that?"

Gnar glanced around to the others waiting and watching nearby before turning back to him. "Some have seen the Flame and the drones from a distance. As soon as they see you coming, they will chase you down."

Axrel closed his eyes and took a long breath. If they saw him coming, so be it. But if the others followed, they would look like a band of fighters, and that might start an attack outside of where the Blood Guard waited. More reason for him to go alone.

"You could go and find yourself in too deep. Or you can hear us out. When I didn't hear back from Kira, we started to talk over our next move. When Zeti arrived with others, we discussed other ways to get off world if the tradeport didn't work. She is confident she can sneak on to one of the vrisha ships," Gnar explained. "If there is a big enough distraction. But it would mean getting inside first."

Crazy. What would make them think that was a good idea at all? He opened his eyes, letting his expression show what he thought. But Gnar was adamant.

"Most of us are willing to try. To fight if we have to. It's all we have now. We know this place won't be safe for long. Zeti informed us once the vrisha destroyed the south port after they set everything for miles aflame along with the city. It's assumed they are planning to do the same for the rest of this land once they leave. They will find us or burn us out." His mouth thinned, venom dripping. "And with the tradeport now confirmed gone as well, we have only this. But we might have a chance if you let us come with you." When Axrel didn't respond, Gnar got up in his face. "If you want to get your woman back, if she is alive, you can't hope to do that if they take you down. Are you really willing to risk it?"

He bared his teeth in annoyance and turned away, pacing before them. He remembered something Charlotte had said back when they had been on the ship. About taking on all three hundred prisoners if he had to. He still believed he could. But his pack was a different story. He wanted his revenge now more than ever. Before, he was willing to die for it. But for Charlotte's life, if she still lived, he knew he could never trade.

With his anger no longer blinding him, he knew now, for her sake, what must be done.

He stopped and turned toward Gnar and the other prisoners standing around him. They were looking to him, he realized, waiting on his decision. He could at least hear them first.

"All right," he said at last. "Tell me your plan."

CHAPTER TWENTY-SEVEN

CHARLOTTE

The sounds of shouting and scuffling woke her from a troubled sleep. The morning was cold and dim as ever, only a soft light above giving hint that a new day had come. A sharp pain rippled up her side as she jolted up. The pain moved up her neck and along her head, making her wince. She rubbed a hand across her temple and groaned, her eyes fluttering open to peer across the wide open area of mats where few now slept. Her eyes drifted over to the noise and, across the hangar, just outside the open doors, she saw groups of prisoners huddling around watching as a pair fought viciously. She watched too for a long moment before she realized one of the fighters was Naba. He had blood dripping down his face and matted in his fur. She couldn't tell yet if he was winning or not.

She groaned again as she shifted where she now sat, her back still up against the large tire of a truck. Her heart leaped in her throat as she swept her eyes over the injured and across to where the soldiers and prison guards were being kept, still being watched by inmates, most now lying on their side, unable to remain kneeling. They were all there still, but for how much longer?

Dread filled her, wondering how long she had been out. Not too long, she was sure, but still enough time for someone to have taken a bad turn in the night. Carefully, she forced herself up, using the truck's side as support. She weaved a little on shaky legs, her energy sapped, the last few days taking their toll. She inhaled through her teeth as the pain shot up her backside again, knowing she had some internal damage from when she was knocked back from the explosion the day before.

She moved toward the mats and hovered a moment, looking over those still left from last night. Naba clearly had recovered at some point and had been dragged into a fight to, as Vraxa said, "prove himself," while a few others had disappeared back into the crowd, likely to watch.

She took a deep breath and turned to one lone skra female. The amphibious, green-skinned alien reminded her of Silf's sister a little, only this one had a set of ridges across her skull which Charlotte had rarely seen on their kind. The woman's full black eyes stared up at her, blinking quickly with inner lids. Last night, Charlotte had determined the skra had acquired a few fractured ribs and bruised organs. She'd told the woman to lie on her back with arms crossed and gave her a pain reliever, but that was about all she could do with the few supplies she had.

She crouched down beside the woman and gently placed a hand on the alien's side, gauging her reaction. Her breath was no longer coming in short bursts nor was she humming which some skra did when in distress. As Charlotte pressed down on the skra's stomach, the woman's hand curled around her wrist. Charlotte froze.

The woman didn't say anything. Not at first. But her eyes almost said enough. She looked afraid. Not angry or wild like some of the others but almost ashamed. Then she leaned up and whispered in Charlotte's ear.

Charlotte listened, her eyes widening. She grew very still as the skra slowly laid back down, releasing her hand. Charlotte stared at her for a second longer before her gaze turned upward, looking around her. There were still many prisoners watching the fight outside, but there were also many lurking about. Some watched from a distance, sitting or standing in groups, talking quietly. Their eyes turned toward her, with an expression much like the skra's. They too were afraid, regret etched in their features.

Charlotte stared back at them, then dropped back to the skra. She squeezed her arm before moving on to the next injured inmate on a mat nearby, this time with determination. As she checked them over, her mind turned over the skra's words.

"We had no choice," she had whispered. "But many don't want to fight. Not for them. We just want to live. Help us."

She wished she had an answer for her. But she didn't. There was no one who could help now. No one who would come in time. And once they were taken off world, they would never be found again.

But the skra's words did leave her with some hope. She'd forgotten that the Blood Guard had coaxed many to come to the Flame. Not all had sought to join them but rather understood they would die if they didn't. Likely, many had been found first, and the vrisha had given them an ultimatum. Which meant not all the prisoners were on their side.

It didn't mean much in the grand scheme of things. The vrisha could still destroy the lot of them. But if there were those willing to disobey—to defy them completely—then there was a chance at some point of working together to escape. Even if the possibility was minuscule.

If all she'd get was that little hope, it was enough for now to keep her going.

The rest of the morning and into the afternoon, she cared for those on the mats. More came as the fights continued. Naba won his but not without hurting himself. He came to her again with a mangled shoulder and gashed up face.

"Just more scars to add to the bunch," he said as she looked him over. "But it's not over yet. The others are still out there. When Gnar finds out what happened..."

"There's nothing they can do," Charlotte replied, cleaning the blood from his face.

Naba went quiet. There was nothing they could do except stay hidden. And only for as long as the vrisha remained in the Flame.

"Kira..." Naba whispered. "She would have fought rather than died. She would have banded the others together."

Charlotte couldn't find words of comfort. Only to say, " I know."

There was a burst of excited roars and cries as another fight finished out, another worthy soldier for the vrishas' army. Charlotte looked around and saw Prisoner One—Roon—amidst the other prisoners. Those who had chosen to side with the vrisha grouped around him, jeering and kicking at the fallen loser. Meanwhile, the winner— a large corax with long head fins and sharp teeth sticking out of his shark-like mouth—was picked up by several and hauled up, half his body being dragged over to the mats.

"Fix him," they hissed, dropping him on a mat next to her. Blood gushed from his back and side. He sat up and leered at her, and Charlotte found herself frozen.

Little did the others know corax anatomy but, judging by what she could see, she knew he was bleeding out from his main artery, leading to his heart as well as into his lungs. He looked stable from their perspective, with just a bad flesh wound, but she knew, without surgical machines or even proper tools, he wasn't going to make it.

Cursing, she stood up and moved closer to him, but the shark growled at her before she could even touch him. He must know too and didn't want her to bother, or he didn't want her touching him regardless. Whatever the reason, she couldn't get close enough to even examine him.

"What are you waiting for?" one of the inmates snapped.

Charlotte shook her head, heat seeping from her body. The corax began to cough up blood, his body shaking.

She stood back as he collapsed in front of her, blood pooling underneath him. He let out two more ragged breaths before he stilled.

The prisoners looked at her with fury. They broke apart as Vraxa appeared, cutting through them.

He clicked his tongue. "You let one die," he said. "I told you what would happen. But it matters not now." He gestured to the prisoners. "Bring the humans. It's time for everyone to gather at the ships."

They forced the soldiers and guards onto their feet and led them out of the hangar. Another prisoner took hold of her and pulled her away, with Naba following close behind.

They brought them out into the wide open space surrounded by the oil refineries and fuel factories, nothing more than a large concrete lot. Around them were the vrisha ships, waiting to be boarded. Several dozen yards away, she could see the walls of the station and the gate, closing them in. The only way out now was up. She noticed many eyes drifting over to the ships, looking wary, desperate.

They set the soldiers and guards with Officer Leslie among them in a tight circle. The vrisha—all sixteen by her count—circled them like wolves among sheep.

"These are the true enemy," Vraxa called out. "And we will show them no mercy. All who oppose us will know our wrath."

Charlotte shut her eyes tight, not wanting to watch as the vrisha drew closer, their tails rising, curling up, ready to strike.

A hand grasped her arm in a sudden bone-crushing grip, tugging her violently. She cried out, eyes popping open to see Vraxa holding her.

"You watch. This is your warning if you do not obey, doctor. You see your fate in them."

Another cry ripped from her, this time furious. She tried to pull away from him, and he swung her around so quickly he nearly dislocated her shoulder. His other hand shot out, grabbing her by the throat, lifting her on to her toes.

"I'll kill you personally. And send your head to your leaders, you worthless worm."

As she struggled in his grip, Xano stepped over, in his hand a black device with an oval-shaped screen. "Not to interrupt you, but there are more prisoners coming," he said. "The skyeyes detected them on the road."

A few seconds later, a shout came from across the lot. Charlotte clawed at Vraxa's hand as he looked around.

Inmates guarding the gate were waving. One was rushing over—a large lygin male with a thick black mane.

"There is a band of more prisoners," he said, a little breathless. "They've come to join us and claim they've found something of value to you."

Vraxa released her, making her drop to her knees. As she clutched her throat, forcing air into her lungs, he gestured for them to open the gate. She heard the groan of the gate opening followed by the sound of engines.

The roar of engines grew louder, and as she looked up, she saw several large military trucks with their backsides covered in a dark green tarp slow and stop in front of them. A band of inmates hopped out from the back of each. She saw Gnar—the old gray-looking grex—drop out from the driver side of one, followed by Silf in the passenger. They were unarmed as they approached.

Vraxa moved into her line of view, his tail flicking just above her head. "You've come to join us."

"We know which side has the better chance," Gnar said.

"A wise decision," Vraxa said. He tilted his head. "And you bring us something?"

Gnar gestured to the others, and they moved to help another group jumping out from the back. Gnar looked back at Vraxa. "We only wish to serve. We knew you'd care for your own. We hope this shows our gratitude."

Several of Gnar's men pulled at something large and heavy from the back of one truck. When they picked up the heavy mass and dragged it around into their line of sight, Charlotte had to swallow the shocked cry that almost escaped her. Blood drained from her face, and a quiet sob stuck in her throat as Vraxa moved out of her view to step closer as the group dropped Axrel on the ground before him.

He was tied tight by a thick set of metal chains around his arms and ankles. Gnar stood beside him. "Some heard and saw an explosion to the north. When they went to investigate, they found him unconscious within the gutted building. The chains were merely a precaution, but we knew he should be brought back to you."

Vraxa glared back at Xano, annoyed. "Detected nothing, eh?"

"Vrisha can survive many things. Explosions are not unheard of," Xano remarked. "He must have found shelter somehow."

Vraxa looked back at Axrel. "Well, brother, you have proved you have the cunning for survival at least. And for that, I am thankful. We have been looking for you." The rose-eyed female vrisha came forward and freed Axrel of his chains. "I hope you learned a valuable lesson. But we are willing to forgive and forget."

Axrel, whose head had been bowed close to his chest, tilted it up to look at him. "Forgive and forget," he repeated. He rose until he and Vraxa were face to face. "I have thought long about my punishment and the perspective it gave me."

The whole of Gnar's men stood before them. Even, to her astonishment, Kira, who was being supported by two others, most of her fur gone from burns. The vrisha didn't seem to notice or care, as they looked only to Axrel, their lost packmate. Behind Gnar and the others, Charlotte thought she caught a shadow move behind one vehicle and disappear on its other side, but it must have been her imagination. Her eyes turned back to Axrel who, despite his unbearably scarred and damaged body, stood tall in front of Vraxa.

"A punishment we did not deal lightly. But it is over now. Almost." Vraxa side-stepped away from him. "I heard some foul rumors of you helping a human. I didn't believe them. But I must make sure you haven't fully fallen. Just one more test to prove you can return to us. Kill the remaining humans. Destroy your true enemy,

Axrel, and all will be forgiven. Then we will return to Queen Theda with our mission a success. And the fighters she desires."

They waited. Charlotte, on her knees, shivered, knowing if he so much as looked at her, he'd give himself away.

"I've longed to destroy my true enemy this whole time, Vraxa. I will relish the chance now." He passed Vraxa to stand before the group of soldiers who cowered before him. Charlotte tensed, her heart pounding. As the vrisha watched him, they didn't take notice as Gnar's men slowly stepped away from the trucks.

Axrel rose his tail, ready to strike the nearest soldier. As he aimed the spiked end of his tail downward, a burst of orange light erupted from the farthest truck, sending it sky high.

Charlotte shielded her eyes, heat licking her skin from the fiery blast. She was knocked back and nearly trampled over, unprepared for the chaos that ensued.

There was a great roaring all around as the other trucks went up one after another. She covered her head, curling into herself.

As the flames consumed the trucks and the ground around them, a low hum made the ground tremble, growing louder as it vibrated through her then all around her. She glanced upward in time to see a ship hovering low to the ground, then dropping back as if unable to properly fly. The prisoners, those not knocked back by the explosion of trucks, were in a battle around her, some making for the ship— those too injured to fight. The rest were fighting each other. She looked around and saw Axrel head-to-head with Vraxa while the other vrisha tried to pry the prisoners off each other. Then the prisoners turned against them. The prisoners swarmed, and with so many, even the vrisha could not keep them all at bay, not unless they were to kill. But that would mean killing those meant for their army and—not seeing the inmates as anything more than expendable soldiers—they couldn't gauge who was on their side.

Charlotte crawled toward her people, still huddled together, prisoners bounding and stepping on her as she went. Silf came out of the fray and picked her up.

"Help me with them!" she shouted. Together, they pried the ropes from their hands and cloth from their eyes.

As they freed the last of them, Charlotte tried to lead them away to safety, but she was knocked down by a heavy hand. She rolled around and saw Xano above her. He hissed in fury and slashed at her, catching her arm with his talons. He tore through her uniform into her skin, making her scream in pain. He went to strike again, then jolted back as a spiny tail whipped out at him.

Axrel stood above her, guarding her. He snarled, talons curled. "Touch her again and die."

Vraxa appeared beside Xano. They each circled him.

"I should have known you'd fallen, Axrel," Vraxa said. "But to choose them over us? You are lost beyond any saving."

"I was lost when you ordered the others to beat me. When you left me for dead!" He leaped at them, forcing them back, away from her. Prisoners attacked Vraxa and Xano from each side, and the vrisha pair cut them down, no longer caring how much they might need them. There were only a few groups still on their side, Roon and his lot being one of them. It was as if there had been a shift in alliance once the prisoners who'd joined out of fear saw Gnar's men fighting back.

Yet, even with the large numbers, the vrisha were beginning to cut them down. Like Vraxa and Xano, they knew it was no use trying to keep them back without majorly harming them in return.

Silf returned to her, leading her toward the ships where her people were also fleeing. The one ship trying to take off hovered again and then dropped.

"Who can fly these besides a vrisha?" Silf said.

Charlotte shook her head. She looked back and saw Axrel still keeping Vraxa at bay while Xano was forced to keep the swarm of prisoners off him. "Axrel. We need Axrel."

The ship dropped for a final time, landing clumsily on the ground. People waiting nearby drew back as the door opened and the fyrien stepped out, looking very annoyed. She had clearly been trying to control the ship without success. Enraged now, she swept by them with knives in hand, deciding to join the fight instead.

With the door open and the ship on the ground, people—both human and otherkin—began to flood inside, unsure where else to go. Charlotte moved with them, then stopped.

"Go, Silf, join your sister," she said. Silf looked at her uncertainly. Charlotte didn't wait to see what he might do. She turned her gaze back to the fray of vrisha and prisoners. The vrisha were gutting them now, and the prisoners were starting to fall back. Those vrisha who had cleared themselves of prisoners were setting their sights on them.

Her eyes swept over and saw Axrel growing farther away as Vraxa pushed him back.

"No, no," she whispered. "Axrel."

She wanted to go to him, as stupid of an idea that was. Because they weren't going to make it. There were too many vrisha. The prisoners couldn't withstand them, and many were starting to run away. They couldn't drive the ships because only the vrisha knew how to. They were stuck, and the vrisha were gaining ground.

She took a step and her head spun. She fell, feeling hands come around her. Her stomach turned, feeling like she might be sick. She dropped a hand on the ground and felt something warm and wet against her palm. When she looked down, she saw the red of blood in a small puddle, dripping from her. Xano had dealt a deep blow to her shoulder.

"I'm...I'm losing too much..." Her words were slurred. She pressed her hand hard to her shoulder to try and stop the flow. There were others around her now. Another pressed their hand against hers to help with the bleeding. Her vision, beginning to dim, saw only Axrel in the distance, Vraxa sending a blow with his tail to Axrel's side. Axrel kicked him back into the growing fire of the vehicles, and Vraxa was momentarily disengaged. In that little time, he searched frantically until his eyes found hers. He rushed for her, only to be blocked by his packmate. Wildly, he fought to get past, but they wouldn't budge.

Charlotte stretched her arm out as if to reach for him. The other vrisha were starting for them, ready to tear them from the ship. Or force them farther inside to take who they could away and deal with them later. Whichever it was, it didn't matter now. They were losing, and if she was taken and separated from Axrel, then she would be content to die rather than be left alone without him, to be forced to help the Blood Guard in their terrible war.

A sudden outburst of cries went up around her. She imagined the others were growing terrified as the pack approached. But then the vrisha began to slow, their heads lifting to the sky.

There was a low hum in the air, and the wind picked up. The others around her were looking to the sky as well, as if seeing something there. Charlotte lifted her gaze and saw nothing but the swirling clouds.

Was it a storm again? No. But there was something. Something there. The humming grew louder, and she saw the clouds breaking apart.

She expected to see the sunlight break through, blinding them, covering them in a warm embrace as if the heavens were opening to take them. She wasn't much of a religious sort, but for a moment, she thought maybe she was about to see something miraculous.

And in a way, she did. But it wasn't the heavens or even sunlight that broke through the clouds. It was the underside of a giant ship with the Grayhart star etched into its hull. And it was descending toward them.

CHAPTER TWENTY-EIGHT

Axrel

The ship dropped past the clouds, hovering over them. He knew it wasn't more of his kind based on its appearance alone. He and Vraxa had paused in their fight to stare upward and watch as smaller ships detached from the sides of the main ship to dive downward.

Axrel turned back to Vraxa who lowered his gaze, fixing Axrel with a death glare.

"I know something for sure," Axrel said. "Even vrisha have a weakness. And one of them is fighting from the sky. You've run out of time, Vraxa."

Vraxa snarled at him. He moved, turning from Axrel to run for his own ship. The rest of the pack were making for them too, hoping to get out and fight back in time.

Axrel ran after him and got in his way, slashing his tail across his chest. Vraxa hissed with rage. He lunged, hoping to land a blow to his neck, and missed.

The smaller, slender ships with narrow fronts and wide backs, made of some shiny steel, flew around, then passed over them. As they did, they shot down at the vrisha. Hundreds of small metal spheres fell around them, and, as they hit the ground, they let off bursts of vapor. One hit Vraxa's shoulder, and the vapor coated his scales in ice. He hissed in shock as his arm suddenly became hard to move. Another hit near Axrel's thigh, and he felt the icy sting. He backed off, trying to dodge the vapor. It was so cold it burned, not in the way of fire. It was extremely unpleasant.

Vraxa shrieked in rage as another sphere struck his back. Enraged, he came for Axrel, sweeping through the vaporized ice. He leaped at him, and Axrel dropped, kicking his legs out, striking Vraxa in the chest, making him fly over him. Vraxa rolled across the ground as another wave of ice fell from the sky. Axrel shot up and made for the cover of a nearby building as the spheres burst open, flooding the area. A few struck his side but not enough to slow him. As he took shelter, he watched as each of the Blood Guard were struck, one after the other, each step making them slower until they were frozen in place.

As the vapor dispelled, the ships flew past one more time before circling then disappearing. Some of the vrisha struggled to move while others were no more than statues.

He, along with others who had taken shelter, moved back into the open shipyard. Some of the prisoners circled the vrisha cautiously, realizing they were stuck. Zeti appeared nearby and stepped over to Xano. She stared the vrisha down before cutting her knife across the warrior's neck. They watched as half of him shattered to pieces.

The prisoners, seeing that, reacted almost instantly. They started for the other members and struck them, breaking them apart. Axrel moved toward the Blood Guard's ships, where Charlotte and the others were, when he spotted Vraxa stuck kneeling on the ground where he had tried to get up before being frozen solid. Axrel approached and stood before him, feeling triumphant.

"Let this be a lesson, brother," Axrel said. "A lesson learned." He shot out his fist, hitting Vraxa in the head, and it crumbled. He kicked Vraxa's chest, and his body fell into pieces at Axrel's feet.

He knew these were not the only members of the Blood Guard. There were others out there in the far systems, but now, they would be at a loss. His pack was no more.

Axrel took one last look at his fallen brother before stepping over him. He started for the vrisha ships, Charlotte finally in his sights. He rushed for her. As soon as he was at her side, he knelt down and picked her up, bringing her to him, holding her tight. He hardly noticed the others around her, who had stayed by her, nor did he notice one of the ships from above dropping down to land nearby. His attention was only on Charlotte.

Her face was pale and her skin cold. Her uniform was stained red. Xano had cut her deep. He placed a hand on the wound, and her own closed over it. She smiled up at him even though she looked on the verge of unconsciousness.

"I'm here, *kissala*," he said softly.

"I know."

"I'm sorry I failed you."

She frowned. "How?"

"I didn't protect you like I should have, and now..." He placed more pressure on her wound.

"It wasn't your fault, Axrel. You did everything you could and more." Her words were only a whisper, her eyes drifting closed. "I'm just glad that you are..."

He shook her gently, keeping her awake. He pressed his mouth to her forehead, and she sighed, her head falling on his shoulder.

Silf, who had stayed close, tapped on his arm and gestured across to where a group of humans ran toward them, some wearing clothing similar to the guards on Fargis with armored padding, shooters drawn. Those close behind them wore light blue and white like the kind of clothing Charlotte had worn before the prisoner ship had crashed. The soldiers halted and raised their weapons, aimed at him. He growled at them while Silf and the other inmates backed away. The humans who had been imprisoned by the Blood Guard, however, began to step out of the ship behind them. They cried out as they saw the soldiers and started toward them, letting the other humans in white and blue take them to safety.

One soldier stepped forward, his gaze on Charlotte. Axrel's fangs slipped from his upper lip, not liking his stare.

"Give us the doctor," he said in xolian. "We don't wish to fight you. Just give her to us."

Another growl rumbled in his chest, wrapping her closer. No, they wouldn't take her from him. Not now. Not after everything.

Charlotte shifted in his arms, her head rising an inch from his shoulder. "Grayson?"

Another soldier stepped closer, lowering his gun. "Charlotte, we're here." He glanced at Axrel with hostility. "Hurt her, vrisha, and you will regret it."

Before Axrel could respond, Charlotte placed her free hand on his chest. "He's all right, Grayson. He's...with me."

The soldiers looked at one another, shocked. "With you?" Grayson asked.

Charlotte nodded her head. She was slipping again. "Don't hurt him...he's with me."

"Charlotte?" He turned toward the other humans in white and blue. "We need medical now!" He turned back to Axrel. "Give her to us. We can get her on board and help her."

He didn't want to be separated from her, but he knew she needed help. And her life was more important than his wants. Still, he couldn't bring himself to give her over. Instead, he rose and took a step toward them. Their guns rose in response.

"I'm not leaving her side," Axrel said in broken xolian.

They seemed at a standstill, until Grayson finally lowered his gun. "I don't trust you. But I trust Charlotte. And if she says you are with her...then I will believe her."

The other soldiers looked between them, then lowered their

guns. The humans in white and blue rushed over, then gave him a wary if not fearful stare.

"The others too," Axrel said, looking to Silf and the remaining prisoners. "They come too. They are all that is left. It's what Charlotte would want."

"They are not our prisoners to take," said one soldier, beside Grayson. Grayson put up his hand.

"Fargis and the prison are destroyed. I'd say that makes them refugees. If they step foot in human territory, however, we can't help them again. They are on their own, agreed?"

The prisoners agreed in unison. With that, the soldiers stepped aside, letting them pass. The medical team followed Axrel close as he carried Charlotte toward their ship, passing by the bodies of his dead pack mates and of those prisoners who sided with them, including the drogin and his ilk, gone with them, their bodies left behind. He gave them one last look and knew, if there were any who deserved to be imprisoned forever in death on this cold world, it was them.

CHAPTER TWENTY-NINE

AXREL

The room was small yet bright, bare of anything but the pod and the machine next to it which beeped softly every few intervals. A window looked out into the endless dark, with nothing to see save for his reflection in the glass. The floor vibrated underneath him, and vents above pushed air in every so often, keeping the room fresh and cool. The lights hummed above, and the pod sometimes made strange clicks and whirs as lights moved across the top panel.

It was strange to be in the position he was in, walking around the room, checking the pod every so often, waiting, because only a little more than a week ago, he had been in the opposite position. He had been the one inside a pod while Charlotte had been walking around, checking on him, waiting. He peered down through the glass panel, and he could see her now, sleeping soundly. But unlike her, he was no doctor. He couldn't tell how well she was doing aside from the assumptions he made from the symbols and numbers on the machine. Vitals the other doctors had called them. Her vitals.

They were stable. She had been like that for a couple days now as they flew aboard the large Grayhart vessel, returning supposedly to Charlotte's home base. The ship, very much like the prisoner ship, carried many onboard, from scientists to Grayhart's own security team. Despite all its many passages and rooms, however, he rarely left the one he was in. Only when the medical staff needed to look Charlotte over did he leave to give them space. They eyed him cautiously if not curiously whenever they came. But they never turned violent or hysterical. At one point, even, a nurse brought him food, noticing he hadn't eaten.

He knew of Grayhart. There were few vrisha who didn't, but his encounters with them had been minimal. He understood now that the people of Grayhart were far different from the military. They treated him differently too. Even when he smelled fear on them, they tried to keep an air of civility, even politeness. They weren't looking to fight, they were looking to understand.

He was grateful for them now. Even if they were a part of an alliance he still couldn't fully get behind. Thankfully, Grayhart didn't consist of just humans. There were many otherkin working amongst them, and they seemed to have their own kind of pact: help one another and learn. Travel together, discover together. It was refreshing in that way.

Despite their so-called compassion, he still felt an outsider. He stayed by Charlotte's side, not just to watch over her, but also because she was all that he wanted. And now, she was all that he had. His pack was gone, and he couldn't return home without being deemed a traitor. There was no one else. The other prisoners, those who had survived, including Gnar, Kira, Naba, Zeti, Silf, and his sister, had worked together out of desperation. But he couldn't call them friends. They visited every so often and gave their regards. The Grayhart team didn't lock them up but gave them somewhere to sleep in spare rooms, allowing them to wander supervised.

They were the closest allies to anyone he had on the ship, and soon, they would be gone when Grayhart dropped them off in the neutral zone, at the tradeport on their base where they could find their own way. Without them, he felt surrounded by people he did not yet trust and old enemies he could not escape. The handful of times he had left the room to wander, he had come upon the surviving humans of the prisoner vessel. He grew angry again at the sight of them, and he could sense their anger in return.

"The prisoners are still government property," one of them said, a so-called officer. "They should be given up at the next landing."

The only thing that kept that from happening was Grayhart security. The one called Grayson, though Axrel could sense the man's apprehension of him and the others, had stood by their decision.

"They are under our jurisdiction now. On our ship. Whatever crimes they committed were under governing law. But we are no longer in the governing systems," Grayson had countered. "If they attack or break Grayhart rules, then we have the right to arrest them. Otherwise, we remain on equal terms. But by all means, Officer Leslie, if you and your men want to try and apprehend them this minute, go ahead. We won't try to stop you. Good luck."

That shut the soldiers up, and they kept their distance after. Axrel had garnered a little respect for the man after that, though he still didn't much care for him.

A bell-like sound went off above him as he watched Charlotte in her pod. A woman's voice spoke clearly overhead.

"Two hours till docking. All passengers should begin preparations for return."

Axrel closed his eyes and took a deep breath. It had been a long time since he had been anywhere familiar, in his own element. He didn't mind ships, nor travel, but he was beginning to miss the warmth of his home. He missed the hunt. And he suspected Charlotte's world might not have those things. He was told it was a terraformed world made up of one of Grayhart's largest bases and docking points, situated in a system within the neutral zone where many traderships passed by and stopped. It was a small city port on a mostly lifeless world.

The door behind him opened. He turned and stiffened when he saw Grayson standing in the doorway. The man had come several times to check on Charlotte, and each time, Axrel had to stifle a growl in his throat.

"You're still here," he said in a rigid voice.

"Yes. I am," Axrel said.

"You're not joining the others?"

"No."

Grayson stepped inside, and Axrel shifted away, to allow him to stand by the pod. Grayson placed his hand on the glass panel, and Axrel felt a twisting in his gut. He'd suspected many times that the man felt something for Charlotte. How strong those feelings were, he couldn't be sure. If they were courting, Charlotte had given no indication of it. Perhaps it was a one-sided longing. Or perhaps not. But it made him feel uncomfortable all the same, seeing the man looking down on her fondly. It took more will than he cared to admit to not step over and get in his way.

After a long moment of them standing near the pod in silence, Grayson slipped his hand from the panel and started to leave the room. At the door, he stopped and looked back at him.

"When we land, we will take the prisoners to the south port. There are a lot of tradeships there that will be willing to take them off world. You could join them."

Axrel didn't respond, his tail flicking irritably behind him.

Grayson turned fully to face him. "You'll have nowhere else to go within the Grayhart base. They won't let you wander alone."

"I'm not alone," Axrel said.

Grayson tilted his head back, studying him. "You two went through something together, didn't you? On Fargis. You were one of the prisoners Charlotte was meant to save on the ship."

"Yes."

"You stayed by her after...why?"

"It's none of your concern."

The man huffed, combing a hand through his dark hair. "You vrisha are stubborn assholes."

"I could say the same for you humans."

Grayson dropped his hand and stared firmly back at him. "Whatever the reason, it's good she had you. I won't bother to understand, not until she and I talk. But I'm glad she's safe." He crossed his arms. "Whatever awful shit she went through, it's over now. She'll be home and can return to the life she had before."

Axrel's eyes narrowed. "You're trying to say I don't belong in her life?"

Grayson shrugged. "I'm saying she might want to keep what happened on Fargis there and leave it behind. Forget it happened. She needed you there then, but maybe now..."

Axrel's hands curled into fists. He wanted to make the man go running with his metaphorical tail between his legs for having the audacity to think Charlotte would want him gone now that it was over. But something kept him at bay. Did he not just think the same of Kira and Gnar and the other prisoners? He knew they were to leave, and he hadn't planned so much as a goodbye. He had judged them not friends or hardly comrades despite what they had been through. He merely saw them as allies in the fight to survive. Who was to say Charlotte didn't feel the same?

He hated Grayson in that moment for putting doubt into his mind and in his heart. No, he wouldn't dare believe it. He was ready to force him out of the room when the man had the nerve to smirk at him with sad eyes.

"You really love her, don't you?"

Axrel tensed, shocked by his unexpected question. Before he could answer, Grayson turned and left.

Standing there, he watched the door slide closed. His eyes drifted back to the pod. He moved to it and looked down on Charlotte again.

All he'd known for so long was anger and vengeance. He had no other emotions in him. At one point, he'd wondered if he could feel anything else. Gazing at Charlotte now, he knew that he could.

He was stunned by that realization. He placed his hand on the glass and knew the answer. He might sometimes miss the warmth of his home and the wild hunts. Or of his own kind and being part of a pack. But he didn't need them. He was a soltari. But he wasn't alone. He had all that he needed right in front of him. And being off Fargis, free and safe, didn't change that.

The lights of the pod flickered to life, whirring and clicking. Charlotte's eyes fluttered opened, her blue gaze turning up to him.

If he had any doubts again about how she might feel, they were quickly snuffed away as her face brightened at the sight of him. He knew her answer then too as she looked up and smiled.

CHAPTER THIRTY

CHARLOTTE

She recovered quickly after her time in the healing pod, only spending another day or two in the medical ward once they had landed. It was good to be home, even better to have Axrel with her. She hardly believed it possible after everything they'd been through on Fargis, when she'd nearly lost all hope. When she was back on her feet again, she rarely left his side. Or maybe it was that he rarely left hers.

They stayed in her apartment once she left the ward, no one questioning that she had a vrisha with her though some gave her odd looks. She worried that Axrel wouldn't acclimate well to the new environment, but he never complained, even about it being a terraformed world which turned many others off. He never hinted to her he wanted to be somewhere else, even when she knew it was not nearly as warm or as wild as his world could be.

Many of the prisoners—now wanted felons according to the military—had already left from the south port, some leaving as soon as they had landed and others waiting a few days to decide where they wanted to go. Zeti had gone the day they landed, only coming to say goodbye to Axrel once. Gnar, Silf, and his sister followed the next day. Only Kira and Naba stayed longer, gifting her and Axrel with a lygin's claw necklace as a thanks for their help. They left two days later.

Each time one of them left, Charlotte worried Axrel might follow. But he never did, and her doubts dissolved away when he made it clear he wasn't going to leave. For her, it seemed, he was willing to stay.

After the others had all left, Officer Leslie and the last band of soldiers of Fargis had called on a military ship to come get them. Before they left, they promised Grayhart would be subject to harsh scrutiny by the governing systems and the alliance council for allowing the prisoners to leave. They wanted Axrel too and threatened that they would come back for him. Charlotte told them Grayhart security would be waiting to stop them if they tried. She would threaten to go to the council about what they were doing on Fargis to fight for Axrel's freedom.

She could not have been more thankful to Grayson and the Grayhart team. If it weren't for them, they might never have gotten away from the Blood Guard.

When she finally had the chance, she went to the security checkpoint at Grayhart's dock to thank Grayson personally.

"I lost your receiver back on Fargis," she said with a sad smile. "Along with my kit."

"We can always get a new one," Grayson assured.

"I'm glad you gave it to me. I guess I needed it after all."

"I told you so," he said.

"I tried it so many times. I thought I'd broken it for good. But you had heard me after all."

Grayson leaned against his desk, crossing his arms. "Well, we heard something. I couldn't get a clear signal at first. It was a jumbled mess mixed with static. But once we got a few words out of it like vrisha...help...prisoners. We knew something wasn't right. It took some convincing to the heads before we finally could get a ship out."

"I'm glad you did. I can never thank you enough," Charlotte said.

Grayson's eyes fell to his feet. "If that vrisha of yours hadn't kept you alive long enough to keep making the call, we might have never made it."

Charlotte smiled sadly, placing a hand on his shoulder. "Probably not."

"I'm sorry, but I have to ask. Can we trust him? He's not...forcing you in some way to... you know."

Charlotte shook her head. "No. He's not one of them. He's good."

"And you are happy with him?"

"I am."

"You'll tell me what happened," he said, looking back at her, his mouth tight.

She sat down by him and told him everything she could, from the crash to their fight across Fargis, leaving out more personal details. When she finished, he merely nodded, his eyes wide and bright.

"I'm glad you are all right," he said, pushing off the desk. "I wish things could have gone differently in so many ways. I wish I had stopped you from going."

She didn't say it, but she was glad that he hadn't. Even after everything she had gone through, there was still Axrel.

They hugged before she left him to his work, returning to her apartment. Back inside, she found Axrel out on their balcony, looking over the city base, the night bringing out what few stars they could see over the glow of the buildings.

She watched him for a long moment, admiring the power and grave beauty of him. When he sensed her behind him, he turned.

"It almost feels unreal, doesn't it? Us being here," she said.

He bowed his head. "Unreal."

He was so calm, she realized. More calm than she'd ever seen him. It was as if a great weight had been lifted from him, his tension gone. Almost.

She approached, wrapping her arms around his waist, letting the heat of him sink into her. He held her close, his mouth brushing against her hair. "Sometimes I wonder," he said, "if I died."

"Me too." She gently pulled back from him, her hand cupping his jaw, bringing his mouth to hers. He picked her up and took them to their bedroom where he had made a pile of blankets and pillows on the floor as the bed was too small for him.

He laid her out, stripping her of her clothes then removing his before he moved on top of her. His touch was slow, as if to savor every part. His teeth grazed her as did his tongue. When he flipped her on her belly, he moved in her deep and slow, savoring every sensation, the scales of his stomach brushing against her back. They had nothing chasing them now, nothing to keep them alert, waiting to fight or run or hide. Just the two of them in a safe place, where Axrel could claim her in all the ways that he wanted.

A week passed, and she was back in the medical bay. Back to her usual self but not without some new scars. She walked down her ward, checking each occupied bed, checking over her patients, scheduling surgeries, and discussing medical treatments. She felt good to be in her element again. She was glad to have all her machines and tools, things that made her job easier, grateful for them now more than ever. She breathed a sigh of relief when she found the supply closet fully stocked and thanked whatever gods there may be for her medical staff. When she found the time on one of her breaks, she made up a new kit, since she lost her old one on Fargis, and stocked it with everything she'd forgotten before, just in case.

Axrel came to visit every day, and they sat and ate meals together by one of the many parks. She worried he was becoming bored or restless with little to do, but he seemed content enough to just be free and by her side for the time being. Some nights, she found him at her computer station looking through the web networks, scouring for any news or signs of the other Blood Guard members or of their mad queen, wanting to keep up with their whereabouts. And some days, he went to the tradeports to watch for any possible agents or signs of threats. Even if he wouldn't admit it, he was still trying to keep them safe in all ways possible. As if there was always a danger lurking, close by.

Sitting in her office one evening, looking over some final reports, she was eager to be off to meet him when a nurse, Synthia, knocked at her door.

"I know you're about to be off," she said, poking her head in, "but there are a couple of security officers waiting for you outside."

Charlotte looked around at the door. Behind Synthia, she could see the officers—one older gentleman with a graying beard and a younger, balding man in black security uniforms—standing close by. She had a sudden hit of deja vu as she cleared her throat and closed out her reports. "Thanks, Synthia, I'll see you tomorrow."

She shut off her lights and locked her door before approaching them. "You're looking for me?" she said.

"Dr. Locksley, we are here to escort you to headquarters."

"Is something wrong?" She looked between them anxiously, fearing it was something to do with Axrel.

"We are just here to take you over, ma'am. What business the heads have with you is their own."

She didn't much like the sound of that, but if the head directors of Larth wanted to see her, she couldn't exactly refuse. "I'll need to make a call on the way if that is all right."

They nodded. Reluctantly, she followed them out of the medical ward and across to the next building to headquarters. As they walked, she lifted her hand, bringing her wristpad up to her mouth to call Axrel. She had gifted him his own wristpad and call number so that they would always have a way to communicate when not together. As she sent the call, he picked up on the first beep.

"Where are you?" he asked.

"I have to go to headquarters. The directors are asking for me."

"I was asked to go as well."

Charlotte stopped, then continued walking when the officers glanced back at her. "Really?"

"I refused to go, but now that I know you are going, I will meet you there." He hung up, and she knew he would get there in record time.

When they entered the main building and walked into the central lobby, they stood waiting until Axrel appeared. He leered at the officers who stood at the lobby's main passage, giving them space. She went to him, and immediately, he reached out and brought her to him, enclosing his arms around her protectively.

"What is this about?" he said, tension in his voice.

"I don't know."

A set of doors opened to one end, and a woman dressed in a fine red uniform with dark, tight curls along her head and sharp black eyes stepped out of a large meeting room. Behind her, the head directors followed. They saw Charlotte and greeted her while eying Axrel nervously.

"Dr. Locksley." The woman smiled. "I have heard so much about you. Please, won't you and Axrel join me inside?"

Charlotte eyed the woman carefully. She looked very familiar, but she couldn't figure out from where. "I'm sorry, do I know you?"

"Maybe not in person, but you might have heard of me. I'm Sia Gray."

Charlotte's eyes widened. She drew out of Axrel's embrace. Sia Gray. Yes, of course, she'd seen the woman many times through the web and on the news. She was a council member of the alliance and cohead of Grayhart.

"I had no idea—I was so busy I didn't check the newsfeed about your arrival," Charlotte said, feeling a little embarrassed.

"It's okay, I didn't exactly announce it." She stepped aside and gestured to the meeting room. "May we talk?"

Charlotte looked to Axrel and nodded her head. "It's all right." He seemed a little skeptical, but he trusted her. They followed Sia into the room, the doors closing behind them.

"Please, sit."

Charlotte sat on one chair on the end of a long table. Axrel did not sit but chose to stand beside her.

Sia took a seat at the other end, placing a large, thin tablet in front of her. "I would start by saying that the other founders and I are very proud of your work. We heard about your time on Fargis and are very happy you made it out of that awful place."

"Thank you."

"And we are very grateful to Axrel for aiding you."

Axrel bowed his head but remained quiet beside her.

"That being said," Sia continued. "I have good news and bad news for both of you. Which would you like to hear first?"

Charlotte glanced up at Axrel, then turned back to Sia. "Bad."

Sia placed her hands on the table, knitting her fingers together. "The governing systems' military leaders want Axrel back. They wanted all the prisoners actually, and right now, we're dealing with quite the headache of a lawsuit for it since those said prisoners are now long gone."

Charlotte inhaled sharply, her body tensing. She felt Axrel grow still beside her. "I thought they were told we wouldn't give them up."

"Oh, they were told. That didn't mean the military wasn't going to go to the council, demanding we change our minds."

Charlotte shook her head. "No, they can't have him. We will leave if we have to. We will go anywhere, and I will talk to the council myself—"

Sia lifted her hand. "It is true you can't stay here." Her gaze shifted over to Axrel. "The council has decided that since you are now no longer a part of the Blood Guard and are on neutral ground, you will not be given over by force. However, the military—and others—have the right to send out bounty hunters to capture you and bring you into the governing systems where they can then re-incarcerate you as they see fit. Since you will then be bound there by their laws, nothing can be done. We can't stop them from trying. But if you become a member of our organization, you'll be given some protective liberties. Which leads me to the good news...if you decide to take our offer."

"And what is that?" Charlotte asked.

Sia tapped on the tablet in front of her, and the screen lit up, displaying a holographic model before them. The model of a ship.

No. Not just a ship. A massive vessel. Larger than the *Tarus*. Larger, in fact, than any Grayhart ship she had ever seen.

"This is *Naviathon*, our greatest ship. You might have heard of it over the years as it was being built."

She stared at it in awe. "I have, actually. But I thought it was just rumors. I didn't know it was complete." It wasn't just any mere ship, she had been told. It was a city, made to float through space. A massive space station that could travel great distances.

"It's scheduled to take off in only a few weeks' time," Sai said. "And it will travel outside of the alliance territories to explore farther out and serve as a base for exploration cruisers." The model turned slowly, showing the massive underside and hull with its front end like the old ships at sea, its back cylindrical in shape with massive solar fans across its side, making it look almost like a great fish, swimming in a dark ocean. Lights glittered like scales and from underneath its belly, smaller ships were attached. "It's made up of both human and otherkin technology, a perfect balance of xolian and gyda and human."

"It's amazing," Charlotte said honestly.

"It is." Sia shrunk the image until it looked like a small toy model in the palm of her hand. "And there is plenty of space on board. I think you two would make a fine addition to the *Naviathon* team."

"You mean...you want us to..."

"You would be head of your own medical sector, of course, and Axrel...well I think he'd make a fine head of security don't you think? You would be out of alliance territory, only subject to Grayhart law."

"And what does that entail?" Axrel said in xolian.

"The main laws are in our contract, the same you have been following here. But, assuming you abide by them, you would make your own judgment on what is fair in terms of justice if they are broken. Do no harm to others, protect those who can't protect themselves. The *Naviathon* will be made of all peoples, human and otherkin. And they will need someone to keep them safe. Who better than a vrisha warrior?"

Charlotte stared at her and the model she cupped in her hand. Then she turned her eyes back up to Axrel. He locked his gaze with hers.

They could leave now and discuss it. Take several days to talk it over. But Charlotte could already tell Axrel's answer. No words needed to be said.

The question now was, would she go? Leave behind this place where she'd already established herself as head doctor? Where she'd called home?

She didn't need to think twice. Yes, Larth was her home. But so were other worlds before it. She could always start again somewhere else. Because home wasn't always just a place.

Charlotte rose from her seat and stood beside Axrel, taking his hand in hers. She threaded her fingers in his and squeezed them gently. "It looks like we have some packing to do."

EPILOGUE

Of all the places he'd thought he'd be several months ago, it was not here. He thought he'd be with his pack, on some suicidal mission, or fighting against enemies who opposed them. Less than several months ago, he'd thought he would be dead. Or imprisoned still on Fargis, being experimented on and tortured.

No, not in his wildest imagination did he think he'd end up here, in a dark, warm house, with the fires lit softly at each corner, looking out at a vast jungle landscape from a wide window before him.

And a woman—his woman—beside him. Wearing silky black clothes, lying on the soft ground mat, her body pressed close to his, her light hair brushing along his arm.

The sun was coming over the horizon, a bright red dot in the distance. Charlotte's eyes fluttered open, and she sighed, her warm breath on his chest.

"You're up?" she mumbled.

"Just watching the sunrise."

She laughed softly. "We fell asleep in the center room again. We never seem to make it to the den."

He grunted, brushing his fingers across her back. "I don't mind."

She smiled, then groaned as she peered at her wristpad. "I'll have to start getting ready. My shift is in a few hours." She didn't move to get up, and neither did he. He closed his eyes and took in her dark, flowery scent as he did every morning, his mouth brushing against her hair, then down to her ear until stopping at her neck, nuzzling deep into the curve of her shoulder. She tilted her head back to allow him better access, one arm wrapped around his waist.

"You were talking in your sleep again," she breathed.

"I was dreaming about our conversations, I think," he said.

"Which ones?"

He turned over the memory. "The time back on Fargis."

He felt her tense a little. "I sometimes dream of that place too. But they are rarely as nice as just a conversation."

"I know. This was one of the pleasant few."

She shifted to her side, curling into him. "It will take time still, to forget."

"I don't want to forget. Not fully." He wrapped his arm around her. "Sometimes, though, I think I died on that prisoner ship after all."

She huffed. "No. Not on my watch."

As if on command, her wristpad beeped. She looked over at it, and her eyes suddenly widened. She let out a small cry. "Oh, that's right now? We can't miss it!" She drew out of his arms and hopped up, walking over to the wall panel next to the window.

Axrel sat up, looking at her curiously. "What can't we miss, exactly?"

She tapped on the panel, and the jungle disappeared from the window, the room changing from a warm reddish color to a soft blue. From the window, they saw what was truly beyond—deep space. But it was not full darkness with the flicker of stars this time, not as usual. There was a brilliant jewel of light before them now, swirling with oranges and purples. The window enhanced the colors while remaining covered by a tinted shield to keep them from being blinded or harmed by any dangerous rays. The rays of a brilliant star.

They moved in unison to the center of the window.

"It's beautiful," he said.

"It's got an interesting name too," Charlotte said.

"Oh?"

She moved again to the panel and brought up the computer screen over the windowpane, which began to map out the various stars and planets already named and the distance they were from the star. The name of the star appeared above the brilliant light:

Axrel's Fury

He looked over at her, stunned. "When did you...?"

She grinned. "I saw a log from the astronomy team of the stars in our path and asked to name it first. They allowed it."

He stared back at the star, then smiled. He grabbed her and pulled her to him. "I suppose it's fitting. But I would have picked a different name."

"Oh, yeah? Like what?"

He took hold of her chin and drew her mouth to his and whispered against her lips, "Axrel's Serenity."

OTHER BOOKS BY OLIVIA RILEY

Dark World Mates Series

Heart's Prisoner
Dark's Savior
Shadow's Chosen
Heart's Keeper

Vrisha Warriors

Xora

ABOUT THE AUTHOR

OLIVIA RILEY LOVES THE FRIGHTENING POSSIBILITIES OF DEEP space, where dark heroes and brave heroines reside. She also loves chocolate and gaming.

Sign up for her newsletter to get the latest updates and visit her page on Amazon for future titles.

Join for her newsletter here:
https://mailchi.mp/2b73fde9127d/olivia-riley-sci-fi-and-fantasy-romance